The Millionaires Cruise

SAILING TOWARD BLACK TUESDAY

The Millionaires Cruise

SAILING TOWARD BLACK TUESDAY

Donald McPhail

Donald McPhail
Mountain View, California
Illustrations by Michelle Imbach Walters

ISBN-13:
978-0-692-36611-0

Originally appeared in 2014 as “The Millionaires Cruise”
(isbn-13: 978-1500475414)

The Millionaires Cruise

SAILING TOWARD BLACK TUESDAY

INTRODUCTION

September 22, 1929

Malone stands to starboard, thick wool collar turned up against the breeze, taking stock of things as he observes the barren headlands and the gaunt military buildings that guard the northern shore. "Early days," he calls these first hours of a new cruise. He calms himself with a glass of sherry, as the adrenaline pumps and the unknowns await. With the instincts of a sportsman, departure-day feels like games-day, getting ready for the big match back in school. But this is greater than a match.

He stands alone down on the main deck next to the gray capstan, newly painted for departure, as the bay breeze blows through his long, dark hair. He prefers it here in the open air, down where the deck crew has done its work of casting off and stowing gear for the next port of call. Now the massive lines are neatly flaked, decks are clear, the working tools packed away. It's quiet. Orderly. Peaceful.

Passengers want the views higher up, and the luxury of ordering drinks and canapés from the waiting stewards. Theirs is a different kind of anticipation, curious to be meeting new people, sizing them up as they sail toward exotic destinations. They gather in small groups, pointing out the hills and landmarks around the bay, chatting comfortably and establishing a sort of hierarchy. Malone is afraid that when they return to port in sixty days, their comfortable lives could be shattered.

For now, they take in this magical view. The sparkling bay, with its rough-neck waterfronts surrounded by cities that expand into the brown foothills, clearly visible in the late afternoon shadows. The bow of the *Malolo* traces across the headlands that separate Marin from San Francisco, completing its gentle arc before cutting into the Pacific chop, then heading to open sea.

People see San Francisco as a charming and rugged frontier town, with its Barbary Coast and wicked past, emerging from the

1906 earthquake as an even more fascinating city. Foreign visitors are immediately attracted to the bay, which feels familiar to them, like Rio or Hong Kong or Sydney, but distinctly different. And the compact size, where they can walk all day, up and down the challenging hills, often ending back where they started: at Union Square or The Palace Hotel or the Ferry Building. Now that he has finally seen it, San Francisco is a place that Malone will remember, perhaps the most beautiful he has ever seen. He will also remember the city as the jumping-off point for the most challenging assignment he has ever had.

This is his quiet time, making mental preparations for the journey. Today's are different, full of contradictions. In this extraordinary time of soaring stocks and unlimited growth, the passengers are flying high. They're the richest of the rich, and their fortunes are multiplying daily. The stock market soars. Business is booming. There's jazz music, ecstatic dancing, free-flowing booze and no restraints. Everyone ignores prohibition and drives fast cars. They dabble in sex, but they invest in the market, borrowing to the hilt.

Malone fears something his passengers don't, and it gnaws at him. They leave port today as millionaires, but by the time they get back they could all be destitute. He's been warned by people who wouldn't lie to him, and he feels the pressure. His job is to keep things smooth, to reassure his clients, and to make this cruise the best they have ever had.

Even on this superliner, this *Malolo*, he feels the turbulence as the bow cuts through the chop near the Farallon islands. Soon they will reach calmer waters, where the long and soothing roll of the sea will take over, encouraging passengers to stroll along the decks and stand against the railing, chatting and looking back at the slowly fading bit of land.

As he climbs the port-side ladder, he wonders about these next sixty days. *How will it hit? How could it happen, amidst this optimism, with all the buildings and automobiles and carefree parties? The surging stock market, with the promise of growth and plenty for all? How can the future be as bad as the Commodore painted it? Aren't these people too rich to be affected?*

Malone knows his job depends on people with money, people demanding a good time, and he worries about his own future. Can he really handle this assignment, visiting ports that he has never seen before, being the expert for people who are so rich and powerful? He has learned how they talk and think. He's sailed the finest ships, dined at the world's greatest restaurants, and stayed in the most luxurious hotels. He knows how to act around them, but because he is far from rich himself, he is still humbled by their wealth.

As the SS *Malolo* sails from San Francisco Bay on a glorious September afternoon, with a bright California sky bursting through the remaining wisps of fog, Malone feels another twinge, one that he can't identify. It isn't the stock market, or the passengers, or rough waters. It's an unfamiliar sensation, with images of vibrant blue eyes and auburn hair, wearing a small nurse's cap. Her eyes sparkle with an incredible intensity, but vulnerable. This young lady seems…

Stop it, man! It's not worth it. He straightens up and looks around, realizing he is very much alone with his glass of sherry. Malone chastises himself for losing focus, and returns to his preparations.

Johannesburg, February 4, 1908

"Does he do this often?" asks the taller man, gazing at the boy across the neatly trimmed playing field.

"Every day, headmaster," replies the other.

"Does he get far? I see he wobbles a bit."

"Twice round the yard, headmaster."

"That far? And then what?"

"Then he halts at the Toryville sign and crosses over to the building. Enters through that door, and proceeds to his classroom. He sits quietly until class resumes."

The two men stand in their crisp summer khakis and watch the boy continue his run around the schoolyard.

"He's a determined boy," sighs the headmaster.

"A sad and determined boy," nods the other. "Poor little chap."

Chapter 1

Theodore Malone was born in Elgin, Scotland in 1872. In 1898, he emigrated to South Africa with his wife, Sarah Wilson Malone, just a year after they married. He had been a coal merchant in Elgin. Once in South Africa, they settled in Johannesburg and Theodore established a claim on the Walthar mine. He was no longer just a merchant, but a mine owner.

The cold and damp of Scotland behind them, Theodore and Sarah soon flourished in the bright South African sun, and with the challenges of creating a new life in Johannesburg. They rented a cottage with a dilapidated stable, a few miles from the city's shops. He slowly rebuilt the house and strengthened the weathered stable walls, so that they were suitable even in the chilly Johannesburg winters. They lived not far from the mine, so Theodore could ride his new dappled mare in half an hour's time, but it was far enough away that the sounds of explosives and digging equipment were barely heard. Sarah packed bread and cheese, and succulent paw-paws or other treats that she purchased from farms nearby.

Angus Robert Wilson was born just after midnight in the new year, on January 1, 1900. He may well have been Africa's first child of the new century. "Sandy, we'll call him," smiled Theodore. "And he will be the first of many!"

"Aye, the first" smiled Sarah, surprised and grateful at how uncomplicated her pregnancy had been, and how skilled was the Zulu midwife who assisted gruff Doctor O'Connell with the birth and the weeks of recovery that followed. Though she fancied Angus as her son's name, Sandy would make a fine moniker.

Just over a year later, Theodore, Junior -- soon to be known as Duff -- was born, but not in Johannesburg. Sarah experienced a difficult pregnancy this time, and for her sake and that of the child, she returned by ship to Scotland four months before the birth. Doctor O'Connell had moved away, and the midwife, whose name was never known, had returned to her village down in Natal. Sarah had family in Elgin, and a familiar doctor to help with the delivery. Even then, recovery was slow following her release from hospital. Sarah was weak, often light-headed when she attempted to walk. The baby, though quiet, was strong and hungry as she nursed him, big brown eyes watching intently. But It was months before she felt strong enough to manage on her own, and two long years before she returned to Johannesburg with young Duff.

Without Sarah to look after him and Sandy, Theodore drifted, drinking his Castle lagers and smoking rough-rolled cigarettes, though the mines flourished. He relied on Funeka to run the house and look after his son. A quiet and sturdy Xhosa woman, she lived with her little boy, Cebo, in a tiny hut behind the stable. Theodore did not know anything about Funeka's husband, or if there was one. Nor did he understand Xhosa, so they communicated with sounds and hand signals. Funeka was stoic and respectful around adults, whether white or black. But around children, especially babies, she was gentle and full of quiet laughter. Funeka smiled shyly, when *baas Teo* laughed at his own clumsy attempts to communicate his request for more of the heavy bread, when he first attempted to describe it, or asked her to fetch his tobacco pouch. But they managed.

Cebo and young Sandy were inseparable and jolly, rolling out in the gritty red dirt during the day, then exploring the main room of the house until they collapsed into deep sleep in the late afternoons. What words they used were an odd combination of Xhosa and English, which Funeka seemed to understand completely.

Theodore maintained the stable and the yard, which was mostly dirt and tufts of dry grass that needed to be kept clipped. Every day, he rode his mare to the mine, returning in the late afternoon to clean the red dust from his tired body, using buckets of cold water from the cistern, careful not to wake the sleeping boys. Then he would don slacks and wool jacket, to take a few drinks and dinner at the private club nearby.

Late each night, relaxed and intoxicated, he sat at the dining room table and composed a brief message to Sarah, wishing her well and sending love to her and their new baby. Then he bundled the notes and posted them at the end of each week, in a single envelope. Though it took several days for the letters to reach her, Sarah sent prompt replies that Theodore eagerly opened and savored. Her letters often contained suggestions about household chores, and cautioned him not to forget her. The time-lapse between his letters and hers made him even more eager to hear the latest chapter of her life in Scotland, and that of young Duff.

Then he put away the letters and slept deeply, gathering energy for another day at the mines, and another evening at the club.

It was September, 1903, when the Union Castle ship carrying Sarah and her two-year-old son crossed the equator and brought them to a gentle South African spring. Theodore had ridden the train from Johannesburg to Durban, a sunny coastal city where white-sand beaches sparkled on one side of a curved and narrow road, and green fields of sugar cane and pineapple grew on the other. The warm climate and safe swimming attracted hard-working settlers, as a place for recreation and rest. Theodore arrived in plenty of time to hire a coach and greet the steamship at nearby Port Natal.

As Sarah and her two-year-old boy were assisted down the gangplank, Theodore rushed to steady her with his hand, at the same time delivering a powerful hug.

"Careful, you," she laughed. "We still have our sea-legs!" Then she lifted the boy so that Theodore could see his new son.

As Sarah watched him watching their young Duff, she could see the eyes and nose of her boy; and the boy had the same little grin as his father. She also saw that her husband had become heavier, much softer than when she had left. "It is good to see you then," she said gently, as she touched his stubbled cheek. "Have you missed me a bit?"

He rubbed the boy's dark hair with a rough miner's hand, then touched her on her thin shoulder. "Very much, my dear. I have missed you very much, indeed. Young Duff is a handsome boy, mother," he said, just audibly. "A right handsome boy."

"He looks quite a bit like you, you know." Sarah smiled and took his hand, as they walked toward the waiting coach.

With the family reunited and the coal business growing, Sarah and Theodore enjoyed a promising life, raising two healthy boys within a rugged and newly prosperous Johannesburg elite. The little boys followed their mother around, Sandy padding after her in the house, and Duff watching carefully with his big eyes.

They constructed a new home in Rosebank, in the Dutch style that they admired, even though they did not agree with the Dutch-Afrikaans ways in politics or religion. They did respect the way Afrikaans businessmen tended to stick together, and share their successes. But the brutal way some of the Afrikaaners treated the Zulu and Xhosa servants and the black men who worked their mines was despicable, and not the way Theodore operated.

Once a scrappy laborer himself, he appreciated the strength and durability of his black mine-workers. To keep them healthy and to reward their labor, Theodore instituted round-the-clock food halls for them, and hot water for showers. It took a bit from the profits, but the daily output increased and, unlike the other mines, workers suffered fewer illnesses and they seldom ran away from the Walthar mines.

During those two years while Sarah was in Scotland, Theodore had found he enjoyed a certain prominence as a mine owner, and he joined the nearby Wanderers Club, where he consumed their hearty meals and good beers. On her return, Sarah attempted to fit into Theodore's routine. She saw that he now spent more of his daytime in the office, working on equipment purchases and bookkeeping, and almost none down the mines with the men.

He had found an able manager, Sean Donnelly, while on a visit to the Southwest Territory. Donnelly was a skilled tracker over in Windhoek when Theodore first met him. Donnelly had also spent time in the coal mines of Aberdeen before locating in South Africa. He was quick to learn, and he got on with the black workers better than any white man Theodore had ever seen. He could communicate well in both Xhosa and Zulu, well enough that he enjoyed the occasional bits of humor that the miners traded each day, despite their difficult and dangerous work. There was also a streak of kindness that strengthened Sean's bond with the men, generating a better quality of work and fewer days off with illnesses than at most other mines.

Theodore welcomed Sean into his home, and was pleased to have another man around the property, learning the business. Sarah was surprisingly distant with Sean, but the boys took to him, and despite their youth they enjoyed listening to stories about his adventures in Windhoek or the veldt.

But the club had become Theodore's territory, and even Sean didn't accompany him there, nor did his wife and young sons. Theodore maintained his appetite for the rich foods and fine lagers, and then reading the most recent newspaper and playing a bit of snooker after his meal. He was at the club when he first heard of the American investment system, and the Dow-Jones stock market. The London Times reported, *The Dow-Jones Industrial Average closed the day at over 100 for the first time.* It sounded important, and he wondered how a man was to go about investing his money in such a system.

Sarah preferred that he stay home and dine with her and the boys. When he did, they joyfully reacted to his presence, vying to see who could sit on his lap and listen to him read one of the little books she had brought from Elgin. It was Duff, especially, who looked so lovingly at Theodore when he rode into the yard after work, and helped him wash off the mine dust. She was saddened for the boys and herself, and not a little angered when he told her that his work exhausted him, then spent his nights at Wanderers. She seldom accompanied him.

At the age of forty-four, when Sandy was seven and Duff not yet six, Theodore occasionally found himself struggling for breath while walking across the mine yards. On a clear day in January, when a fire broke out in one of the sheds, he dashed to the cistern and grabbed a water bucket. As he dragged the bucket through the water and rushed toward the fiery building, he suddenly dropped it and fell to the ground, into the muddy puddle that slowly grew around him.

Sarah was devastated by Theodore's sudden death, and she was badly confused. *How could this happen?* She felt he would always be here, running the business while she tended to Sandy and Duff, and to their new home. She knew nothing of the business or finances, like paying the merchants and such. Theodore had taken care of those things, along with Donnelly. She had always looked after the staff and worked in the garden, and she helped her boys to dress themselves and keep their shared room in an orderly state.

Sarah felt totally alone, overwhelmed. The mines, the boys, a large home. Seven-year-old Sandy was a determined boy, methodically continuing with his schoolwork. While Funeka and Cebo did the housework, Sandy fed the animals and went to the office when he was allowed. Sean Donnelly took over the mining operations. He was sound and smart, and had proven to be a trustworthy friend to Theodore, though Sarah stubbornly avoided contact. Little Duff remained at home and played with Cebo, but he had become strangely quiet after his father died. He looked to his mother, his eyes seeking a response.

But Sarah became quiet as well, withdrawing into her bible and showing little affection to either boy. God's will became part of her conversation. She took to sipping from the brandy that Theo had kept in the cupboard, then replacing it when the bottle was empty. As she sipped, she grew more sullen. The boys saw how her faced hardened and the anger crept in. She wept, and said cruel things to Sandy and Duff that seemed to come from someone else. About how her husband was gone, and how much she had loved him. *"And you two! Look at you! You're alive, and he's not!"* Pummeling them with her words. Somehow, his death became their fault. This wasn't their mother. It was another woman, one that frightened them.

Duff was confused, wondering where his loving mother had gone, angry and humiliated when the following day she would not remember her own outbursts, what she had said so bitterly. She needed help sorting through daily tasks, and was often short with

Funeka when she offered assistance. Days passed, and her anger resurfaced with verbal blows that hurt like heavy fists. While it did not happen daily, the boys grew anxious and edgy, not knowing when the anger would reappear, nourishing the growing sense of unworthiness that Duff held within his little body.

Often agitated and shaky, she needed help for her boys, at least for Duff. It would simplify things. Sandy seemed to understand. He was a friendly boy. He didn't need much attention, and he knew how to take care of himself. He was different from Duff. He went with her whenever she visited the mines, and he was eager to be alongside Sean Donnelly when he descended into the mine shaft.

But Duff withdrew, and she had nothing to give him. Though once he was her special favorite, Duff was different now. He seemed angry with her, and he showed no interest in his chores, or the mines, or the ways of business. Sometimes he took to the books in their den, sitting on the chair next to the little table where his father's photo sat watching, while his own soft, dark eyes looked around the room. Duff liked the books with photos of ships and far away cities.

Sometimes he sat completely quiet, staring into the distance. Saying nothing. *Was he thinking nothing?* This worried Sarah, and she knew she must do something to change their lives. There was money from her parents set aside to send Duff off to boarding school, and enough to keep him there through his school years. Their savings would help as well. She would get Sandy and their home back together, and then send for Duff.

It had been over a year since Theodore died, and Sarah decided that Sandy would remain at home with her. She would teach him what he needed to know, and they could call upon occasional visiting tutors. In a few years he would know how to assist with the mines operations. Duff would go alone to board full-time at Toryville School; then in a few years he could become a resident student at Jeppe High School. The schools were near enough, located in the city, but far enough away to create the distance she wanted. After that, she had no ideas.

Sarah expected resistance from the boy. She was surprised when he agreed to go. Duff was nearly seven years old, and independent. He told Sandy, "I want to leave." He didn't seem angry, not sad. He just seemed determined.

What do you do when your father dies? He didn't understand why she blamed them. That they were alive and he was not. It frightened him when she drank. Though he was glad to get away, he felt that his real mother had disappeared, abandoned him.

Toryville suited Duff. He lived in a nice room with a roommate, a farmer's son from Transvaal. His teachers were strict and fair, and he had no difficulty following the rules about studies, and cleanliness, and punctuality, and behavior in class. The food was decent, and he didn't mind sitting attentively at the dining table while older boys took the largest portions. There was enough to eat, and the boys seldom bullied him. Though a younger boy, there was something about his dark quiet that caused them to leave him alone. He had no special passion for studies or people. Aside from occasional outbursts, he seemed to have no feelings at all.

Encouraged by his instructors, he wrote short notes to Sandy and his mother, telling them about the books he was reading and the competitive games that interested him. Or a teacher who had become his favorite. Their occasional replies were also brief, describing work at the mines, and how Sandy was diligent with his mathematics, and Cebo was getting tall. Soon there was little left to say to each other. It was as if by mutual agreement that Duff wrote less frequently and they seldom wrote to him. As he reached the third year at Toryville, Duff had grown away from his past life and his family, settling into a solitary existence, allowing only a few school friends and teachers into his life.

Over time, he found that he enjoyed the structure and the ideas in his studies. He learned of the crusades in Europe, and the power of the monarchies. He was intrigued that a new country like America would break away from the king of England and declare independence. When he finished at Toryville and moved on to Jeppe High School, he continued on his path. He did not question it, and he was satisfied. He still sought his quiet times, staring into the distance. And when he went to bed, he often had his dream.

"Young man. Do you have any questions for your father?" The instructor says, as he stands rigid before his classmates.

"I have no father," Duff replies.

"Nonsense, young man. Everyone has a father. Go on, now. What will you ask him?"

Duff has questions that no-one can answer. "How would my life be different, daddy?" he asks. "Would I have loved mom, instead of hating her? How would she have been if you had lived?" Duff sometimes asks if he might have become worthy, not so ashamed.

He lay awake and wondered. *I don't remember him now, a photo in the living room, of a man like God. He is kind. Stares at me, into me. I can't remember now. Once he was there, like air or sky. He looked like God, whose love I wanted. And like God, I distance myself. Not thinking about him, or feeling. I accept his existence. No meaning to me. I cry when I try to find the answers.*

Duff made new friends at Jeppe, mostly among the athletes -- the boxers and his teammates for cricket and rugby. Competition stirred him, and it allowed him to unload his feelings. After a particularly good catch during the cricket match, the sting of the heavy ball against his outstretched hand felt good. In rugby, when he outran the blindside flanker, then bowled over the final tackler and pressed the ball down for the winning score, he was elated. He dreamed of playing for the Springboks, the national team.

As a boxer, he could stay within the rules and still punish another boy with all his might. Duff had agile feet and an uncanny ability to leave a small opening, luring his opponent to begin a blow, then lash-out with his own damaging punch to the unguarded nose or lip. His hunger to win made him dangerous. He was surprised at the satisfaction of flicking his left hand and bloodying a boy's nose. At thirteen, when he found himself pummeling another boy -- his right hand smashing the boy's bleeding face until he finally went down in mucous, blood and tears -- Duff was frightened by the rage. He turned-in his gloves, and he didn't box again.

Cricket and rugby were different. These team sports drew his interest, using controlled speed and strategy, and working together in order to win. He was always chosen first for the school teams, and the older boys welcomed him as an equal, not just in sports. Yet he continued to feel surprise at his success.

He eventually met his friends' families, and even went to their homes on holiday from time to time. When he was fifteen, his friend Mattie Cole invited him home to the family's farm near Ladysmith, where he met Mattie's older sister, Lynette.

"Come on, Duff!" challenges Lynette. "Race you to the pond! Mattie went with mum and dads for some shopping or other. You take Jango, the speckled one."

Because she's a girl, and older by at least two years, Duff hesitates, "Won't they be back soon?"

"Not for hours. Now, can you keep up or not? There's cakes and water in the saddle bag."

"You just watch me!" he dashes to the waiting horse and hoists himself onto the saddle.

Leaping onto her brown mare, Lynette is slim and attractive, but powerful as she kicks the big animal into action. She surprises Duff with her quickness.

Jango is stubborn, and she moves slowly, walking at first, then trotting down the familiar dirt path, shaking her big head when Duff kicks her in the ribs with his hard leather heels. Finally she trots faster and moves to a slow, rolling gallop, but they remain far behind Lynette and her swift horse.

As they crest the low hill, the pond looks more like a big lake to Duff. Lynette is already off her horse and at the water, britches off and pulling her shirt over her head. She tosses it on a rock. Duff has never seen a girl in her underwear before. He slowly follows suit, dropping his boots next to hers.

"Race you to that dock. You have five seconds, slow poke, or I'll leave without you!"

Embarrassed, Duff turns away and removes his trousers, then slowly unbuttons his shirt. Finally, he drops them and runs down to the water in his underpants. She has already gotten a head start, and Duff dives in where the water seems deep enough. Soon he is stroking furiously and catching up. But the dock is further than it looked from shore. Duff blinks through the splashes and sees Lynette just ahead, but he isn't sure he can make it. He thinks of turning back, but knows it is too far.

This can't happen! Duff panics, his exhausted arms slowing. He is helpless and embarrassed, and knows he is sinking, coughing with each desperate breath, his nose and mouth filling. As he settles under for the last time, resigned to what is happening, he feels pressure around his chest, lifting him, dragging him along. Now his hand is on an object, solid. He feels himself pushed up onto the rough surface, resting his chest against the edge, then up onto the wood planks. Shivering and still frightened, he feels Lynette's weight on top of him, calming his shivering body with her warmth.

Slowly, the weight lifts and he feels her hands rubbing his back. She gently turns him and massages his chest, his face. When she reaches his stomach, her hands creep further and she slides his underpants down, crawling back onto him. She moves slowly, so that their slick bodies slide together. His hands touch her shoulders, then down to her back and hips.

Instead of feeling exhausted, he responds and helps roll down her thin pants. They move together, her lips on his, and Lynette helps guide him, probing with her tongue and moving slowly.

Though it is quickly over, they cling together for a time, not speaking, then quietly lie side by side on the dock. Then she touches his face and smiles gently, a lovely, freckled smile. Suddenly, she jumps up and challenges him to swim back to shore with her there to help.

Duff never forgot his fear, and how he had accepted death. His relief when she saved him. The surge that fills him now, when he thinks of her. It was more than her slim body and his first kisses. He could never forget her gentleness. He could never love anyone else. From then on he would connect sex with love, and love with Lynette.

At school, he couldn't stop thinking of her, finding ways to ask Mattie about her without revealing what had happened. He traded letters with Lynette for the rest of the school year, writing weekly, and anxiously waiting for her response. He worried when her letters slowed, and was deeply hurt when she stopped writing altogether. Her last letter said that she was being sent on to a private school in England. It was an awkward letter, filled with excuses, apologies and promises. He longed for Lynette. It hurt when he wondered why she abandoned him.

He turned further inward. Duff's instructors were dismayed that he did not go home on holidays or year-end break, nor did his mother or brother visit him at Jeppe. His mother wrote to him, of course, telling him of changes to the house and expansion of the mines, and of how Sandy and Cebo were advancing in their different schools. Sandy was quick at mathematics and was helping his mother with bookkeeping. Cebo loved numbers, too, and rapidly learned other languages. Sandy now scrawled short notes on scraps of paper, and included assurances that "ma is fine", or "ma is trusting Donnelly with the mines work". Duff's eyes hardened when Sandy told him "ma misses you, you know. I think she changed when you left for school."

Duff responded with his own general descriptions of teachers and sports, and of his different school subjects. And he told Sandy about his friends, and how he loved rugby. But he never said he missed them, or about Lynette. He didn't tell him of his smoldering anger. And he never asked to come home.

He told his headmaster that he preferred life at school, and requested assignments from his coaches, tasks for him to carry out when school was not in session. Alone in his room during the holidays, he sometimes wondered where Lynette was and what she might be doing just then. *What must England be like? Why does she never write?*

Duff became the quiet overseer of athletic fields and equipment huts, and was accepted everywhere on campus. This gave him access to the library, where he absorbed Kipling's "Kim", and his epic poem "If", that was inspired by the famous South African battle two decades earlier, between the British forces and the Boers.

> *...if neither foes nor loving friends can hurt you, If all men count with you, but none too much; If you can fill the unforgiving minute With sixty seconds' worth of distance run, Yours is the Earth and everything that's in it, And - which is more - you'll be a Man, my son!*

He was excited to discover America's Jack London, fascinated by the heroism and independence in these books. He was drawn to the isolation and rugged terrain in "Call of the Wild", so different from his own land; and the heroic dog Buck, who survived hardship and rejection, but won out in the end. Duff felt he understood the unfairness that London described.

Duff's athleticism led to strong relationships with his coaches. When he was a new boy at school, they treated him like all the others, so he held back and wasn't certain he would like playing for them. But they were patient, and in time they seemed fairer. Eventually the coaches encouraged Duff and chose him to play, even if he made an occasional mistake, when he couldn't grasp a new technique for lofting the ball at the rugby line-out, or snatching it from the ground among all the thrashing legs and feet. But the coaches made suggestions and remained confident in him, encouraging him to play on and to hold his emotions inside.

He loved cricket, too, knowing the ball's heft and its welcome sting, the way he knew his own hands. Though the most competitive boy on the team, Duff never competed against a particular boy to beat him at the position. He never thought about their size or skills, or feared that they would take his spot on the starting team. He simply concentrated on what the coaches wanted him to do, determined to be the best who ever played, and he worked harder than anyone else. And he always won.

Duff was honored when coach Scott told him he was a team captain fully two years before he was to graduate, a feat never before achieved at Jeppe. "You earned it, son," coach Scott told him. "Accept it for what it is. Don't be awed by it." Then, like a father, he cautioned Duff to bury his anger, to channel it toward competing. Duff listened, and he felt even greater admiration toward his coach. He wanted to make him proud.

Duff became a diligent student, performing well in language, both written and verbal. He had been raised to speak Xhosa and Zulu, with their complex click-sounds, conversing with Funeka and Cebo. Like most South Africans, he also spoke some Afrikaans. So he enjoyed learning German and French.

He was best at sports, twice earning Jeppe's annual athletic award. From his earliest years, he loved the grace and ritual of cricket, where he was a talented bowler. He also relished the quickness and violent contact of rugby, and was scheduled to audition for the Springboks, South Africa's famed world-class rugby squad. But a cracked ankle shortened his final season at Jeppe, and because it did not heal properly, he lost the extra bit of quickness that had given him such promise as a potential Springbok.

This was a setback for Duff, because sports and competition were his passion. With graduation approaching, he recognized the immediate need to decide between coaching young men in the sports that he loved, or starting another career that might take him outside of sports, beyond the limits of South Africa. He would never go back to the mines. It was 1919, and most of the world was still celebrating the end of the Great War. For Duff, it was a serious time, a time of change.

He longed to know more about Great Britain, and Scotland where he was born. He was also intrigued with America, from reading London, and Zane Grey. This sounded like a young and vigorous country, much like his own. It was founded by adventurous souls who escaped from old ways, who sought hard work and opportunity, and new lands to conquer.

Born in Scotland and raised in South Africa, Duff felt fragmented -- more a part of the entire world than of either country. He felt no more apprehension about leaving South Africa than he had of leaving his mother and brother more than ten years before. Beyond the few special places that he had come to know and love, there was little to keep him here. He was now fascinated with foreign countries, and the open seas that would carry him there. With the encouragement of a favorite professor, and to the disappointment of coach Scott, Duff turned his interests to a new kind of business, called travel.

South Africa was settled by seagoing explorers and adventurers. In the fifteenth century, the Dutch East India Company established refueling and provisioning posts at the Cape. And they settled its vast, rugged land through grueling physical labor. Then other European settlers arrived and slowly moved inland, on horseback, afoot, and in covered wagons, creating farms and towns along the trek. If tribal villages were in the way, they were eliminated, creating another harsh component to South Africa's history.

By the start of the twentieth century, when Duff was born, steamships were essential to the social and economic lives of this expanding country. Passenger ships carried new European immigrants into South Africa, and residents back to London or Antwerp or Holland, to visit their families or to attend school. They also carried laborers and merchants from India, who brought new goods and pungent aromas and flavors in their foods, along with a new business class to the growing country. Cargo ships carried food, medicine, building material and other supplies. And along with a few hearty passengers, they carried precious South African gold and rare diamonds to European and Asian markets.

Eventually, the wealthiest South Africans chose to extend their visits in the more interesting ports of call en route to Europe. With the foresight of growing travel companies like Thomas

Cook and Sons, and American Express, shore excursions became luxury experiences, with prepaid sightseeing tours to interior cities. Comfortable lodges and hotels were built, and special menus created for the well-traveled. All of this was embellished by the growing availability of African and Indian labor, trainable and able to speak English, which was the language of tourism in South Africa and the major ports of call.

It was 1919 when Duff entered this emerging profession. Increased demand for experienced travel planners created the chance for a young man to use his imagination, creating special itineraries for wealthy customers, and possibly seeing more of the world himself.

Initially a clerk in the Johannesburg office of Thomas Cook and Sons, after a year Duff was asked to lead a tour for two wealthy farmers and their wives. They wanted to sail up the east coast of Africa, stopping at Mombasa for a shore excursion to Nairobi, and at Port Said for a private tour to Cairo and Giza. They would eventually disembark in Holland. It was in Nairobi that Duff learned an important lesson, that he never forgot.

CHAPTER 2

She hasn't taken her eyes off me, worries Duff, glancing through the cigarette smoke at the blonde woman across the main dining room, converted to a dance venue following dinner. It's late, and most of the hotel guests have made their way off to bed, but surprisingly, the attractive Mrs. van Flek remains seated with her friend at a table near the dance-band. Duff notices an unshaven young man in a tan safari jacket standing at the bar, who seems interested.

Duff saw their husbands excuse themselves nearly two hours ago, to smoke cigars and play cards. Middle-aged farmers from Bloomfontein, the men drank brandy with dinner instead of wine, and took half-filled tumblers with them, staggering a bit as they left.

Hulda van Flek has seemed interested in Duff ever since the ship departed from Durban, gazing at him whenever her husband was not around. Something about her kind eyes and healthy freckles reminds him of Lynette.

She and her friend Syl Hoeffer are much younger than their husbands. Both healthy farm-girls, it is clear from their many questions that neither has been far from home before. Hulda van Flek is pretty in an unpolished, schoolgirl way. Once they reached Kenya, the ladies had squealed in joy at the multitude of giraffe, zebra and elephants roaming free between the train station and their hotel. There are many wild animals in South Africa, but here in Kenya it all seems like an adventure.

This trip is a pilgrimage of sorts, a meeting with in-laws in Amsterdam and The Hague. Duff learned this earlier in the evening over dinner. The meal went well enough, with the ladies conversing together while Duff was at the opposite end, chatting with the men about sports and farming. They were interested in his rugby experiences, and excited to hear that he had boxed competitively, for they had also boxed for a local club back in their school years.

When van Flek and Hoeffer announced they were going to the card room, Duff politely excused himself.

Now, as he returns to the terrace for a beer, he sees Syl leave through the swinging doors. Hulda makes her way past the small bandstand where a skilled African quintet is providing lively dance music, and she walks straight toward him. The man at the bar follows her with his eyes.

"Good evening, Mr. Duff," she laughs as she sits down next to him. "I hoped you might return for a dance." she says in an encouraging voice.

"I just stopped in for a nightcap. Are you enjoying the entertainment?"

"Very much. But I would like to dance, and I would like it if you called me Hulda." Holding his eyes, she adds, "My Jaapie is too drunk by now." She giggles, and raises her eyebrows. "He and Karl prefer their brandy at night and their wives in the morning."

Ignoring her innuendo, he concedes, "Well then, a dance it is."

The band has softened its tone, and is in the middle of a familiar slow tune, as Duff places his right arm around her waist and maintains a safe distance.

"That is not dancing, my dear," she murmurs, "Come a bit closer." Placing her cheek against his chest, she rubs her hand against his back.

As they move around the half-empty dance floor, Duff slides his right leg forward with the music, and finds her legs parted slightly, touching his thigh. As he moves away, guiding in another direction, his leg again bumps her waiting thighs. Then the song ends and he steps away.

"That was very nice, Duff," she continues to stare. "You are a fine dancer."

"And you, Hulda," he responds, avoiding her directness. "So are you. But I must apologize. I need to prepare my reports for tomorrow's courier. May I escort you to your room, or will Mr. van

Flek return here for you?"

"Jaapie will be snoring by now, so no, he will not return for me," she pouts. "And I am disappointed, you know. You seem to work much too hard." She takes his arm, and as they walk out of the bar, her breast rubs against it.

Duff carefully extracts his arm as he reaches to open the door leading to the lobby, and he remains at a slight distance until they approach her room. She hands him the key, and as he turns it in the lock, Duff is startled to feel her arms around him, hugging him from behind.

"I don't want to go in just yet," she murmurs.

"I…uh," Duff struggles for words, knowing how easy it would be to guide her to his room. "Please, Hulda. I really must go."

"Ach. It is just a thought. Of course you must go." She releases him and steps away.

"Well, it is goodnight, then Hulda."

"Goodnight, Duff," she takes his hand and smiles hopefully. "We shall dance again, I hope."

Carrying his valise down to the lobby after taking breakfast in his room, Duff sees the stocky van Flek storming toward him. "Just a moment, Mr. Malone. I must have a word."

Gesturing to the sitting area, Duff sets his bag down and leads the way.

"I won't have it, Malone," he huffs. "I just won't have it! I'll contact your superiors."

"I can see you are unhappy," he responds carefully, his face calm. "But I don't quite follow. What's bothering you?"

"My wife, Malone. It's my wife and you. That's what bothers me."

"I still don't follow."

"I turn my back, and there you go sneaking off to the

dance floor with my wife. I heard all about it from Hoeffer's wife."

"I'll be happy to talk about dancing with Mrs. van Flek, but I know nothing about Mrs. Hoeffer. She wasn't with us."

"Watching through the door, she said. Watching you dance some romantic dance with my Hulda. *A right attractive couple*, she said."

Duff listens quietly, never losing eye contact. "So that's it. I can see the misunderstanding."

"Misunderstanding? You say sneaking off with my wife is a misunderstanding?" Van Flek's face is red with anger.

"Put that way, I do. Please, let's sit for a moment." They take chairs opposite each other.

"First of all, perhaps it was I who misunderstood." Duff's face is calm and his eyes direct.

"What do you mean? You know Hulda is my wife. Little to misunderstand there."

"It's my job to entertain our guests, Mr. van Flek. Aboard ship, I help people to meet other passengers, arrange special seating arrangements, that sort of thing."

"Yes. Yes. What's your point?"

"When husbands and wives are sitting near the dance floor, sometimes the men prefer not to dance. But their wives often do, and so I am encouraged to ask them to dance. This is part of their expectations, part of my training. Naturally, when I returned to the bar and saw your wife alone, I knew it wasn't right for her to sit unattended in a Nairobi dance-lounge. This is quite a fine hotel, but Nairobi is not a small town, and one occasionally runs into rough people."

"So you were looking after her?" Van Flek's face softens.

"Until you returned for her, that was my intention. But when I spoke with Mrs. van Flek, she said you wouldn't be back. Since she appeared to enjoy the dance band, I thought she might want a dance before adjourning for the night. This is what we did, and then I escorted her safely to your room. Had you been sitting there with her, this is what I would have done, with your permission, naturally. It's a courtesy to you and your wife. That really is the whole of it."

"I don't know what that girl was thinking, Malone. Syl Hoeffer and her stories. Never traveled before, that's her problem. Doesn't understand the world, you know?" Reaching out his hand, he says, "You seem a direct fellow. A man of your word. I apologize to you for the misunderstanding."

Shaking his hand and looking him in the eye, Duff replies, "As do I, Mr. van Flek."

Duff is able to avoid Hulda's advances aboard ship as they sail on to Egypt. Daytime is easiest, since the two couples spend most of their time together, and Duff can carefully move about the ship. Hulda and Syl usually adjourn to the upper deck sitting room at tea-time, and the men go to the bar. For five nights, he arranges most of his meals in his stateroom and absents himself from the evening festivities. Though he might avoid entanglement on the ship, the Cairo itinerary will prove more difficult. Thank God for Herim.

Ten years older than Duff, Herim is a *dragoman*, a freelance guide who works for all of the larger tour companies. Small and slim, with a trim dark beard framing a serious face, Herim works long hours, and never turns away an assignment. On their arrival in Cairo, he immediately senses Duff's dilemma with Mrs. van Flek, and diplomatically inserts himself as the group leader throughout their stay, something he would ordinarily share with a cruise director such as Duff.

The final day, when they motor out to Giza to see the pyramids and sphinx, they ride in two chauffered cars, their convertible roofs in place to protect them from the sun and the dust. Herim has asked Duff to accompany the Hoeffers, while he escorts the van Fleks on the short journey. As they ride, they pass through modest cement and stone homes, then traffic nearly stops as they make their way through a crowded outdoor marketplace. The smell of animals and dung combine with welcome aromas of cinnamon, cumin and onions grilling in nearby stalls. They find relief as they reach the Nile, traveling along the vast river for a few minutes before crossing over to open land and the short, unpaved road that leads to Giza.

Emerging to the bright sunlight, Duff brushes aside his hair and shields his eyes, then assists the Hoeffers out of their touring car. Hoeffer stretches his legs and looks around for the following car, as Syl clutches her large hat to keep it from blowing away in the crosscurrents. A short distance away stand six camels, stoic and disinterested, topped by worn saddles. The scruffy animals are loosely held by an old man in worn white robes and a filthy headdress, who is equally unfazed by their arrival. Another man, similarly dressed, waits in the distance next to what appears to be an old tripod and camera.

As the second car pulls up, Herim steps gracefully from the front seat and opens the passenger door for the van Fleks. Hulda emerges first, looking quickly over to her friends, then locates Duff with a smile. As van Flek hefts himself out, Herim gently takes their elbows and walks them to the camels. The camel man lowers one of his animals by motioning downward with a rough stick, then gestures at Hulda to place her foot into one of the waiting stirrups, and then seat herself sideways atop the large saddle. Climbing aboard, she tugs down on her long dress to cover her legs, then lets out a squeal as the camel lurches forward onto its front knees, rising abruptly on its long hind legs, then regaining its balance by straightening onto its forelegs. She seems both giddy and worried as she sits high in the air. "This creature is as tall as a giraffe," she cries, as the camel man moves to the next animal.

Soon the four of them are seated uncomfortably on the smelly creatures, and the owner leads them to a space not far from the photographer, just in front of massive broken stones, which look to be the damaged entrance to an ancient temple. Random, shoulder-high piles of huge hand-hewn stones form a rough barricade. In the distance, centering the background for the experienced eye of the old photographer, stands the solid peak of the Great Pyramid, intact and stunning; to its right the Great Sphinx, its regal countenance deformed from nearly three thousand years of wind and sand and harsh weather.

The camel man approaches Herim, who gently waves him away. He murmurs to Duff, "I already have too many portraits of myself and these ungrateful beasts. I certainly do not need another."

As the camel-man walks further along, no longer holding the camels' tethers, the animals follow diligently, obviously familiar with the well-worn path. Despite the blasé attitude of their desert guides, Duff is excited at the prospect of exploring these ancient structures. Who might have thought that he would actually visit the pyramids, the same ones he saw in his schoolbooks all those years ago?

As he and Herim follow behind, Duff asks, "Do you ever get tired of this? Of visiting this amazing place?"

"Never, my friend," he smiles. "The people I accompany may change, and the camels are a regular nuisance, but it is always breathtaking. These pyramids never change. They are now older than life, thousands of years, and the accomplishment of more than twenty years of unthinkable labor. For me, they remain larger than this world. I will bring you here to this spot for your own photo, on another day."

"Do not be so afraid, my friend," Herim chuckles in meticulous English, as they sit in the corner of a tiny, very clean café near the hotel, his voice low and soothing. "That is a woman, of course, but not such a worldly one."

"What difference does that make, Herim?" Duff winces, "Worldly or not, she is still a woman, and it isn't quite so easy as it seems. The trip to the pyramids was safe enough, but what do I do on the final leg of our cruise?"

"Are you not up to this simple challenge, young man?" Herim chides gently, as he rises and smiles, "Ah, here is Nafre, to dine with us. Welcome my dear. Please meet my friend Duff

Malone, about whom I have spoken. He is escorting the two couples from South Africa."

As tall as her husband, and dressed in the simple, tailored black uniform of a museum guide, Nafre's regal features are striking, with long black hair pulled back and secured by a dark comb. "Duff, of course. Herim has certainly told me of you. Welcome to Cairo."

"Thank you, Nafre. I'm honored to meet you."

"Excellent timing, my dear," Herim says as he nods to the nearby waiter. "Duff and I were just arriving at a point where your woman's wisdom could be quite valuable."

As the waiter appears with a glass of sweet tea, she responds, raising her eyebrows, "And are there times when our wisdom would not be valuable, may I ask?"

Herim smiles calmly, enjoying the good-natured exchange, "Always, my dear. It is always valuable. Please excuse my misstatement."

She strokes her husband's hand, "Well, then. What is the conversation?"

"Duff was just acknowledging that, while a rather attractive young lady is presenting herself for his personal attention, he wishes to avoid that attention while continuing his friendship with her and her husband, who are traveling with him to London."

"And do you find this woman attractive, Duff?" inquires Nafre, in a serious tone.

"A man would be quite cold not to find her attractive. That is certain," stammers Duff. "And I admire a woman with her spirit. I once cared for someone like her back when I was in school. At the same time, that isn't it. It simply isn't right. And I happen to like that husband of hers, van Flek. Hulda is very nice. I can see she is just naïve, and overwhelmed by romantic settings. I just want them all to enjoy their journey, and to let me get on with my responsibilities."

"This is good, I think," she continues. "Your admitted

attraction is honest, so you are not misleading yourself by sounding noble. Instead of hiding, then, I suggest that you find a time to tell her your feelings, such as they are, and your respect for her and her husband."

"I understand, I think," Duff responds, rubbing his forehead, as if to smooth away a headache. "I will speak with her when the opportunity arises."

The van Fleks and Hoeffers have returned to the hotel, tired and in a happy mood. It has been an hour since their dinner, and the men quickly excuse themselves to the bar. Syl goes to her room as usual, leaving Hulda alone in the spacious lobby, in a thin and revealing dress.

"Hulda, may I have word?"

"Of course, Mr. Duff," her face brightens. "Shall we have a drink?"

As the waiter carefully sets their drinks on the low table between them, Duff looks up to see that Hulda has tears in her eyes. "Hulda, what is it?"

"I'm so embarrassed, Duff. But I'm also disappointed in you. You avoided me all the way from Kenya, and the entire time here."

"I believe I can explain," he begins carefully. "We are both in a sensitive position."

"You feel this, too?" she exclaims, recovering her composure.

"Of course, I do feel something, Hulda," Duff assures, concerned that she is emotional, and that he may have admitted too much. "You are an attractive woman. We are in romantic places."

"But,"

"Ah, but there is a 'but', I'm afraid." He lifts his glass, and tips it toward her, "We know there is an attraction between us. But I've given it serious thought. I believe this is more important than just an attraction."

Hulda remains quiet, watching cautiously as Duff continues, "I believe we are good friends, would you agree?"

Nodding slowly, Hulda whispers, "I think I agree."

He looks directly into her brimming eyes. "Do you have many friends, Hulda? Close ones?"

She slowly shakes her head, still quiet.

"I believe that a good friend is much harder to find than a lover. Do you understand what I mean?"

She nods.

"I believe that I want to be your friend, Hulda. As much as I admire you, I want to be your friend, and not your lover."

Hulda reaches into her handbag and finds a kerchief to stem the tears.

Reaching over to touch her hand, Duff asks, " Do you think we can do this?"

"So what did she do?" Herim asks, as they meet for breakfast. "How did she take it?"

"She surprised me. First, I was surprised, and worried when she began to cry. I had no idea what she was expecting. Then, when I explained about true friendships, and how valuable they are, I think she was stunned. Then, thank goodness, she seemed relieved."

"You are thoughtful, Duff. And quite fortunate, I should say, that she recognized your honesty."

Over the remaining three days -- when the van Fleks and Hoeffers are dining at local restaurants or are at leisure in their hotel -- Herim and his driver take Duff to out-of-the way cafes or restaurants, for special meals and private conversations. Or they tour to a bazaar, where they examine fine jewelry of woven gold and tiny scarabs carved from ivory, and they haggle with accommodating vendors for mysterious vials that are said to contain the exotic essences of fragrant perfumes. Another day they visit the Museum of Egyptian Antiquities, and the new Coptic Museum a few kilometers away, then a return visit to Giza, where Duff is placed on a clean and healthy camel, for his own photo with the sphinx and pyramid in the background. Over time, they become fast friends. Herim and Nafre lead him to special places to visit and dine, establishments that are not well known to other travel companies, and he teaches Duff how to negotiate with local merchants.

Herim is deeply impressed with Duff's way of listening and observing, of putting people at ease, respecting them whether they are merchants, drivers, hotel managers or simple workers. Duff has quickly mastered the fundamentals of creating sightseeing programs in a crowded and challenging city such as Cairo. With his friend's experience in escorting visitors from many different cultures, Duff also comes to understand the nuances of guiding and informing without lecturing; of observing and adjusting his presentation, depending on the reactions of his listeners.

Herim also notices how Duff wants to please people, and from his occasional comments to Nafre and him, how shy Duff is about his relationships with women.

Chapter 3

He can't wait to strip off his clothes and stand beneath the outdoor shower after walking home on a hot Johannesburg day. Though Duff's rented room is just minutes from the Eloff Street office by tram, he prefers to have a fast-paced half-hour walk to ward off the effects of the heavy meals and regular cocktail parties that are part of his cruise escort job.

A scattering of envelopes lies beneath the mail slot, as he closes the heavy door to the rooming house. Separating his mail from all the others, he recognizes the distinctive black symbol of American Express on a blue airmail envelope postmarked "New York, NY, USA". The return address says American Express Headquarters. Duff wonders who might be writing to him and how they found him in far-away Johannesburg. When he reads the letter from Commodore Walter F. Patterson, he learns of Herim's influence:

20 November, 1921

Dear Mr. Malone,

You have been brought to our attention by my overseas agents in London. They were recently in Cairo for negotiations with the Egyptian government in connection with newly discovered tombs and artifacts, and they met with your friend and colleague, Mr. Abdul Herim.

Mr. Herim advised them of your extraordinary work with South African tour groups, and your unique professional skills. We are looking for young men with your expertise and character to join our company as cruise directors.

We are offering you a position in our New York office, to escort groups of elite clients on steamship tours to Latin America, Europe and the Mediterranean. We are prepared to offer you a reasonable salary, and want you to begin as soon as possible.

If you are interested, please advise by return post, and we will wire the necessary travel documents and tickets. Naturally, we will pay for your travel and expenses en route. I look forward to hearing from you right away.

Sincerely Yours,
Commodore Walter F. Patterson
Managing Director

Duff's answer is short, in the form of a question: *When do you want me there?*

New York City is more than the other side of the world; it's the opposite of everything he knows. Although both New York and Johannesburg were settled by the Dutch, the cities could not be more different, geographically, culturally and economically.

Johannesburg is a vast and dusty city, a mile high and far from the sea. It is pocked with hundred-foot hillocks of yellow residue from the gold mines, and populated with nearly two hundred thousand people, half of them Bantus, mostly Xhosa or Zulu. Most of the whites are rough miners and adventurers from all over Europe. New York is a compact seagoing city of over six million people, of many colors, cultures and languages. Its vast harbors link it to the rest of the world, and to inland American cities via the powerful Hudson River and overland railroads.

Johannesburg is a rough stew of modest houses interspersed with small farms, and a few grand estates. New York is a city of huge apartment buildings and row houses with stark exteriors, where poverty might be revealed by flapping laundry or broken windows; and wealth displayed by clean, orderly lobbies where doormen stand tall and orchestrate the movement of residents, workmen and delivery boys.

Located on the high veldt, or prairie, Johannesburg weather is moderate in winter months, hot and humid in summer.

Automobiles are limited to the very wealthy, so there are more horses and carts than motorcars. Most businesses are family owned retail shops or places where craftsmen work with wood or stone, with occasional *apteeks*, or pharmacies. Mine owners mingle downtown near the American Express office, with bankers and visiting traders for gold and valuable jewels. Nearby farmers bring daily produce into the city, for sale in food stalls and meat markets. Bars and restaurants are available, but plain. And surrounding the ruling white businesses are thousands of Bantus performing the labor, as they watch and learn. Johannesburg is nothing like New York City.

February in New York is freezing, and when his ship lands Duff can see his breath as he steps outside the warmth of his stateroom. Looking beyond the pier, he sees that the streets are deep in snow. He disembarks into the covered pier and locates his steamer trunk and hand luggage, but he sees no waiting taxis or trams. Nor is there any sign of the company's representative. He hopes the staff has gotten through in this weather, or that his British pounds will be accepted by a local lorry driver. He is glad he changed currency from South African pounds during his London stopover.

"There you are, Mr. Malone." A large young man approaches, in a gray overcoat and dark hat, and two scarves wrapped over his chin. His lips are not visible, but Duff sees part of a mustache and hears a muffled tenor voice.

"Glad to see you," he responds. "I'm Duff Malone. What do I call you?"

"Ah, I'm sorry Mr. Malone. I should have introduced myself. I'm Charlie Kline, from American Express." The large man hefts the trunk and suggests, "If you will take one end, I'll take the other, along with these suitcases. You take the small valise, and we'll be off."

"Don't the porters object?"

"Not enough porters today, I'm afraid. Most of them

couldn't get to work in this weather. Welcome to New York!"

"Welcome, indeed!" Duff hoists his end of the trunk and grabs two suitcases. "You just take that one. How far are we going?"

"Just over there. See that car with the steam coming from the back?"

As the two men slog through the snow and reach the car, Kline opens the back door and slides the large trunk inside. "If you can hold one suitcase, I think I can jam the other bags in the back. You're booked into the Cosmopolitan."

Once again, Duff pulls the light blue envelope from his jacket pocket. It is badly worn from rereading during the long journey. 25 Broadway, it says, so it must be nearby. He's proud of the return address, *American Express Worldwide Headquarters.* Duff knows this is an important day, and he didn't come all this way to fail.

As he makes his way along the icy sidewalks, he is stunned by the skyscrapers and massive office buildings, side by side, block after block. *There's the Cunard Building with the famous lobby!* Then he steadies his back against a pillar so he can look up toward the top of the Standard Oil Building. Even the smaller structures are much larger than the biggest ones in Johannesburg. It feels like London, but looks taller and brighter. Even this early in the day, the city hums with the activity of masses of people. You don't see them all, but you know they are there, on the telephone, pounding away on typewriters, poring over books and lists and timetables. He can't wait to get started.

During his first days at work, he quickly memorizes the vast American Express network around the globe, recognizing most of the cities but none of the managers. Their reach into Asia, Africa and Latin America is unmatched by other travel companies, even Thomas Cook and Sons.

Duff is excited to learn that the company has stationed him on their featured cruises, including two trans-Atlantic crossings during the next six months. He will assist a veteran cruise man named Werner Bergen.

These first months in America are exhilarating and only mildly confusing, and Duff is enjoying his new life. Charlie Kline, the associate who picked him up at the terminal, recently introduced him to the fascinating American game of baseball. They sat together one sunny and memorable day in Yankee Stadium, eating American hot dogs and watching in amazement as a good-natured player called Babe hit the ball high over the center field fence, for what everyone around them proclaimed to be his thirtieth home-run. They say he is the greatest hitter in the game.

Duff is attracted far more to a young player named Lou Gehrig, a first baseman. Duff read in the New York Times that he had hit two long home-runs in one game early in the season. Gehrig's humility epitomizes the things Duff admires about America. The son of German immigrants, the first baseman seems honest and hard-working, never taking a day off for rest during the grueling season. Duff was initially distracted by the use of leather gloves by the fielders. As a cricket-man he feels that the large, stuffed glove must be quite restrictive. Sitting in the bleachers with thousands of vocal fans, he is stimulated to be around sports again.

In 1924, Duff escorts trans-Atlantic crossings to Dover and Marseilles, and makes his first sailing to Rio de Janeiro, where he met Ruth and Anna.

"What will you do when you graduate?" Anna asks her friend, as they lie on their cots in the darkness, eyes searching through the open window, hoping to glimpse a shooting star. These were favorite times for the girls, best friends since they met at Bryn Mawr early in their freshman year. Ruth had joined Anna and her parents at the cottage for three straight summers. This was where Anna had spent every vacation as she was growing up, and Ruth immediately sensed her friend's comfort here, her sense of belonging.

"An attorney, of course, like my father," she giggles. "He wouldn't want any other career for his only son!"

"Oh Ruth. Don't tease yourself like that," laughing gently. "You're his only child. His only daughter!"

"But he truly wanted a son. He once told me so. So now I'm a better tennis player and baseball tosser than he is. One day I will be a better attorney, too."

"Will they allow a girl into law school?"

"Penn Law will. It's dad's alma mater, and they will find a way, even if I have to study with a private tutor. Besides, I plan to be a swimmer there, too. I'm faster than most of the men."

"I love our summers here at the lake," Anna could almost hear Ruth smiling her brilliant smile. She envied her full lips and confident ways. She worried that she herself was too inward, too shy and too slim to be strong enough for a girl like Ruth.

"I do, too, Anna. It is so peaceful. And just smell the dark fragrance of the forest. This place is so much like you, and it suits me greatly."

*Nine years later, in 1925, Ruth treated them both to a luxurious cruise aboard the famed "*Italia *to Rio" from New York to South America. Anna was able to switch enough days with her friends at the New York University library, to have four weeks off of work. It would take forever to repay them. Ruth advised her clients not to do anything rash for at least a month, then she would be back to help them untangle any legal problems. Specializing in detailed contracts between construction companies and the banks that provided financing, she knew her regular clients would get along without her for at least this long. The girls knew that their cats were in good hands with the neighbors below, and that the two cagey felines would even gain some weight while they were away.*

The Italia *was highly recommended by their travel planner, who told them that their cruise director would be a quiet and handsome South African, who was "perfect for two sisters traveling together!" Though they had no romantic attraction to men, the girls decided it would be wise to rely on an experienced cruise expert, who might enjoy the friendship of two sisters who love to dance!*

Their experience on the Italia *was extraordinary. It was smooth sailing the entire trip, and the food and comforts were delightful. Not only was the South African an accomplished dancer, but he was a charming and interesting man, who exclaimed that he spent a great deal of time at the University Library, and in future he would keep an eye out for Anna. Over dinner, Anna and Duff spent hours discussing T. S. Eliot, Somerset Maugham and Virginia Woolf. Afterward, Ruth and Duff enjoyed the dance band, which specialized in smooth versions of "Avalon" and "I'll See You In My Dreams". She understood when Duff preferred to sit-out the faster numbers. Anna and Duff agreed that Proust was daunting, and both swore they planned to read him one day. They split on Scott Fitzgerald, and never could reach a conclusion on Joyce's newest challenge, "Ulysses".*

When Ruth and Anna confided that they were not sisters, and that they considered this a sort of overdue honeymoon, Duff ordered the best champagne and insisted that they sign-on for another of his cruises.

Chapter 4

The wild and woozy Twenties are filled with flappers, fast cars, hot jazz, and jargon like "bee's knees", "bootleg" and "bushwa". Prohibition is the law, and everyone ignores it. Cops and criminals belly up to the same private bars as bankers, brokers and lawyers.

Reason is ignored, too, as uninformed investors jump into the glorious money game, joining the smart set, who are forever in the know. They are certain that stocks will always go up, because every American wants one of these new electric toasters and refrigerators and coffee makers. Few know about the swindlers and syndicates who manipulate the financial numbers, hiding risky loans in family trusts.

Professors from Princeton and Yale are in high demand, providing insider's advice for wealthy cronies who move and manage the markets. All the smart ones are in, because the markets will never stop rising. For twenty per cent down, even the office boys and girls are investors.

This is a time of action, and of conflicting feelings. The Great War was won and business is booming. Cars are fast and plentiful, women have been freed from their Victorian restrictions, and styles are exploding. Modern girls wear anything from short skirts and garter-flasks, to trousers and manly jackets made from sexy silks and linens that emphasize sheer undergarments, if any are worn at all.

Bobbed hair and cloche hats are all the rage. Men sport padded shoulders on their snazzy suits, with braces to hold up their trousers and sharp neckties to make a bold statement. Tailored jackets leave room for elegant flasks of silver and pewter, neatly tucked away. No-one worries about tomorrow, in this frantic, manic, dynamic time.

Speakeasies and jazz clubs provide the daring places and

wild music that people seem to crave. Despite prohibition, for every thriving speakeasy there are cops or politicians who turn their heads away, with eager money-hands stuck out behind them, waiting for the scratch.

Some have invested all they own in the ballooning stock market, then they borrow even more for another thousand shares. Others worry that the balloon could burst, that things might be getting out of hand, and that hard work and discipline never hurt anyone. Newspapers and newly popular radio stations give conflicting information, and these confusing reports serve to heighten the excitement and the chaos.

Still a loner who prefers an independent path, Malone feels like an outsider in New York. For the past seven years he has sailed the world, serving elite travelers and learning from them. His clients seldom become personal friends, though many are friendly acquaintances who invite him to stop by if he is ever near Stockholm, or Oxford or Buenos Aires.

His few close friends are within the travel industry. Even with them he seems to maintain a distance, as if he senses that the relationships might not last. Most are with American Express -- other cruise directors and office people -- or they manage hotels and restaurants on his stopovers in places like Brussels or London or Valparaiso.

He often spends holidays alone. If he is overseas during Christmas or Easter, the ship's captain or a hotel's general manager will invariably invite him to join him for a special meal aboard ship or in the hotel. He often meets women, but most of them are clients and he is careful not to get involved.

Early in 1926, Duff escorts two important groups. First, fifty business executives on the refurbished *Mauretania*; then an elite group of educators and socialites aboard the *Bremen.* These are elegant ships, considered the finest in the world, filled with palatial furnishings and priceless artwork, and featuring finest European dining and vintage wines. It was when the *Bremen* reached Marseilles that Duff took three days off to explore the countryside, ending up in Arles. This is where he happened upon Justine, and that unusual man, Count Giovanni Sorvini.

It was a dusty day on the shores of Lake Como when Antonino Scarpini was born. A midwife came across the lake from Varenna to assist his mother, Lena, who was just fifteen years older than the newborn baby. It was a painful pregnancy for the frail girl, and when she died the midwife handed Antonino to his grandmother, Adelina. Just thirty-three herself, she was a busy hostess in the main dining room at the Grand Hotel. Rushing to get back to work for the busy dinner service, where wealthy patrons often left sizable gratuities for her, and the men occasionally suggested places where they might meet later on, Adelina handed the baby to her mother, Rosalina, to look after.

A great-grandmother at fifty-two, Rosalina loved the baby right away, and a bond was formed that helped Antonino to survive and grow into a wiry and determined ten-year-old. Antonino was somber and observant at Rosalina's funeral mass, a corner of his mouth twitching as the prayers were said. Then he slipped away and joined his fifteen-year-old friend, Giussepe, both of them living in an abandoned storage building on the outskirts of Bellagio.

By the time he arrived in Lugano, he called himself Rico and said he was a chef. Now nineteen, he had worked aboard the ferries that shuttled people from Bellagio to Varenna, Cernobbio and Como. He washed dishes and chopped vegetables, and kept a close eye on the main cuoco, *so he felt no shame in proclaiming to the owner of the little cafe at Lake Lugano, that he was qualified for the chef's position. He was a taut, energetic boy, far from handsome, and toughened by his years of hard work.*

When they hired him to assist an older Swiss who had retired from his own small inn, Rico surprised them with his facility in preparing vegetables with a french cut, and trimming veal and chicken, preserving the scraps for gravies and stews. He quickly learned to prepare sauces, with the sticky bits from grilled meats, adding inexpensive white wine and chicken stock, and dabs of butter and garlic to enrich the flavors.

From Lugano, Rico found his way to Milan, then on to Florence. Now in his twenties, he was an accomplished chef, slim, with smooth black hair and an occasional smile that softened his pocked face, and the slight twitch when he was agitated. When the owner of Mandolino, a popular restaurant near Palazzo Vecchio, sampled his roasted meats and his simple preparations of vegetables and pastas, with just the right touch of herbs, he brought Rico to Florence and paid him frugally.

Rico left for New York in August of 1921, just thirty years old, working his way across the Atlantic as the chief cook on a tramp steamer. His years in Lugano and Florence had exposed him to different languages and inflections, including shards of English. He practiced his English with some of the veteran sailors who gathered in the galley, trading stories with Rico before and after standing their overnight watches, grateful for his hot coffee with warm milk, and his fragrant, cinnamon-laced pastries.

He loved working at night when the captain slept, allowing time for the crew members to relax with him and share their knowledge of America. They told him about opportunities for restaurant work in New Jersey, in a city named Newark. "Not New York, but New-Ark" they told him. Seventh Avenue was where Italians went to live, and there were dozens of Italian restaurants. Though they were mostly owned by Sicilians, his way with inflections would likely make him acceptable.

The papers he bought in Florence were in the name of Giovanni Sorvini, and he liked the new name "Gio", because it set him apart, since everyone in America seemed to call these immigrants "Tony". Gio began as a janitor, cleaning the restaurant late at night, a schedule which closely matched his shipboard routine. Sometimes Regazzo, the owner, would ask him to help the chef in the morning, when cleanup was done. When he recognized Gio's cooking skills, Regazzo eagerly accepted his suggestion to open the kitchen for him during the night, so Gio could prepare slow-roasted meats and sauces that could be added to the lunch menu.

Soon, Regazzo found that Gio's creations were drawing businessmen from New York, and the name Sorvini became recognized throughout the Italian section of Newark. When Regazzo proposed to enlarge the dining area and make Gio a partner, the new restaurant emerged as Rosalina's, named for his great-grandmother.

Arnaud's touring car is already running and the roof is opened, so Duff hops onto the running board and tumbles backward over the rear door, piling artfully into the cushy back seat, trying not to land on top of Justine. The two of them giggle while Arnaud, still wearing his apron, and dark-suited Gio contrive to navigate the powerful automobile onto the roadway. Two bottles of grenache with lunch, and a chilled glass or two of champagne with dessert, have set a jolly tone for these four new friends. Fortunately, there is little traffic at this time of the afternoon.

"How far to the farm?" Gio asks, as Arnaud releases the clutch and chugs into motion, "and who are these people, may I ask?"

"Of course you may ask, but you must trust me, my friend. I promise you will not be disappointed."

Justine draws Duff closer, clasping her blue straw hat with her left hand, protecting against the breeze. Three hours ago none of them had met, and here they are motoring off to visit Arnaud's cousin in the outskirts of Arles. Arnaud left his bistro in his wife's care, insisting that they see Clément's vineyard before dark. In fact, why not bring a leg of lamb to roast on the spit while they view the fields? He will prepare dinner while Clément shows them around.

Filled with tipsy appreciation for their new friendship, they accepted his generosity and are off on an adventure. As they ride along, the quiet and the lull of the road creates a mellowness. Duff gently removes Justine's hat and places it on his knee, safe from the breeze. Her flowing hair is fragrant and soft, as he gently kisses the top of her head, realizing how forward this must seem. She snuggles-in and murmurs something he cannot hear, and he welcomes the warmth of her soft body. Soon she is puffing quietly in gentle sleep, as they leave the city and enter fecund and peaceful farmlands.

Arnaud makes a gentle right turn as they approach Le Baux, onto a wide dirt road. He admires the long row of pink and peach roses, and then the scent of lavender from fragrant fields of grey, green and purple. Justine wakens and wrinkles her nose in appreciation of these new aromas, as she and Duff exchange silent smiles. Sitting up and stretching her long arms, she settles back against him, opens her brown eyes and proclaims, "I must find a toilette, if you would be so kind, Msr. Arnaud."

Chuckling to himself, "Of course, *mamselle*, I see one just ahead." Pointing, "See that olive grove on the right? Or there are some oaks just beyond."

"The olives, I should think," Justine responds in a serious voice, then laughs again. "There is the matter of time, you see."

"Ah, I do see *mamselle*. The olives it will be."

Arnaud pulls to the side nearest the trees. Justine opens the door and steps out with dignity, then she dashes toward the trees, her elegant high shoes flitting over the rocky soil, as the men walk across the road to admire distant hills.

Soon Justine is back in the car and they take in the beauty around them. "If you look there," Arnaud points with his left hand toward a structure just visible beyond more orderly rows of lavender. "Just beyond the grapes. That is Clément's farm. We shall be there in a few minutes."

He drives past the house and toward the faded red barn. As he pulls up, a stout man in dark work pants and green plaid shirt steps from inside the structure, looking confused as he wipes his hands on his thighs. "Arnaud. A nice surprise. What brings you here today? It's a work day for you"

"My friends, Clément. Come, meet my new friends." He walks over and encases Clément in a powerful hug. "I brought a piece of lamb for your spit, if Marina can spare some potatoes and carrots, and a bit of garlic and thyme. Some olive oil, perhaps."

Clément laughs and waves the passengers over for their own hugs, "Come! Introduce yourselves, and we will go and find Marina."

A simple dinner turned into a noisy evening with dozens of neighbors and friends. Impromptu music, and many bottles of rich, red wine, now standing empty on the different tables. After hugs and multiple kisses, everyone has said their good-byes and left for home.

And they must go soon, he and Arnaud and Gio and lovely Justine. Duff is full and content, and he's had just enough wine. He isn't drunk, despite all the wine. Instead, a subtle anticipation sharpens his senses, a feeling of *rightness*. It's not simply Justine. This would be easy to explain. She's a beautiful, magical woman. It's much more. The time and the place, the new friends. And the glow of an unexpected moment.

He stands out near the fire pit and peers at his pocket-watch. It's after ten and the sensuous aromas of roasted lamb and rosemary remain, mingled with sweet scents from nearby gardens. *She went inside to help Marina with the washing up. But where are Arnaud and Gio? We must be going.* Duff knows that she must be back at her hotel for an afternoon train to Paris. His own train is not until evening, down to Marseilles.

"There you are, Duff. Out here with all the bottles." Justine sounds weary, but she is radiant in the light of the old railroad lamp that she carries. "Shall we walk a bit? It's a beautiful evening, and we'll be able to see with this."

Preferring her company and happy to delay the ride back to Arles, Duff takes the lamp and offers his hand. She appears to know where she is going, leading him through a little garden near the back of the house. "Careful. Don't step on the plants."

"Aren't we waiting for Arnaud, to get back to Arles?"

"Arnaud is snoring soundly in one of the guest bedrooms, so we won't be driving back tonight. That's why I have the lamp." He hears her giggle, "We need to go this way."

Enjoying the warm night and Justine's soft hand, Duff asks, "But what about Gio? He was adamant about visiting another restaurant tomorrow morning."

"Let's not worry about our friend Gio, either." She moves his arm up around her shoulder as they walk on. "He is also snoring. He's in another guest room."

"And what about us? Where will we snore tonight?"

Soft laughter, "Just follow me, Duff. I spoke with Marina, and she has put us into the guest house down the way."

Stopping and turning to face her. "You are a mind-reader."

Justine turns and places her arms around Duff's neck, lifting herself up close to his lips. "I believe that Marina is the mind-reader. I hope you don't mind." Releasing his neck and taking his hand again, Justine continues to a door, which opens with the turn of a handle.

Duff covers his eyes from the bright sun, careful not to wake her. Exhausted and energized, he marvels at this incredible woman. Quiet on the surface, but so fierce and giving beneath. He turns to admire her as she rests. But she's gone. The bed is empty and her clothes are missing. Quickly, he locates his trousers and pocket-watch on a nearby chair. Nearly six o'clock. Where would she go?

"Duff, my friend," Gio's voice outside the cottage. "Are you sleeping the day away?"

"I'm awake, Gio. I'll be right out." he slips his pants and socks on, and pulls his shirt over his head. Then splashes water from the bowl on the dresser. Then he sees the small note: "A perfect moment. You are a gentle and loving man. *Au revoir cheri,* Justine."

Chapter 5

New York, September 10, 1929

Something is not quite right, thinks Malone, as he makes his way through the elegant corridors of American Express headquarters, past open doors with executive names embossed on shined brass plates, finally arriving at the Executive Office. It's unusual for Commodore Patterson to send for him. He has no idea what Patterson thinks of his work, and wonders if he may be in for a dressing-down. He hasn't felt this uncomfortable since he was a schoolboy, the first time he was called-in by coach Scott after losing the ball in a scrum.

Though they have exchanged casual conversation a few times, Malone doesn't know the Commodore on a personal level. Only that he is a retired navy man and was quite a hero in the Great War, and everyone is aware of his continued connections to the government. He seems cordial and businesslike with people, but like a skilled negotiator, he seldom shares all that he knows.

"Sit down, Duff," the shorter Patterson gestures toward two chairs overlooking Broadway, and his pink face is taut. "Glad you could join me."

"A pleasure, sir." Sitting erect at the front of the chair, Malone's neck is tense, and he feels a drop of sweat rolling down his back.

"Call me Walt, son. First off, let me thank you for your careful treatment of my friend, Francis Farley."

"Farley? The wonderful chap at Global Bank? The pleasure was mine, I would say." The tension begins to leave his neck and shoulders.

"I won't go into detail, but he contacted me not long ago, to thank me. His wife is no longer an issue, and he'll continue doing business with us."

"Well, that's good news. But you look serious, Walt. That can't be all of it."

"Is it that obvious?" He smiles, "Sorry Duff, there is something else, and I need to ask for your help. You wouldn't be aware just yet. We've been behind closed doors for the past three days, rearranging plans for a major program. You may have heard of it around the office. It's that millionaires cruise."

"Surely. We all know about it. The Matson liner, *Malolo*. It departs later this month. Washburn and the Los Angeles people are assigned, are they not?"

"They were. And that's one of the recent changes." Patterson stands and walks to his desk, retrieving a folder. "Washburn is a good man, but we need a different approach now, because there are several pieces to this puzzle. Here is the latest file on the trip. Take a close look tonight, and ask me any questions. But do it soon. This cruise is a big investment on our part, and it's beginning to unravel a bit."

"Word is, it's sold out," Malone responds, raising his eyebrows. "I recognize some of the names from my past assignments."

"The cruise will be sold out, of course. But some of our top clients have dropped out, and we've added from the waiting list."

"Is there a cause for the cancellations?"

The Commodore slowly pushes himself up and walks gingerly to the window, showing signs of aging joints, and looks out, gathering himself. Finally, he turns, "I don't know any other way to say it. We're going to be in the shit very soon!" Returning to his chair, he sits again and leans toward Duff, clear-eyed and serious. "I mean the whole economy. Wall Street is nervous, and some of our clients, insiders, have withdrawn from the cruise. They're saying that sixty days is simply too long a voyage right now. They can't be away from their investments and businesses for that amount of time. Two weeks may be too long."

"But the stock market is soaring! Everyone I know has invested, and is looking to buy more."

"That's the public, Duff. They hear what they want to hear. But the signs are ominous. Discipline and good judgment were gone months ago. Most of this was good for our business, of course. Money to spend. Jazz music and nightclubs, the need to get away and see the world. The new ships get faster, more elegant and comfortable. It's our job to help people to enjoy them."

"But you're serious?"

"Dead serious. From our contacts in Washington, and confirmed here in Manhattan. Stocks are likely to drop, and when they do, banks are next. That's why some of our clients have dropped out. That brings us back to your cruise. The sailing is set. We just need to prepare ourselves for the worst. Our passengers will demand information, and they deserve help, whatever that might be. We don't know when it will hit, or what it might look like. That's where you come in. People know they can trust you. I've watched your progress, and seen you with clients at receptions. You're quiet and reserved, but passionate about your work. And you listen. Everyone sees that. You're a good fit for this group. Whatever happens while the *Malolo* is at sea, we need a calming influence out there, someone who can make decisions without startling our passengers -- and without needing close advice from headquarters. That's you."

"I'm flattered, sir, and surprised. But I have reservations."

"Tell me."

"I've never worked in the Pacific, for one. Never even been out there. How will I handle the shore excursions without the personal contacts and local knowledge?"

"We considered this. You know Werner Bergen?"

"Bergen? Of course. He's a genius."

"He'll join you when you reach Honolulu. He's been there finalizing all the downline shore excursions, and he will brief you before each port of call. You provide the client knowledge and relationships, while Bergen provides the on-shore knowledge and contacts."

"So he creates the programs, and I carry them out? It sounds workable. What about communications? I assume you will want me to stay in direct contact with you."

"I'll get weekly updates via the west coast office. Anything more urgent you will communicate directly to me. Your only shipboard communications will be via RCA radiograms. And on shore via long distance telephone. But the ship's radio officer must not know the full story. He'll see every message and we know he'll talk to the other officers, who talk to all the passengers. Your day-to-day contact will come through Los Angeles. You remember Monte Roberts?"

"LA Chief? I remember him. Monte and I worked a Mediterranean cruise together."

"Roberts will provide periodic updates for you, from newspaper headlines that seem appropriate to help camouflage our information. He'll send the latest stock markets, theater, sports. We don't want to appear nervous about the market. You can read the numbers and decide what to tell our passengers. Some of it may be too disturbing to share. But always keep in mind, these clients are not like ordinary people."

"Far from ordinary. Will they also use the radiograms to receive or send information?"

"In a very limited way. It's ship's policy that they are to be used for emergencies, and for our internal operating information. We know that some of the steamship companies are trying to install ticker tapes aboard their vessels, but that is some time away. For now, the radiograms are the fastest method, but we need to limit them and keep them brief. When you reach port, Roberts will expect your telephone calls when possible. You will update our passengers in the usual way, through the daily briefing sheets that you duplicate aboard ship."

"So cooperation from the captain and ship's radio officer is paramount."

"It is, but deal with them carefully. We don't want them to inadvertently share information that might panic people. Then there is the frustration-level. Our clients are mainly investors or bankers, accustomed to picking up the telephone and getting immediate answers. You will need to anticipate their frustrations about the lack of phones, radio and newspapers, and help them to be patient. At the same time, you will need to have the latest facts at your disposal, and communicate them calmly, and with good judgment. Not all the news is likely to be good."

"This is a lot to digest, Walt, considering how high the market is flying. Everything we read is about easy money, shiny new cars, and good times. Everywhere, we see dancing, speakeasies and wild music."

"I agree, Duff. I read the news and see the reckless mood of the people, and I'm damned disappointed. Exaggerations from financial types, then conflicting assurances from politicians! It's dangerous. They are setting this country up for real trouble, with lies or partial truths. Insiders tell us the production figures are down lately, to a startling degree. So is employment. Corporate executives we talk to are increasingly cautious about earnings. Our overseas offices hear similar rumblings from their governments. England, France, Spain."

"And if we know this inside information, why don't our wealthy passengers know it, as well?"

"That's the odd part of it, Duff. Many people don't want to believe what they hear. I mentioned that some of our guests withdrew. But others, the remaining passengers, have done so well with their investments, that they haven't listened, or choose not to believe it."

"I accept your information, of course, but there'll be hell to pay when the market does come down."

"It's unpleasant, but there it is, son. There is one last item. It's another confidential one, just the two of us. It involves a personal friend of mine, and it is important for you as well."

"I'm ready."

"When you reach Pago Pago, believe it or not, there is a friend who lives there much of the year. A local, you might say. He will meet you in the village bar -- there is only one in Pago. I want you to listen to his information, and take it very seriously. He's an aeronautics man, an inventor of sorts, name of Martin Bradley. His nickname is 'Wings'. When you hear what he has to tell you, I want you to think very carefully about your career."

"My career?" The tightness creeps back to his neck and shoulders.

"That's right, son. It shouldn't worry you. In fact, it could be quite exciting," he pauses and gazes out into the winter sky. "I wish I were fifteen years younger, ten even. I would volunteer to go over and meet with old Wings myself."

As he walks to the door, he smiles and extends his hand, resting his left one on Duff's shoulder, in a fatherly way. "You will do just fine, Duff."

Walking slowly down the long corridor, Malone's mind is racing.

CHAPTER 6

New York City, September 13, 1929

Malone quickly scans through a *Herald-Tribune* article about the new high-speed tickers at the New York Stock Exchange. Just last week the Dow-Jones reached an all-time high at 381. Today's market is down to 366, about four percent below. Malone wonders what people will do if the bubble really bursts.

Once again, he pulls out the instructions to make absolutely sure he doesn't forget something important.

5PM, booked on the *Twentieth Century Limited* from Grand Central Station, bound for Chicago, then transfer to the *Santa Fe Chief* to San Francisco on the following day. On arrival, transfer to the Hotel Mark Hopkins before joining Matson's SS *Malolo* two days later.

The *Malolo* sails on September 22 for a sixty-day Pacific cruise, returning to San Francisco on November 20. This special voyage is referred to as "The Millionaires Cruise", because of the exclusive group of participants, who are all certified millionaires.

While the ship's capacity normally exceeds 600 people, the *Malolo* will restrict capacity to only 325 passengers, affording maximum comfort and the finest possible services for each individual. Twenty of these special guests are under the special care of American Express, and you, as cruise director.

Clients will receive the highest level of service, and you are there to ensure total satisfaction. The 325-person limit assures the type of privacy and special services that such travelers have every right to expect."

Thank God for Werner Bergen, the red-headed wonder, Malone says to himself. *He had better be in Honolulu when we get there.* For now, Malone's main concern is the stock market.

How quickly will he receive information and pass it along to the passengers, and how much will it fluctuate? The Commodore made it quite clear, he is to reassure their passengers, make everyone aboard feel comfortable and special. At the same time, he must update them on what's happening in America and try to hold their frustrations down. And his job is on the line.

Men in pale linen suits stroll by in the large terminus, some with arms linked to glamorous women in thin silk dresses. Others walk swiftly past, obviously lone businessmen with newspapers and briefcases in hand for the overnight rail trip to Chicago. The weather is hot and humid in these latter days of September.

Malone carries a tan suit jacket over his arm, following a negro in a red coat who struggles with his luggage. Despite the stocky porter's obvious strength, he grimaces as he hoists the massive trunk onto the luggage cart, followed by two leather suitcases, then wheels them diligently down to the departure track.

"I'll need that one in my compartment, if you please," directs Malone, pointing out the smaller suitcase, and handing him a five dollar bill.

"Thank you kindly," responds the porter, eyebrows raised appreciatively. "Your car is number twenty-nine, just there on the end." He points to the rounded pullman car.

"Thanks for taking care with that trunk," adds Malone. "It contains everything I own."

Stepping over the portable step, directly onto the elevated stairs, he quickly boards his car. Then he turns down a narrow corridor to locate the correct door. Knocking once, out of habit, he pushes the door and enters. He's impressed with the large suite, complete with a leather-covered swivel chair positioned next to the spacious viewing window, and a fold-out bed, tucked neatly into casings at the end of the compartment.

Spying a fruit basket, he reads the card. *'Bon Voyage Duff! Wishing you a successful journey. Cheers! The Commodore'*

That's a bit odd. Malone senses the train losing speed shortly after leaving Grand Central. A knock and a calming voice outside his door, "Just a scheduled re-coupling, sir. Nothing to worry about."

As he opens it, a paunchy man in his dark conductor's uniform smiles and continues a well-rehearsed description, as he removes his black cap and wipes his forehead with his kerchief, "The big engine can't come into the terminal, so they ferry us out with a smaller one, just like a tugboat, and then disconnect and hook-up to the steam engine out here at Harmon. Now it's a sixteen-hour run to Chicago. You should be quite comfortable." He braces as the train moves again. "There, we're already underway." Then he sways down the corridor, nimbly adjusting his step, as a sailor does in rough seas.

Sitting back as they pick up speed, Malone is stunned as he watches the dark golds and flaming crimsons of the passing terrain, hungry to capture as much as he can with the remaining hour or so of daylight. *How could there be so many trees, and such rich colors?*

The rolling motion has become smooth and comfortable, and his ears easily adjust to the humming wheels. He's never been west of New York City, so every tree and hillock is a fresh look at America. As they roll north alongside the massive river, he sees grasslands and miles of lush forests. He is surprised to see such rugged and wild terrain so near to the big city.

Removing his jacket and leaving it on the chair, he decides to explore the train. Entering what must be a viewing car, he sees the friendly conductor. "What river is this, may I ask?"

Looking up, he pulls a printed folder from his jacket and hands it to Malone. "It's the Hudson, and it's pretty amazing. Three miles wide in some places. Seems like an ocean, with large boats and small ships plying their trade. Just keep your eyes peeled and you'll see colors like nowhere in the world, and some fabulous mansions. This is the land of the extremely wealthy. There's a bit of history there in the flyer. And I'll call out at West Point, the famous military academy."

Malone shields his eyes against the reflections on the window, to get a better view of the massive stone cliffs along the western shore, *The Palisades,* they are called in the brochure. Taking a wide chair, he remains at the window, watching intently as they glide past thick forests, interrupted occasionally by beautifully maintained estates. *I can see why they choose this valley,* Malone marvels.

From Chicago, the muted landscape unfolds like the pages in an atlas. For hours, they pass through flat farmlands of Iowa and Nebraska, and cities with names like Cedar Rapids and Omaha and Lincoln. The fields are dry and shorn of their spent crops, but Malone can sense the millions of acres of fertile land that helps to feed this growing country. The look and feel reminds him of farms in the Transvaal and the Orange Free State, only ten times bigger. South Africa isn't small -- twice as large as France -- and it contains multiple geographic and temperate zones. But this America, with its broad plains, high desert lands and massive mountain ranges, it's endless.

Malone remains in his seat for hours, watching through the observation window. He is intrigued at the hundreds of tiny towns along the route, where youngsters wave from schoolyards and older people from shops and automobiles, grinning at the passengers and the engineer, as the long train passes swiftly through. And he marvels at the endless, empty flatlands that soon lull him into a gentle sleep.

Light pressure in his ears wakes him, and he is startled by the tracks that are visible far ahead, snaking up the steep mountain and disappearing into dense forests. As they climb higher, he gasps, looking down into a steep chasm, toward rough ridges and overhangs. They remind him of the Drakensburg Mountains east of Johannesburg, but these frightening drops are deeper and darker, with wild rivers raging far below.

How could there be such dense forests? Colorado, Utah, Nevada, California. Endless blue-green layers of trees, interrupted by sparkling lakes and topped by jagged mountain peaks, with snow atop the very highest. Eerie gaps appear, charred clearings where lightning-fires must have burned away hundreds, perhaps thousands of years of cones and needles, along with decayed pines and firs. As a seagoing man, he compares this deep, rolling mass of forests to the ocean, extending further than the eye can see, making a human feel insignificant.

Reluctantly, Malone opens his briefcase to prepare for the assignment. There is a file for each passenger, with multiple fact-sheets about the ports of call. He is excited to learn more about Japan and China, two countries that seem so foreign. He has absolutely no vision of what cities like Yokohama and Shanghai might look like. Are there proper houses or tiny structures with sliding paper screens, like those he has read about in *The Mikado*? He has visited the mud huts that Zulus live in not far from Johannesburg. Might the Chinese live this way in their poor country towns? As for Hawaii and Pago Pago, he imagines that they are quiet, barely populated tropical islands, as in the Robinson Crusoe story or the paintings of Paul Gauguin that he has seen in books.

And what of the ship?

Malolo is Matson's newest vessel, considered the fastest and most glamorous of any ship ever built. All first class sleeping accommodations have private baths and nearly all are outside staterooms. There are three electric elevators to carry passengers to elegant dining rooms and lounges. The promenade and sunning areas are spacious and comfortable, and the ship boasts an indoor swimming pool that is the talk of the industry.

There are no ordinary staterooms on the *Malolo,* so Malone's millionaires will have large and richly appointed accommodations. Matson blocked thirteen suites for American Express, providing first-access to these special spaces. They know that the *crème de le crème* of society, both in the United States and abroad, will book with them, and this will give Matson a huge boost over its Trans-Atlantic competitors. For years, European cruises on the *Mauritania* and *Ile de France* have dominated the steamship scene, and this special cruise throughout Asia will be just the thing to place Matson at the top of the industry.

By the time he arrives in San Francisco, he is familiar with the ship and can't wait to be on board. He also has an entirely new vision of Yokohama and Shanghai, and for their long and complex histories. As for Honolulu and Pago Pago, they still sound tropical and uncrowded, and very peaceful.

Arriving in San Francisco at dusk, Malone has no sense of direction. Taking a taxi from the ferry terminal and riding along the bay, Malone feels he is on an island. Streets seem to veer at all angles, and multiple hills interrupt any sort of direct routes. His short ride involves steep climbs and abrupt drops, dodging the many trams and trolleys that line the streets. He sees that the sidewalks are as full as the roadways, as the car makes its way up one final hill.

Once at the top, Malone arrives at the elegant *porte-cochère* of the Hotel Mark Hopkins, a *chateau*-like structure that has achieved a fine reputation after just three years in operation. The tall, ageless captain, dressed in elaborate uniform and gold epaulets, directs a well trained staff. A quick one, a young boy it seems, grasps his luggage and stands quietly while Malone signs in with the night clerk, then the boy escorts him onto the elevator, easily carrying the bags to his room high in the towering structure. His steamer trunk will be stored overnight at the bell desk. Too tired to be shown around the suite, Malone hands the boy two dollars and thanks him, then retires for the night.

Awakening early, Malone is drawn to emerging daylight, that unveils a most beautiful city beneath him, and quite a large one beyond, across the bay. On this clear day, he stands and takes in the bay view, shining in the distance and dotted with three dark islands, the biggest over toward the eastern side. The water's surface is busy with ferry boats crossing in all directions. Shielding his eyes from the sun, he looks beyond the water, toward forested foothills. Far below the hills, buildings and houses extend down to the waterfront, where ships and barges stand at busy piers. He must have disembarked over there yesterday afternoon, in Emeryville, before taking the ferry across to San Francisco.

Wanting morning tea, he walks back through his suite. It's

magnificent, but too big for a single occupant. Certainly more than he needs. The richness of heavy comforters and thick bath towels impresses him as a professional travel man, but he never quite feels comfortable with the opulence. He sees fresh flowers on a silver tray next to a crystal bowl of fresh fruit, and an elegant candy box.

Malone strolls to the larger room and picks up an envelope addressed to him.

Mr. Malone, Welcome to the Hotel Mark Hopkins.
We hope you enjoy your stay.
We have confirmed your luncheon reservations at the Bay Point Oyster Co, twelve noon. We recommend it highly. Please let the hotel operator know when you are ready for breakfast.
Most Sincerely, John Bowden, General Manager

There isn't much time to take it all in, he thinks, as the bell captain holds the large front door for him. He steps into the courtyard and looks across at the famed Fairmont Hotel. Damaged by the earthquake some twenty-three years ago, the Fairmont is considered one of the nation's finest. These two luxury hotels atop Nob Hill make this neighborhood one of the most elegant in the world.

It's a pleasant morning, and Malone is glad he didn't bring his overcoat. Mansions and apartments are mixed here atop this tall hill, connected to the rest of the city by cable cars and slippery cobblestones. Autos slip past him, having successfully crested the hill, while horse-drawn carts struggle toward the top.

Except for the hills, of course, this is much like Johannesburg. He sees men dressed rough, in workingman's clothes, walking beside tycoons, or at least men dressed like tycoons, with dark business suits and carrying walking sticks. Nearly rebuilt following the great earthquake, San Francisco seems as much a frontier city as his own.

He walks carefully down California Street, not wanting to slip on the steep slope. The cable car has just left, but he can ride it back up after lunch. California Street is wide and the sounds of people and passing autos lighten his spirits.

He locates the restaurant, and pushes through the swinging doors, hearing a familiar tune on the piano, as it reinforces the laughter and loud conversations.

“Mr. Malone, welcome,” says the tuxedo’d *maitre de*, as he shows him to the center of the elegant room.

“If you don’t mind, I’d prefer something more private.”

“Of course. We felt you would like this one. It’s our very best,” his eyebrows raise, suggesting he may wish to change his mind.

“Thanks, but as I’m on my own, something quieter would be fine. How about that corner booth?”

“Excellent, Mr. Malone. Will anyone be joining you?”

“Not this afternoon, thank you. And if possible, I’d like to begin with a whisky.”

Chapter 7

The next morning, as the taxi brings him down Nob Hill and hurries toward the bay, Malone spots the distinctive reddish-brown hull of Matson's SS *Malolo*. An elegant white superstructure displays two tall funnels, smokestacks painted bright-yellow and bearing the dark Matson "M". He knows this is one of the world's newest ships. *Malolo* is also reputed to be the most elegant and the fastest, some say twenty-seven knots.

As the taxi leaves him at the pier, a black-sweatered porter approaches to quietly receive his trunk and cases from the driver, hefting them onto wheeled carts and trundling them away. Documents in hand, Malone steps up the gangway, shivering in his light tropical suit and matching Panama hat. On this day, it is not the sunny California that he had anticipated.

An early arrival, he sees no passengers at the entry-way, and only a handful of crew members. As the cruise director, he is greeted enthusiastically by the duty officer. Then a young man in crisp white trousers and blue blazer, with a blue-and-white muffler around his neck, escorts Malone to his stateroom. With the ship limiting its full passenger count to only half of the normal 600 or so, he has an outside cabin, more spacious and luxurious than he is usually assigned.

There is much work to do before the passengers board, and the first task, after locating a wool pullover to ward off the chill, is to meet the ship's staff. Malone will seek out the captain and his officers, then the head chef and chief purser. In time, he also needs to know the key working staff, like cabin stewards, waiters, junior officers and medical staff. Remembering the Commodore's cautions, he will take special care to meet with the communications officer and his people.

He takes his time moving about the ship, stopping in to see his new colleagues. Captain Christian greets Malone tersely, and allows a brief chat. His quarters are minimal and elegant. A direct man in a distinctive dark beard, his suite is neat and tidy, and displays a handful of impressive furnishings from China and Japan, with ebony tables and cinnamon-red vases painted in delicate patterns. In contrast, the handful of paintings depict ships in ancient battles. The absence of photos or personal material tells him that the captain is unmarried and that he, too, is independent and prefers his isolation.

After the visit, Malone locates the galley, and is startled at its size and modern fixtures. It is a classic kitchen, fit for a gourmet restaurant and filled with burbling pots and tempting aromas, both savory and sweet. Though the chef, a tall Swiss dressed in pure white double-breasted jacket and toque, is too busy to spend personal time with him, he introduces a plump assistant, similarly dressed and with a kerchief around his neck, soaking up obvious perspiration.

Back in the public areas, the large dining saloon impresses him. This *Malolo* is far different from the older European ships. It's shiny and bright. All white bulkheads and gold trim. Now that's an elegant ballroom. He peers into a large space with a parquet dance floor, punctuated by four white columns, one at each corner. It's called the *Malolo* Lounge, according to the steward. He stops short and admires the large mural, a fearsome rendering of the open sea. No paintings of stuffy old monarchs here.

He walks through the lounge area, where gold trim highlights pale grey bulkheads. This is where we must hold our private receptions. It's elegant. It provides privacy, but accesses the main dining room nicely. We must block it for departure night from every port of call. And for crossing the dateline.

Malone hears familiar music coming from the lounge, where the band must be rehearsing. It's the new Rodgers and Hart tune, "You Took Advantage of Me." As he moves aft along the main deck, Malone notes a bulkhead marked with a small red cross on a white background. He steps over the hatchway into a clean space smelling of rubbing alcohol, containing three hospital beds and a variety of jars filled with swabs and cotton objects. Looking around, he observes white-uniformed medical staff seated on straight-backed chairs, intent upon a lecturer at the front. A small sign affixed to the door advises that a briefing is on, from the ship's doctor. "Leo L. Stanley, MD", it says.

Perhaps I shall come back later. Then he spots an attractive young woman with auburn hair, cut short and covered by a smart nurse's cap. Placing his hand gently on her slim arm, not wanting to interrupt the presentation, he whispers, "Excuse me miss," and she looks up, smiling confidently and showing the clearest blue eyes he has ever seen. "Here is my card. Would you ask Doctor Stanley to contact me when he is free?" He reads "Christy Miller, RN", on the small brass name-tag on her uniform. She nods gently, accepting his card and watching intently as he retreats back through the hatch.

Chapter 8

Ever since she could remember, Christy took the morning walk to the beach, her dad holding her hand as they navigated the path from their nearby cottage, her bright blue eyes fixed on him, and her tiny legs churning to keep up with Pete's long stride. The sandy streets were already warm and felt good between her toes.

Pete Miller worked nights at the nearby shipyard, and he always arrived home before Doris left for her job at the hospital a few blocks away. While Doris was at work, Pete sat on a boulder while Christy played in the sand. This was his way of unwinding after a long shift, preferring to spend time with two of the three things he loved most: his four-year old daughter, his wife, and the sea. No need for sleep until late afternoon, when Doris was home again.

Doris had worked at Long Beach Memorial for nearly ten years. She knew filing and typing, and enjoyed her job. Doctors and staff let her know how much they liked her positive attitude, and appreciated how she knew exactly where a patient's records were. The supervisors allowed her to bring baby Christy to work during the years when Pete was away in the navy. While hospital friends saw her smart and administrative side, only Pete knew how passionate and loving she could be. He loved her, the radiant, natural beauty of her face, with dark eyes and shy smile. He loved her slim body, so soft and welcoming. He dedicated his life to protecting her, and the bright, beautiful daughter that, except for her blue eyes, was so much like her mother.

Though Christy was always welcome at the hospital, Doris knew that Pete's time with her was special, and that this energetic four-year-old was better off in at the peaceful beach they both loved, more than in the sterile confines of an office.

From the beginning, Christy and Pete were comfortable together. He taught her how to swim with him, first in a small inlet and later in the surf. She learned to always respect the waves and sense the pull of the undertow, but not to be afraid of the water. After swimming, they reserved time to explore the tide pools, identifying tiny creatures: limpets, turban shells, bat stars. She always remembered the specific names. Sometimes they even found an empty abalone shell to take home and display on the back step. Christy was fascinated by undersea life, whether it was learning where kelp and sand crabs came from, or hearing about the creatures her dad had seen far out at sea, like sharks, porpoises and whales; and birds like gulls and pelicans, and his favorite of all seabirds, the powerful albatross. These were joyous days for Christy and Pete.

When she started in school, he walked with her as far as the metal gate, then waved goodbye as she trotted off with her sack lunch in hand. He greeted her each day as school ended, asking about her classes and reviewing new words or numbers that she had learned. She was eager to read, and her penmanship was clean and graceful from the beginning.

When she reached high school, Christy realized just how much Pete and Doris had taught her at home. While the history books described the heroic settling of America -- about Meriwether Lewis, George Washington, Thomas Jefferson -- Pete shared what he knew about how nations expanded and took new territory for sources of food and natural resources. He talked about the settlers who moved across country from places like New York and Pennsylvania, seeking space for farming and ranching, and he didn't mince words when he told her that buffalo and elk were slaughtered and replaced by cattle and sheep and horses. They discussed how American soldiers removed the Indians from their villages, relocating families to distant and unfamiliar places, often killing them, as they had the buffalo and elk.

Sometimes Pete talked about his time in the navy. A peacetime sailor, he made two trans-Pacific cruises, visiting Shanghai, Sasebo, Sydney and Manila. He told colorful stories of those far-away places and people he had met. And sometimes he described the raging typhoons that battered his small destroyer as it was flounced and pounded by the fearsome sea. Christy loved the soft blue robe from China that hung on the living room wall like a piece of fine artwork. She saw exotic dreams stitched into the gentle silk.

As a teen, Christy read Edith Wharton and a sort of namesake, Agatha Christy, whose new detective character, Hercule Poirot, amused and intrigued her. For a time, she thought she wanted to be a writer. Then she came upon Florence Nightingale, reading about her extraordinary career, and how she had lived in the most austere and daunting circumstances. She was like the nurses Christy met whenever she visited her mother at work in the hospital. She became fascinated by Nightingale's work with sick and injured soldiers, how she steadfastly refused to accept primitive and filthy surroundings. Christy read of nurse Nightingale's travels through Egypt and Eastern Europe during World War I, and of her influence on military hospitals in the Crimea, demanding improvements that made modern hospitals like Long Beach Memorial so safe and healing. Already an avid reader, Christy now knew she would study science and mathematics, and would become a nurse who would one day make a difference in the world.

CHAPTER 9

Long Beach, August, 1929

Pete raises the shade a few inches and quietly turns the latch tight, allowing in some daylight while keeping the summer heat outside. He entered quietly, careful not to wake Doris and little Mary. He positions himself so he can see the mailman as he approaches, to keep him from rattling the mailbox. Though Pete has reminded him about Doris and the little girl, Frank is getting on and he sometimes forgets. He hopes for a letter from Christy.

August in Long Beach can be hot if the overcast has burned away, and he knows how uncomfortable Doris is with her congestion in the heat. Her breathing is labored, and she tires so easily. Neither of them wants to miss work and lose a day's pay. And they need to stay strong for Mary's sake. Christy is about to graduate from St. Luke's, and they send her a few dollars each month.

There he is. Pete lets himself out, leaving the front door ajar and carefully closing the screen. "Hey Frank," he whispers, holding his finger to his lips.

The postman returns the signal with one hand and waves the letter with his other.

Taking it, he mouths a silent "Thanks."

Frank continues up the sandy sidewalk, peering into his leather pouch for the next letter.

Tempted to open the envelope and sit outside for a few minutes, Pete decides to read it inside instead, in case Doris has awakened. She'll want to share it, and he enjoys reading quietly to her.

"I thought you might have heard me," he smiles, speaking softly and kissing her forehead. "You always seem to know when Christy writes."

"And I thought you wouldn't wait, that you'd sit out there and read it without me!" she teases. "You're a very thoughtful man."

"So here goes, love...

August 20, 1929 *San Francisco*

Dear Mom and Dad and Mary,

How is Mary? I miss her so. And how are you? You must get very tired. I'm studying harder than ever tonight. It feels strange to be graduating at this time of year, or graduating at all, but I'm determined not to let you down.

I have two finals tomorrow. By the time you read this, I will have passed them (I hope!). And I did get that job, the one I applied for, on the ship! The pay is twice what I would get in a regular hospital. It's just for two months, then I'll come home and become a real mother again.

The ship is called "Malolo" *which means flying-fish. I don't know if that is a good-luck fish or a bad-luck one. Maybe dad can tell me. It's big and new, and supposed to be very beautiful.*

That's all for now. Have to finish studying. Started at the feet, and I'm way up to the thorax now. Only a few hundred more to go!

I hope Mary is behaving like a good girl, and that mom's feeling better. I love you all!!

Christy

"So she got the job, love."

"She did, Pete. And wouldn't you know it would be on a big ship. Just like her dad. And for good pay."

"A better one than I was on, that's for sure. I hope it's a big, stable one, if she got my stomach," he smiles and looks out the window. "I don't think I told her how seasick I used to get in rough weather."

"You told her, Pete." She ruffles his hair, "About a dozen

times."

"Oh," he takes her hand. "Good, then. At least she'll know where she gets it."

"Let's go wake Mary, and I'll take her down to the beach."

Chapter 10

Malone stops in the Veranda Cafe, empty except for the tall and jovial bartender who is busy setting up for departure time, slicing limes, lemons and oranges, and skillfully skewering the olives, pickled onions and juicy chunks of pineapple. Malone asks for a tonic and lime, and the bartender quickly obliges. Prohibition laws prevent the barman from serving alcohol in port, but he courteously disappears while Malone loads his tonic with a pour from his silver flask.

Malone loves this life as a seagoing man. It's the open ocean and the unique ports of call, and the unexpected moments with clients. He's respected as the leader, and that's a large part of the attraction. Crew-members consider Malone a member of the ship's-company. Waiters, deck seamen and ordinary crew-members might resent some of the other cruise directors, fancy dressers who ignore them aboard ship and fail to recognize them ashore. But Malone is different. Aboard ship, he always knows their names and asks for their opinions on anything from weather to the best shops at the next port. Ashore, he recognizes them and stands them to drinks at whatever bar happens to be nearby. In return, they get to know him and share stories. They confide in Malone, inviting him to their own informal crew gatherings.

He spreads the client file across the shiny bar top, reviewing his plan. We have nineteen people in our charge -- nine couples plus my friend Gio. They're millionaires, so the greetings should be simple and respectful. They may be in a hurry to settle-in, so they won't want to hear much from me, and they will likely want a snort from their liquor supply.

He reviews the passenger list. Anna and Ruth, his two delightful friends from the *Italia*. Ruth's the dancer, and Anna will want to talk books. It will be nice to see them again, friends to spend comfortable time with. Once we reach Honolulu, Bergen will join me and become the expert on each port of call. God help us, I'd better be a good student!

He steps from the elevator and walks to the starboard side and aft, looking for the right suite. Approaching slowly, Malone sees the stateroom door ajar. He starts to knock, then quickly withdraws his hand as he hears shattering glass.

"Damn you!" barks a male voice. He hears what sounds like shoes crunching against crushed shards. "Damn that vase! You nearly hit me! You can take this blasted cruise. I don't have the time. I need to be back in New York!"

"For God's sake Jason. You can't leave now! What will I tell people?"

"If I'm not back in New York this week, there will be no more cruises. No more nothing!"

Malone pulls away as the door swings open, avoiding a short and very angry man in a dark suit. Striding away with what looks like a briefcase in his left hand, he glances up at Malone, then bumps past, scuffling the bottoms of his shoes across the decking, and darting out onto the passageway where he disappears from view.

Malone recognizes the scowl and the pencil-thin mustache on an otherwise ordinary face. Jason Gibson is one of the richest bankers in America, and his photo is often displayed on the financial pages of the *Times.* Somehow, he never looks pleased. He and his wife, Gwendolyn, are on the guest list and Malone was stopping in to welcome them. As the stateroom door slams shut, he continues past and decides to return in an hour or so, realizing how awkward any sort of greeting might be just now.

He moves to the railing and looks down toward the gangway, to see the dark suit becoming smaller. Then it turns, shifts the briefcase to his other hand, and Malone watches him slowly retrace his steps back to the suite.

As the Chairman of Worldwide Bank in Manhattan, where

he has worked for twenty-two years, Jason Gibson is an active member of the New York Athletic Club, ranking thirty-seventh in the squash rankings.

He still remembers his days as a teller at the Philadelphia Charter Bank, while he was a bright and serious undergraduate at the University of Pennsylvania. He had hoped to enter Wharton School after graduation, but his father couldn't pull together enough for tuition. Instead, he remained at Philadelphia Charter, working his way through the ranks, becoming the youngest manager in the bank's history, at twenty-eight.

Gibson attended a conference in Princeton and met Oscar Childress, director at Worldwide Bank in New York. They struck up a conversation between sessions, and without expecting it, he was interviewing for his next job. When he returned home, Gibson gave two weeks notice at Philadelphia Charter and turned over all of his files to the new man.

When he arrived in Manhattan, he rented a room close to the bank, near Lexington and 49th Streets. He immediately captured the attention of his superiors, as a meticulous, serious and hard working manager. He introduced morning briefings to the organization, where he received oral reports from each department supervisor and set goals for the day, stipulating that they would provide him with day-end summaries of transactions and goals accomplished.

At the end of each day, he patiently gathered written summaries from each supervisor, as he wished them well and locked the doors behind them. He then remained for ninety minutes, to enter the numbers into his ledger, reviewing them for inconsistencies. Then he carefully checked the safes and the door locks before leaving for a solitary dinner at a Greek café on the next block. Friday nights he allowed himself a glass of beer with dinner, and treated himself to a show at the Fourteenth Street Theater, where the famed Lillian Russell occasionally starred.

Oscar Childress was quietly proud of his protégé. Like himself, Gibson was reserved and uncomfortable in social situations. Childress also noted his tenacity and strict regimen, and the accuracy of his ledgers. Gibson's computations were impeccable, thorough and on time. When Childress moved to a senior vice president position in 1910, he appointed thirty-four year old Gibson as his successor. Childress advised him to delegate the ledger work to his replacement, and counseled him to look for a new home out in Westchester County.

Soon, director Gibson appeared in more tailored suits, always with modest ties, a smart black hat, and carefully shined shoes. His hair was neatly trimmed, and he sported a small black mustache. Gibson continued to be the first to arrive each day, though he now commuted by train. He used a two-hour lunch to engage the businessmen he met at his club, many of whom became sizable depositors.

Gibson's Friday evenings were dedicated to quiet dinners with one or two clients or business colleagues. He occasionally accompanied them to clubs in the Bowery, where the music was lively and the shows a welcome distraction from the pressures of work.

In 1921, shortly after prohibition began, he was a vice-president, and well-respected in the banking industry. One night he found himself with two friends from the Athletic Club, in a speakeasy over in Queens. He was strict in the office, and in most aspects of life, but he despised the prohibition laws.

He was unfamiliar with the neighborhood, though he recognized Fordham University when the taxi sped past en route. Fordham became his landmark, as he was often to return on his own, to visit the speakeasy and observe its tall lead dancer, Gwendolyn Ames. He admired her elegance, with dark hair swept back to emphasize a beautiful face, almost unapproachable.

One night he called the little waitress over, "Send a bottle of champagne, would you? To Miss Ames' dressing room. Best you have!" To his surprise, he was invited to a table next to the dance floor, where he spent that night and every Friday and Saturday night, chatting with this magnificent woman. She was a willing listener, and laughed easily. She eventually allowed him to escort her to the rooming house after her late show.

They married in September, 1923, at the country club near his house, before twenty of his friends. She was stunning, and the guests could not help but admire this smaller man as he beamed up at his radiant bride. Two years later, when Oscar Childress retired from Worldwide Bank, Gibson was named senior vice president. Soon he and his wife moved into an estate near White Plains, with hopes of raising children and settling into a family life.

By 1927, Gibson had grown serious again. There were no children to capture his attention, and Gwen became busy with volunteer work at the club, while the bank demanded an increasing amount of his time now that he was its president. He took to staying over in Manhattan several nights each week. Gwen joined him occasionally, to attend the theater, but she preferred to dine with other women friends at the club.

Gibson now spent much of his time analyzing investments, especially the movement of stocks on the Dow-Jones exchange. He was aware that investment groups were often formed, guided by finance professors from major institutions like Harvard, Columbia and Wharton. They assessed the different stocks and made confidential recommendations to the investors in the group, in return for significant monthly stipends.

With more people buying automobiles and the latest electrical appliances, like refrigerators and toasters and clocks and vacuum cleaners, investments in the companies that produced them were natural. Zenith Radio and Remington Rand were early favorites. Companies that provided materials like steel and copper attracted investors, as did the utility companies that provided electricity, or fuel companies like Standard Oil of New Jersey. There were more speculative opportunities, but Gibson concentrated on the soundest ones.

Thanks to his foresight, Worldwide was one of the earliest banks to offer attractive loans to individuals who wanted to invest in the stock market. For special investors, ten per cent down payment was enough to buy the stock, with ninety percent loaned for the balance. With nearly every stock gaining value, more people were borrowing even more money, and Gibson became a powerful force at Worldwide. When the board insisted that he take over as chairman, he was honored and quite proud.

He enjoyed the friends he had made, heads of other banks and investment firms. He was still proud to be seen with his stunning wife on his arm, as they entertained in their home or attended grand events in the city, riding in their new Pierce-Arrow touring car, which was driven by a middle-aged man in a dark uniform.

In April of 1929, the Gibsons received a telephone call from their travel man at American Express, inviting them to join a special cruise offered only to acknowledged millionaires. "The Commodore wants you to be the first to hear from us," he had told Gibson.

Fully aware of his current worth, he was eager to join this distinguished group of business leaders. He had earned his money through hard work, and this bit of recognition by his colleagues was a small reward for him and his wife. An adventure like this might help restore some of the warmth.

In August, a month before the sailing date, Gibson received another interesting call, from a man named Alfred Thompson of the Chumbly Corporation, wanting to discuss an arrangement with his family trusts. This was a new opportunity for Worldwide to stabilize its control in the investments field, extending loans to wealthy families whose certain gains would bring greater profits to the bank.

When they met over lunch at Thompson's club, Gibson listened carefully to his descriptions of family trusts, and he came away convinced that trusts were a clever way to protect investments. He was aware, too, of the term used by Thompson, that of "selling short". Gibson was certain that Chumbly was the first of many family companies that would be drawn to him.

As he was leaving, Thompson mentioned something that drew Gibson's interest. Thompson's family trust, located in New York, was part-owner of a company in the Hawaiian Islands called Waikele Land & Pineapple, that was looking for investors. All they needed for certain profitability, was a loan from Gibson's bank, issued to the family trust in New York. Though the land was in Hawaii and the bank in New York, Gibson was certain he could convince his board that Chumbly's New York holdings were more than sufficient to secure the one million dollar loan. America's agriculture had been booming and Hawaii was no different. This new company, Waikele, was adding macadamia nut farms to the mix, with seven thousand acres in an area called Kaka'ako. He pointed at The Hawaiian Pineapple Company and Del Monte Corporation for graphic evidence that such a venture couldn't fail.

Realizing the Malolo's *first port of call would be in Honolulu, Gibson would personally visit Waikele and interview them about the loan. Thompson willingly arranged a meeting with Carl Knauss, Waikele's operating partner.*

This was a fortunate coincidence, he thought, and one that he would pursue during their stopover. By securing Thompson's investments, and this new Waikele company, word would spread about his specialized knowledge of stock transactions, and he felt that, by December when he returned from this cruise, scores of other wealthy clients would be approaching him. He also had a few ideas that would be useful if the market began to falter.

Chapter 11

Next will be Mr. Aubrey Kirsch, and then Camille and Emile DuPris, if they ever get here. It says here that they are late arrivals. As he ascends the starboard ladder, Malone thinks about what he read in the Kirsch dossier. *He's a star, they say. Or nearly so. Some sort of comedian. But it seems his last few films have done rather badly. Something's not right with Mr. Kirsch.*

When the baby was born, Marla Kirsch was forty-one years old and ailing. An unwilling cowboy's wife, she was worn out, and not at all interested in having a child. Jesse was the cowboy, and he spent most of his time traveling from rodeo to rodeo, scraping together enough money to buy whisky and to pay the rent for the piece of land down in Fallbrook, where Marla was. Jesse didn't much like Marla any more, since she let herself go and got mouthy when he was home. But she was his wife, and he owed her now that she was going to have the kid.

Perez lived next door to Marla, in the old squatter's cabin that was part of the ranch property where the dozen or so shacks were set. Perez lived alone and was mostly quiet, raising his few vegetables and trading some of them for meat and liquor. He was over fifty, with a furry black mustache and a large belly. But he wore clean work-clothes, and was always polite.

Jesse was glad that Perez was there, because his rodeo swing would keep him away, up into Salinas and Redding, then to Pendleton, Hermiston and Calgary. It would be eight months before he could get back down to Fallbrook. By that time, the baby would be six months old, maybe older.

They named the boy Aubrey, or Marla did, because of some British actor she saw once in a play when she lived up near San Francisco. That was over twenty years ago, back when life was better. Aubrey was surprisingly plump and healthy, and he was a smiler, no matter how bad Marla felt, or how much she left him alone.

Perez looked in every day, and as Aubrey grew, Perez was the face he saw when he awoke and went to bed. Jesse quit coming home after Aubrey turned eight. His legs pained him, and he wasn't able to get around the way he wanted. He sent letters from someplace called Wallowa, up in Oregon. But he never said when he would be back.

So while Marla went to town and cleaned some of the bigger houses, Perez taught Aubrey to ride the mule that roamed the fields around the shacks. They didn't have a saddle, so Aubrey was a bare-back expert, never minding the boney spine that ground up between his legs and pounded his young frame. Perez also noticed the boy's unusual voice, sort of garbled like a sore throat.

By the time he turned twelve, Aubrey could ride any horse bareback, even the rancher's best stallion. He also knew how to bring him in and cool him off, humming and rubbing the big horse down, getting him ready for the stall. He was a tall kid, good-looking enough to attract attention from the high school girls down at the soda shop. His voice didn't bother them any. Mostly, he was quiet, respectful, and stayed out of trouble.

When he was fifteen, he asked Perez to drive him up to Temecula. A movie company advertised for men who could ride and jump onto horses, and to pretend they were some famous cowboy actor while doing these things. Perez drove him the seven miles to the interview, such as it was. A large, bald man in a plaid suit lined the fourteen candidates up by height, weeding out the gangly and the short, and making marks on a clipboard. This left eight. The large man checked their teeth and skin, excused five of them, and asked the remaining three to mount a horse and ride. Aubrey was one of the three.

Aubrey waited until last, watching, as a punk kid about six feet tall, who looked to be at least eighteen, quickly climbed onto the animal and kicked it into action, whooping and showing off for the observers. When he returned, he slid down and smiled over to the large man. "How'd I do, mister?"

The man nodded and waved him back with the other two. Then a grizzled man with a noticeable limp, who must have been over thirty, strode to the horse, patted it gently and hoisted himself gracefully into the saddle. Before he set off, the large man said, "Hold on mister. You been in movies before?"

"Yes sir, I have," he responded.

"Was you the one who fell out at Pomona, hurt pretty bad?"

"Might have been."

"I'm sorry mister. We can't be taking chances on a injured man. Company won't allow it." He shrugged and looked up at the rider, "This is a real physical job we're about to do. I'm sorry. You got to dismount."

Aubrey watched the man lower himself off the saddle, graceful and strong until he stood on the ground. Then he limped over to the line of rejected men.

Aubrey approached the horse, walked around it, looking from its head down the left flank, and stepping around the backside, rubbing the muscled skin and talking calmly. He stopped at the withers and in front of the dignified head, rubbing the bristly muzzle. He returned beside the stirrups at the left side. Then he easily stepped up into the saddle, gave a small nudge with his heels and moved smoothly away. He trotted the animal gently in a large circle, sitting tall and comfortable, returning to the original point. Then he stopped, dismounted, lifted the reins over its head and handed them to the handler.

"I'd like the job, mister. Let me know what I need to do."

The rough sound of Aubrey's voice didn't bother the man. "How old are you, son? Aubrey, it says here?"

"Eighteen, mister. And ready to go to work."

Movies were silent, and besides, this was a stunt job, with no on-screen lines. So long as he could ride, that was all that mattered. "No more questions, son. See me in ten minutes over by that car. Just in case, better bring your daddy, too," winking and nodding at Perez.

When Aubrey and Perez signed the papers, the man handed Aubrey a check and a photograph of the cowboy actor, and told him to find his way to El Centro in ten days. That's when filming would begin. "That's for transport, and to buy yourself a new pair of boots, plain black ones like these in the picture."

Ten years later, Aubrey was done with stunt-riding and cowboy movies, and was a comedy star. The great Harold Lloyd picked him when he needed a rugged masculine character, to contrast with his own frantic persona. When they climbed up skyscrapers, and entered oversized cuckoo clocks, or swam across raging rivers, Aubrey did his own action parts, and he remained calm and handsome, and never intruded on the great man's manic role.

As the star's onscreen friend, Aubrey brought in more money than his mother in Fallbrook would have believed, if she were alive, and he developed an interest in different kinds of roles. He missed the horses and cowboy parts, but the talking pictures were coming in, and that voice of his was a major concern.

Midge was his steady girl. They met in the dressing room on one of the movies. She was doing small chores for the actors, including the makeup they had to wear in front of the cameras. The actors never remembered her name; they just called her Toots.

She was eighteen when she first met Aubrey, ten years younger than he was, but she had been on her own for the past five years. Her parents were gone, and she drifted to California from Reno, and signed up to work makeup for the actors. She liked the way Aubrey treated her, and how polite he was to people, even though he was almost the lead actor.

She sat with him sometimes at lunch break, and soon they had dinner together. When Aubrey told her his manager had gotten him an unusual job, as entertainer on a cruise ship, to do small comedy bits and tap dance a little with the band, she was excited. Then when he asked her to go along with him, as his girlfriend, she actually cried, which frightened Aubrey. He thought he had hurt her feelings or something. She told him she always cried when she was really happy, and he was relieved.

Knocking at the Polynesian Suite, Malone stands quietly and scans the hallway, which is far too wide to be called a gangway. He admires the fledgling palm trees in their immaculate turquoise pots. As the door opens, the grin from a cherubic young lady, with glossy lips and a revealing sundress, elicits a smile of his own.

"Hi there, Mr. Handsome," she purrs, then a giggle. "Want to come in?"

"Who is it Toots?" Malone hears a gravelly voice in the distance.

"A tall and beautiful man, baby! What do you say we invite him in?" Her eyes are clear and kind.

"Does he have a lady friend with him?" asks the voice, in need of a throat-clearing.

"No, baby. But it's not a social call. He's carrying important-looking papers."

Malone looks across the room, at a cheerful face that is quite familiar from the movie posters. Dressed in a dark green dressing gown, Aubrey Kirsch is one of America's best-known comedians, usually appearing in the silent films opposite Harold Lloyd. His wide eyes and bushy mustache have become a trademark, almost as recognizable as Lloyd's round glasses and innocence.

"Hello, Mr. Kirsch. I'm Duff Malone, your cruise director. May I welcome you aboard the *Malolo*?"

"Malone. Malone," a raspy response, clear enough to understand if you listen carefully. "Malone of the *Malolo.* Are you Irish, then?"

"Ah, yes, the accent," says Malone. "No, not from Ireland. I am from South Africa, though born in Scotland."

"Scotland to South Africa! You don't say? Do they speak English over in Africa?"

He laughs gently, "Very much so, Mr. Kirsch. My

schoolmasters were all from England, though some of my classmates spoke a sort of Dutch."

"Would you like a drink, Mr. Malone of the *Malolo*?" Laughing now, and sounding to Malone a bit like the great jazz musician, Louis Armstrong, Kirsch continues, "Toots, that is, Miss Beeson will pour you one? Will whisky do?"

"Not just yet, but thank you, indeed. May I accept later this evening?"

"Absolutely. I believe there's a *soiree* planned, to launch our journey?"

"That there is, at five o'clock in the lounge. We have a special space set aside." He smiles down at the striking Miss Beeson, whose loose dress reveals more than soft curves. "Drinks and *canapés* together, and a wonderful dinner in the main dining room, followed by a little dancing with a marvelous band."

Kirsch pauses and shows a frown, "Can I ask a straight question, Duff? I want to get off on the right foot."

"Of course, Mr. Kirsch. Anything at all."

"I'll level with you, we -- Toots and I -- we're here as working types. We aren't part of the millionaires crowd. You never know, though," he raises his eyebrows and crosses himself, lifting his eyes to heaven. "If Miss Evangeline Adams is right -- she's a famous astrologer, you know -- and if I listen to these financial guys on the ship, we could be big-time investors after this trip."

"You are fully part of the group, Mr. Kirsch. The cruise line asked us to look after you as a special client. We are pleased that you agreed to provide entertainment three or four times each week. But you truly are an honored guest, with full entitlements." When Malone reaches out his hand, Kirsch grasps it while Miss Beeson gives him a friendly wink. Then Malone adds, "And whoever your Miss Adams is, I hope she can make more sense of the stock market than I can. Astrology is as reasonable as anything I have heard."

"You're a gent, Duff. Toots and I look forward to spending some time with you." He pauses, "And I'm not kidding about what she told me about the market. How will we keep up with it when we are out at sea?"

"We'll receive RCA bulletins from my Los Angeles office -- telegrams. I'll include them in our daily briefing sheet, with the latest newspaper headlines and stock information as often as we receive them."

Chapter 12

As he is admitted to their suite, Malone knows very little about Lloyd Winston and his wife, Alita. The company's profile was limited, mentioning his previous appointment in China and a current "United States Government" job. No title. The steward leads him into the main room, and his eyes are immediately drawn to Alita's quiet beauty. In a silky cream-colored jacket and slacks, she has an expressive face, clear blue eyes, and a halo of blonde hair with soft darker tones. As she stands with her husband they are an imposing couple, looking tan and fit, and welcoming. He is tall and athletic, dressed in a light blue cotton shirt and gray slacks. Observing them together, Malone feels a sense of competence and trust.

Though the family estate was in Kenilworth, Lloyd Winston was raised since the fifth grade in a series of private schools near Washington, D.C. When he was ready to enter high school, Harris Prep in Potomac, Maryland was the place to attend if you planned to go to Annapolis, and this is what his father intended. The curriculum was designed around the Academy's rigorous engineering courses and military environment, and the entrance fee was steep. Modest in appearance, the school was run by a retired navy commander from the Annapolis class of 1866. It was popular with wealthy families who lived outside of the Capitol area.

Alita Fowler attended Mount Vernon College for Women in Washington, D.C. A respected school that attracted independent and intellectual women, Mount Vernon also prided itself in the number of graduates who married Naval Academy graduates. It was during spring of 1892 that she met Lloyd Winston at Annapolis. He was not yet a midshipman, but was on campus for a final visit before accepting his congressional appointment for the approaching summer.

As they walked through the rotunda, coming from opposite

directions and each admiring the photos along the wall, Lloyd bumped Alita and stopped to apologize. As they were caught in conversation, the campus walking-tours to which they had been assigned went on without them. Instead of catching up with their groups, they strolled out of the front gate and found a small restaurant downtown, and proceeded to talk for two hours.

Immediately, Lloyd knew that he did not want to spend four years away from this wonderful girl. He decided to withdraw his application for Annapolis, turn down the appointment, and attend George Washington University, a school that offered a path to diplomatic service. More important, George Washington was near Mount Vernon College.

Alita, two years older than Lloyd, immediately knew that he was the one for her. His thoughtfulness and courtesy were as attractive to her as his handsome and athletic features. He was intelligent, and seemed to know what he wanted in life, and he was willing to make decisions and not equivocate.

After college they lived in Chicago, where Lloyd worked for a law firm specializing in international trade. Alita, though she was from a wealthy family herself, decided to accept a job at Marshall Field, as a buyer. They lived in Evanston and were actively involved in community work, volunteering at the local hospital, a small theater group, and the Art Institute. Lloyd sang in the theater's chorus, and loved the work of Franz Lehar. Alita, a fine soprano, played the lead in "The Merry Widow" and was quite a success.

Lloyd distinguished himself in the field of international trade, and his calm manner and handsome appearance always attracted attention from the politicians. Their combined friendships in Georgetown and nearby Alexandria brought Lloyd and Alita to the capital for meetings and social events; and his father's personal friendships with President Taft, and President Roosevelt before him, were an added benefit.

They were excited when the appointment of Envoy Extraordinary and Minister Plenipotentiary to China was extended to Lloyd in the fall of 1911. They arrived in Nanking early in 1912.

Lloyd, now forty and Alita forty-two, realized that this was a sensitive time in world relations, and particularly in China. The newly established republic was a dramatic shift from dynastic rule, and many Chinese remained loyal to the overthrown Manchu dynasty. After just a few months in Nanking, the capital was moved to Peking, and that is where they lived and worked until 1916, when President Wilson politely ended their assignment and brought them back to America.

During their time in China, they experienced the World War through Germany's occupation of Tsingtao and its neighbors; then they monitored fierce naval battles, as the Japanese fought alongside Great Britain to retake Tsingtao. It was clear that Japan had its own aspirations in China.

Naturally, Alita and Lloyd traveled back and forth to the United States several times, disembarking at the ports of Los Angeles or San Francisco, then traveling by train to Washington, D.C. They always regretted that they could not visit some of the exotic ports en route to America, like Hawaii, Borneo, Sydney or Pago Pago.

While they were proud of their diplomatic service, and they had come to admire much about the Chinese culture, the day-to-day existence was unacceptable. The stench of raw sewage was abominable, transportation and heating were impossible, and they were appalled at the atrocities that they witnessed. Craving a quieter existence, they returned home, and Lloyd remained a trusted advisor to President Wilson. As a sideline, he built on his father's experience in speculating in gold and silver.

When their invitation arrived for the Malolo, *Alita and Lloyd each expressed excitement at the prospect of a leisurely Pacific cruise, to see the peaceful and sunny islands that they had missed before -- fully enjoying some special time together now that the world was at peace.*

"Mr. Ambassador and Lady Winston, so glad to meet you," Duff begins.

"Call us Alita and Lloyd," she responds gently. "We shall have many days together, and we prefer first names from the start. For the record, my true title is mother or Mrs., but I was never quite as grand as to be a Lady."

"Then please call me Duff, Alita. An honor to meet you, Lloyd. May I welcome you to our very special Pacific cruise?"

"You may, indeed," Lloyd responds quietly. "This is our first time back on the Pacific after many years. And for the record, I was an envoy or minister to China. Never quite an ambassador."

"Well noted, Lloyd, thank you. You have sailed this route often, I'm sure," Malone offers.

"Many times between China and America," Alita responds. "But not such an intriguing itinerary as this, and never such a magnificent ship. Lloyd was posted to Nanking, and then Peking when the capital was moved there. On our other trips, we were never able to stop over in some of these wonderful places."

"Would you care for a gin and tonic?" Lloyd raises a glass.

"Thank you, I would," Malone responds, surprising himself. He wants to know these people better.

"So it is, then. Ice?" As he nods, Lloyd pours from a heavy decanter into matching highball glasses, and adds the lime slices and tonic.

Alita accepts her glass and raises it, "Here's to a special voyage, Duff. And to you, my dear."

As glasses clink, she continues, "Are you a married man, Duff?"

Malone hesitates at the unexpected question. "I am not, Alita. I have a few years I suppose, before I can settle down." He smiles, "But one day -- that is my hope."

"This cruise work must keep you away from home. South Africa, is it?"

"You have a good ear," he chuckles. "Not many have seen or heard a South African speak, at least not many Americans."

"Our work around China and Hong Kong brought us into contact with South Africans, usually dealing with diamonds or gold," says Lloyd, adding, "Were you educated in Britain or down home?"

"In Johannesburg, but by British university men."

"Good education. I know something of your recent history. The Boer War was a difficult time for your country. I'm sure it left plenty of scars."

"It did, indeed. The war ended when I was born, but those scars are visible to this day."

"That man, Hertzog, seems very dangerous to me," notes Lloyd. "I much prefer Mr. Smuts."

"As do I, Lloyd. Prime Minister Hertzog is a divider in a badly divided country, and certainly not a man for all of our people. He disregards the Africans, and so do his supporters. They often refer to the blacks as animals, but the natives are some of the smartest people I know. The Hertzog government would do well to realize what a marvelous resource they are, and not merely laborers."

"How brutal that is, to call them animals. And ignorant. This is something I should like to discuss during our voyage, because our country is not entirely free of prejudice against negroes. Asians, too, in many places. Germans, Irish and Italians, even. The inevitable bias of the rich against the very poor. Or the poor against one another. So make note, that we shall talk further before too long. In the meantime, you are thoughtful to look in on us. We'll see you at the reception?"

"That you will, and I look forward to hearing your points of view, both of you. There will be ample time."

As Malone rises to leave, he wonders if this is a couple that can help bring the group together, to create the courage they may need if the worst happens. It's a lot to ask, but if they can help set the tone, it could make a world of difference.

Chapter 13

It's just before noon, and Malone is worried about Emile and Camille DuPris. He has checked with the radio office, and no messages or telegrams have arrived for him. There are few alternatives. He knows that another vessel, the *Pemberton*, is sailing in two days from Los Angeles to Hawaii, and the DuPris couple might catch up with them in Honolulu. Or, they could sail directly to Yokohama in another week, but this is an unlikely option. He will need to leave word with the port authorities.

Heading toward Ship's Communications, he spies a large black convertible down at dockside, with a young couple spilling out of its back doors, a confusion of white linen and bright pinks and greens. They clasp hands and run together, laughing up the gangway, clutching their hats as they make their way safely aboard. The slim girl's yellow frock is nearly lost in the breeze, before she grabs it and traipses onto the ship.

He quickly descends the two levels and sees the couple, breathless and giggling, as they look around for their luggage. Approaching them he offers his hand to the young man, "Emile, is it?"

"Why, yes it is." He lightly grasps Malone's hand and transfers it to the young lady's chiffon-covered arm, ignoring him. His eyes are cold and distant. Then, "Uh, this is Camille. Help us with our luggage, would you?"

Ignoring the rudeness, "Mr. DuPris. Miss DuPris. I'm Duff Malone, your cruise director. Your luggage will be taken care of directly, by the porters. We shall have you signed on and comfortable in no time. May I offer you refreshment?"

"Champagne, dear," sighs Camille, her cheeks flushed. "And oodles of it. This has been far too exciting for us, but champagne may help." Her youthful face has dark lines beneath sunken eyes.

"French bubbly, if you please," Emile adds, looking around him, slightly disoriented.

"Not here, I'm afraid," cautions Malone. "Prohibition is still on in port." He raises his eyebrows and continues, "But in your suite, we may have a chilled surprise package from France."

"That's a good fellow!" Emile abruptly takes his sister's hand and leads Malone to the waiting elevator.

The boy's room is dark and quiet, the shades drawn against the early sun and muting the colorful baby elephants that dance across the bedroom walls. They speak in whispers so they will not wake his younger sister next door.

"Place your hand here, cherie*. Just here, and move it as I have shown you." She murmurs, encouraging the boy. "That's right. Now then, I will just do this for you. Lie still."*

"Are you sure, mamsell,*" the boy pronounces it in the French manner that she has taught him. "What will* maman *say?" lifting his hand away.*

"Ah, not yet Emile. Please do not move just yet," she gently replaces his hand on her. "She will be proud of you, just as I am. They are far away, and they wish me to teach you these things." She wipes the perspiration from her upper lip with her finger, "That is right, Emile. Just right."

"How have I done, mamsell*?"*

"Well done, Emile," she sighs and takes his hand, as they stand and she leads him to the door. "Now let us share with Camille this nice thing we have learned."

Malone shows them to their location and gauges the time it might take to complete his introductions. As they arrive at the DuPris' suite, the young couple flits inside and disappears, shutting the door without further words. Duff speaks a polite "Until tonight," then he smiles and continues to the elevator. He has one more guest, a very familiar one, located two decks up on the starboard side. The ship's manifest indicates, "Count Giuseppe Sorvini, from Newark, New Jersey". But Duff knows Gio from their special adventure three years before, in Arles.

He locates the number, then knocks and waits, hearing a powerful symphony from within, Rachmoninoff.

"Ah, yes. May I help you?" in an Italian accent.

As the door opens, Malone is surprised at the darkness within. Then a familiar firm handshake, as a slim gray man emerges from the dimness, accompanied by cigarette smoke. Duff says, formally, "Count Sorvini, I believe?"

"Yes, of course." A brief silence, then, "Is it you Duff? My friend from Arles?"

Malone pauses, surprised that he seems so pale. It must be the attire. His gray hair matches a carefully tailored shirt and flannel trousers. Only black shoes and alert, dark eyes offset the rest of his presence.

"I'm here to officially welcome you, my friend, as your cruise director."

The slight smile twitches at the edges and the eyes soften. "I'm honored and pleased Duff, and look forward to spending time together," He pauses and laughs gently, "as we did in France. And please excuse the dark. It was a long journey to San Francisco, and I have been resting here with my music."

"Your music? Ah, yes the gramophone. Marvelous sound."

"And in the darkness, one can almost see the instruments." Pausing, "All of your shipboard arrangements are marvelous. I must thank you for including me."

"I was so glad you could schedule this cruise. We have so much to catch up on. I believe you will find the accommodations comfortable, and the food quite interesting. How are your restaurants?"

"We are doing well, my friend. We now have restaurants in New York and Boston, and two in Canada. Soon, we hope to open a new one, possibly in California."

"Then I shall enjoy your thoughts about the cuisine aboard the *Malolo.* The chef is Swiss, and he has added many elegant touches."

"Ah, I shall pay my regards to him. I once worked in Switzerland, as a boy. Lugano, do you know it?"

"I do not, but I intend to visit northern Italy one day, Lago Maggiore, Como. They all sound so beautiful."

"They are beautiful, as are so many places. I do look forward to visiting Asia. Perhaps I will learn from the Chinese and Japanese cuisines."

"We have some fascinating ports of call, and I will enjoy visiting them with you." Rising, "In the meantime, I need to excuse myself and welcome one more couple. I'll see you at the reception, my friend."

Malone raps twice on the door and stands back.

"Come in, please come in." A surprisingly tall and stunning woman gestures for Duff to enter, watching him with a curious expression. Her lovely face is wise and watchful. She is dressed in a silky grey trouser outfit, and the sheer blouse shifts gently with her movement. As he lifts his eyes he sees a determined smile, with lively green eyes and auburn hair pulled back beneath a multi-colored headband.

"Jason," she calls, and her husband appears, dressed in his tuxedo. It is well cut and carefully sized, but he looks uncomfortable. "May we offer the gentleman some champagne?" She pauses and looks Malone over. "Or would you prefer something stronger?"

"Champagne is fine," he responds, nodding toward her husband.

"Champagne all around," she smiles. "And it's Gwendolyn. Please call me Gwen."

"I'm Duff Malone, Mrs. Gibson. Mr. Gibson. Your cruise director. May I welcome you, and offer you my services?"

"You are very kind, Mr. Malone. Jason and I are looking forward to a wonderful cruise," looking toward her silent husband, she continues, "aren't we dear?"

"We are," smiles Gibson through thin lips, but his eyes are hard.

As Malone looks back, her smile has softened, and her eyes have become moist. "Thank you for your welcome, Mr. Malone. Please excuse us." Then she drains her glass.

They quickly down their drinks, and Duff moves toward the door, followed by Mrs. Gibson.

"Duff, I thank you for being charming...and for not coming in when my husband dashed off."

Six hours at sea, and Malone has received nothing yet from Roberts in Los Angeles. He doesn't want to face his guests at dinner without the most current information. There will be plenty of small talk, likely to focus on famous athletes like Babe Ruth or Big Bill Tilden, or which motion pictures they will miss during the voyage -- things they have just left behind, more than what lies ahead. *You can bet these wealthy travelers will want to know how high the stock market has risen. The further they get from America, the more their thoughts of home will fade -- except for those addictive stock market numbers. And the further away from communications, the more frustrated they will get. Then they will look to us for help. Damn! Where is Roberts' telegram?*

As he finishes dressing for dinner, the expected knock finally comes.

"Well, young man, I am glad to see you," he smiles, trying not to show his irritation. "Did this just come in"

"It did, sir. Radio room sent it up right away, sir."

The messenger's eyes widen as Malone hands him a dollar and says, "Thanks, son. Well done."

Opening the envelope, he reads intently:

News for Sunday, September 22. Major speakeasy fire in Detroit. Twenty people killed, including cops. Babe hit another homer, Yankees win again. Little change with stocks. Dow at 362 on Friday 20th, down slightly. New Warner Baxter cowboy talkie "In Old Arizona". More later. Roberts.

Surprisingly, Malone ignores the old stock news and concentrates on the movies. Aubrey Kirsch will be interested in this. He sounds quite rough enough to be one of those cowboys in the cinema.

Chapter 14

Dressed in his newest tuxedo, with crisp white shirt and black bow-tie, Malone is in the main dining room at four-thirty sharp, reviewing the setup for their opening reception. Though the crew is capable, experience tells him that he should recheck everything in advance, or some detail could go wrong.

They have the private salon just off of the main dining room. Following the reception, his clients will rejoin the other passengers for the regular dinner seating. As he scans different sections of the room, Malone is impressed with the originality of the *Malolo.* Except for the *Ile de France*, most of the Atlantic ships seem like old English manors or German castles, with elaborate frills and plush furniture surrounded by dark wood panels. This new ship gleams with the lightness and warmth of the tropics: simple bamboo, teak and mahogany, along with expensive highlights that are obviously designed for the new-money crowd.

The simple pastel walls are livened with contemporary artwork, giving the lounge a spacious feel. Modern cocktail tables and chairs are neatly arranged in one corner, near a comfortable section where guests can stand together and chat, enjoying cocktails and extraordinary hors d'oeuvres served to them by a team of tuxedo'd waiters. For privacy, the charming lounges are shielded by pillars, allowing passengers to sit if they choose, facing slightly aft where final sunlight plays with the darkening ocean.

Ship's officers arrive, extending Captain Christian's welcome to Malone, and indicating that the captain himself will be with them shortly. *Damned disappointing!* Just after boarding, Malone had asked the captain to join him at this event, to personally greet his clients on the first evening at sea. These initial impressions are critical, and they set the stage for the rest of the voyage. In addition, he knows that the choppy waters just off the coast occasionally bring complaints from passengers. It helps to have seasoned veterans to reassure them of a smooth cruise.

The first arrival is Mrs. Gibson, looking stunning in a silky, light-green full-length gown. Emphasizing her height, it clings to her shapely body, revealing enough to draw admiring glances from the men. Mr. Gibson releases her arm and shakes hands with the officers, including the captain who has just arrived. As she receives an enthusiastic welcome, Malone positions himself near a waiter who is holding a silver tray with two fluted glasses of champagne.

"Mrs. Gibson, Mr. Gibson, I am so glad to see you," smiles Malone. "Welcome, and may we offer you champagne?".

"How delightful, Mr. Malone...Duff. Will you join me?" They touch glasses with a light chime. Then, remembering her husband, she turns and tilts her glass in his direction. He smiles and leaves for the outer deck.

"May I show you the ocean view?" asks Malone, escorting her toward her silent husband.

The Winstons are next to arrive. Alita wears a creamy white floor-length dress, with a jade necklace that matches the modest bracelet on her left wrist, and a delicate jade ring on her right hand. The emerald green color emphasizes her flawless tan. Lloyd's tuxedo is perfectly fitted, and has a small American flag on the lapel, just above a tiny red rosebud. "Hallo, Duff," he calls, as he waves amiably before greeting the captain and his officers. Alita seems to be chatting among old friends, as she shakes hands, patting them gently on the arms.

Malone takes Alita's hand and touches Lloyd's elbow, "Let's just move over here a moment, and the waiter will bring us refreshments. Whisky?"

"I would like a very dry martini, if you please," Alita says pensively to the waiter, then winks and adds, "and a twist of lemon."

"Same for me, Duff," adds Lloyd.

Malone nods and the waiter moves away swiftly, to the nearby bartender. "Are you ready for some new experiences?" Malone asks, as another server brings canapés.

"If you mean, are we glad to get away from the madness in Washington," laughs Lloyd, "the answer is 'yes'."

"Hawaii sounds glorious," offers Alita. "They say that Waikiki beach is the most beautiful in the world."

"I must admit," responds Malone, "that I have not seen Waikiki, and I have heard that as well -- considered even nicer than those along the Côte d'Azur."

"Our experience is limited, I'm afraid," says Lloyd. "Alita and I have been to Tahiti, and found those beaches to be quite spectacular. And several breathtaking places in Malaya and Indo-China."

"Beauty includes the moment, don't you think? And the one you are with." Alita nods at her husband.

As the waiter returns with their frosty stemmed glasses, Malone takes a moment to admire the obvious affection between them. Then he excuses himself and returns to the greeting line, as he sees a gray-haired couple he has not met, but he recognizes from their file, Austin and Marjorie Clark.

"I'm Duff Malone, your cruise director," shaking his hand and then hers.

"It's good to meet you, Duff," says Austin, gently releasing his hand. "I heard from friends that you may be a young fellow, but you have seen almost everywhere a ship can sail."

"And you, Mr. Clark, I have read of your travels, and that you are from the Carolinas."

"Well done, Duff. Yes, near Durham. Marjorie and I are partial to steamship travel. We have cruised the Atlantic on some of your past ships -- *Mauritania*, for example. I'm surprised we have not crossed paths before."

"I, as well. Have you been on the *Italia*?" asks Malone.

"Not yet," purrs Marjorie, in a surprisingly deep voice, "but we are booked to Rio next year, out of Miami.

"Perhaps we will be on that one," he responds. "The *Italia* is one of my favorites, and I'm likely to take two groups next year." His eyes widen suddenly, "And speaking of the *Italia*, Austin, Marjorie, I believe I see the Swanton sisters just over there. They sailed on the *Italia* with me two years ago. Quite charming women." He pauses, "I will just bring them over."

As Malone returns, each arm is held by an attractive young lady, one who is petite with soft eyes, set off by a short aqua-colored dress and wildly patterned head scarf; the other, taller, in beige silk pants and matching jacket, with short black hair and a wide smile. Matching ropes of pearls adorn their necks, and despite their differences in size and appearance they each exude gentle humor.

"Ruth and Anna," introduces Malone, "please meet Marjorie and Austin Clark. They want to ask you about sailing on the *Italia*." He smiles mischievously, "You won't tell them everything, will you?"

"Why Duff, you rascal, of course we won't. The fun we had on the *Italia* is our little secret!" Laughs the smaller girl, "I am Anna Swanton, and this is Ruth."

"I won't promise anything of the sort, Anna," Ruth swings her pearls coquettishly, and feigns a serious look. "The fun we had should be passed along to others who are willing and able!"

Moving smoothly away, Malone approaches the bar and scans the room for guests in need of attention. He sees that all the men's eyes are on the dance floor, watching a well-dressed couple move to a jaunty version of "Blue Skies". Their eyes are on the tall woman with an actress's confident smile and a stately grace. Duff admires, too, while Mrs. Gibson maneuvers her husband past other couples, his face cold and stoic.

Three levels up, Emile strikes a match and touches it unsteadily to the tip of his dark cigarette. *Lounges. Meals. Dances. Drinks. Conversation. God! Why can't we just sail on by ourselves? A private yacht next time. Portofino. Corfu.* He looks to see if there is another stairway to carry him higher.

Instead, he remains shivering outside the stateroom, smoking his nightly cigarette, thoughts darting like little night creatures. *Cami is agitated. Blames the orchestra or something. Always starts this way. New surroundings. Needs to settle.*

What's there! Moving to the rail, he stretches over to see as far as he is able, looking past the horizon. *What is over there?*

He straightens and stretches his arms wide against the railing, caressing the brass fittings, now cold and moist from the sea spray. As he rubs his hand through his hair, the dampness mats it down and chills him. That familiar sea-scent stays on his fingers, a reminder. *It's still her smell.* Tonight he can't avoid the salty attraction of Camille. And the sea. And all the lessons learned.

Chapter 15

MALOLO DAILY REVIEW

Port of Call Honolulu, Territory of Hawaii

Tuesday, September 24, 1929

SS Malolo, Matson Lines

Pacific Cruise

SHORE EXCURSIONS

Our first port of call is Honolulu, the largest city in the Territory of Hawaii. We arrive tomorrow morning, 0800 hours. The Hawaiian Islands are an American protectorate, and a tropical paradise. Hawaii was founded by Polynesians nearly 1,500 years ago, and over the years was influenced by many Pacific cultures. In 1820, Christian missionaries brought education and religion to Hawaii, and it became a territory of the United States in 1898. In 1920, the population exceeded 80,000 people. Last year more than 15,000 people visited the islands.

For the past century, sugar cane and pineapple have been the major industries. During the three-night and four-day stay in Honolulu, *Malolo* passengers will be guests at the Royal Hawaiian Hotel on Waikiki Beach, a new and luxurious resort for guests of Matson Navigation Company. During our stay, we will provide sightseeing excursions, which may be arranged at the hotel. We will feast on local delicacies, including a gala welcome banquet or "luau" Friday evening, offering bountiful native roasts, seafoods and fruits. We end with a Farewell Banquet on Sunday evening. The finest wines will accompany our meals, and a full bar will be available at all times.

"Blast!" exclaims Malone, a bit louder than intended. What does this mean, 'Loo-ah-ooh'? How do I speak this bloody language?

"L-U-A-U," he says aloud. He reads from the information sheet and "An easy Hawaiian word, that means picnic, or outdoor buffet or banquet." *Ah, like a* braai *in South Africa, meats and vegetables cooked over a fire.*

As he prepares for his first Hawaii experience, Malone notes how quickly these millionaires accept each other. They seem to interact like business partners. Members of the same club. The first few days, he is their leader. They treat him like a new-found friend. Then, once they get to know each other, most of them gravitate away, and back among their own people. Not everyone, of course. Anna and Ruth, for example. They are true friends. And the Winstons are genuine like that. Alita and Lloyd. Nice people.

Malone reopens the itinerary sheet. Back to the Hawaiian foods. What is it I need to know?

"Lots of fresh fruit," he reads, "with roasted pig and local fish, cooked moist inside a banana leaf. A variety of local vegetables, and a purple paste, called *poi*, pronounced 'poy'. The descriptions remind Malone of some of the exotic foods he has had to try. *The goat's eyes in Morocco were the worst! This should be much less challenging. Must have been the pink gins beforehand, that helped me get them down. And lots of them afterward. They were a primitive lot, but thank God they had English gin!*

Malone reads another word, "Kupuna: a leader, a respected tribal elder." Sort of how we talk about our Werner Bergen, "Bergen-san". There is another word they use for 'king', pronounced 'ah-lee-ee', *ali'i.* He pauses to think, and continues, *kupuna* is the one we would use. A spiritual connotation. Werner Bergen, indeed. Respected elder describes him exactly. I can hardly wait to see him again.

He can't help but think about the embattled Gibson couple yesterday. *He always seems so angry. And why would she put up with this? Besides, she's so attractive. Maybe it's the market.*

Malone realizes that many customers can invest cheaply, putting down just ten or twenty cents on the dollar. The banks loan them the rest. Every time the market dives, the bank has to go back to their customers and ask for additional money to strengthen the deposit. Gibson could be just worried.

And what about that nurse, Miss Miller? She's a lively girl when she's off duty. Pretty, too. She was having the time of her life out there on the fast numbers, dancing with Captain Christian. But I'm a slow-dance sort of chap. I believe she is too high spirited for me.

CHAPTER 16

"Here's another letter. Frank left it when you were out to get the milk. Come and read to me while I fix breakfast. Mary is up, and in playing with her toys. You must be exhausted."

"Not too bad tonight, love," he walks into the kitchen and removes the letter, going over to his usual living room chair, knowing Doris can hear him in the kitchen. "We had a safety meeting first, so the shift went pretty fast. Here's what Christy has to say,

September 21, 1929
Departing San Francisco en route to Hawaii

Dear Mom and Dad and Mary,
Thanks for "loves" from Mary! Glad that she is being such a good girl. I miss her very much. More than I can tell you.

I'm glad to hear that mom is feeling good again. I hope you both are not working too hard. I'm mailing this from San Francisco just before we leave on the big cruise. The ship is huge! I will tell you about it next time. It's quite exciting!

We sail this morning for Honolulu. Then we go to Yokohama, Japan. (I forget. Were you ever there dad?) Then to two ports in China. First is Shanghai and second is Hong Kong. Then we come home, stopping in Samoa en route. The port has a funny name -- Pago Pago. We will be gone for sixty days.

Did I tell you that our passengers are all millionaires? Can you imagine an entire ship full of millionaires? Maybe I will meet one and he will sweep me off my feet! (Don't worry, dad, I'm just joking. I'm aware of my responsibilities.) I don't know how I should act around these wealthy people. I better not make any mistakes, or it might be my last job ever!

We had a class yesterday, and a surprise, you could say. It

was a first-aid lecture from Dr. Stanley. A man came in to see the doctor, but the lecture had started. The man had some kind of English accent. His calling card says he works for the travel company, American Express in New York. He was quite nice, tall and sort of handsome.

I have to hurry to get this into the post.

I love you both!!!

Christy

"So she is meeting people?" eyebrows raised. "And wants to meet a millionaire?"

"I'm sure she was teasing us, dear. You, especially. She knows how you feel about men."

"Particular? Me? He better be more than a millionaire. He better be smart, and decent to my daughter, or he'll have an old sailor to deal with."

"Calm yourself, Pete. Christy inherited a lot of common sense from both of us. She'll be fine."

VIA RCA RADIOGRAM VIA RCA

WEDNESDAY SEPTEMBER 25 1929

TO DUFF MALONE

LARGE STOCK SELLOFFS EXPECTED,

RUMORS RAMPANT.

$200 MILLION TAX CUT EXPECTED.

YANKEES MANAGER MILLER HUGGINS DIES, NEWS HALTS YANKEE GAME.

$25 MILLION INVESTMENT TRUST CREATED IN CHICAGO.

TODAY'S MARKET UNCHANGED AT 352.6

MM ROBERTS

Chapter 17

Malone reads the news and doesn't know what to think. *Obviously the selloff rumors will worry people. But what does the tax cut mean? Or the big investment trust? Those should be good news. Should I share any of this, or stick with the unchanged stock market?*

I don't own stock, and haven't borrowed money from banks. I really don't believe in it. What in hell should I tell them? If it were up to me, I'd say hold-on, if you bought your stock for sound reasons. If you hear rumors, check your broker for the facts. Stay with your reasoning until facts tell you to do otherwise.

He decides to publish only the unchanged Dow industrials prices in the daily bulletin, and the Yankees' manager news. Then, on shore he will help people communicate with their advisors and families.

Approaching the Veranda Bar for the evening's party, the noise level seems higher than usual. Three stewards stand by, ready to provide cocktails and canapés. By now, the stewards know the drinking preferences of each client, and smoothly order from the bartender as the guest approaches. Malone sees Ruth and Anna seated at the open-air section, looking serious, with empty martini glasses on the table, their expressions contrasting starkly with their colorful dresses. They are usually the soundest and most positive people in the group.

"There you are, Duff," says Ruth. "We hoped you would be here early. Have you heard the news? It is so distressing."

"What have you heard?" he asks, wondering how it may have gotten out.

"It's all over the ship. Don't you see people just chattering away there, in the ballroom? The communications clerk told the couple next door to us. Some people are talking of selling-off! Selling their stocks, right away. Those young dancers, the DuPris, are simply beside themselves. We are not usually worriers, but that rumor is terribly unsettling. "

"I did just hear, Ruth, but it's conflicting news. Is it stocks or is it banks? On the good side, there is also a big tax cut, and a new trust company was announced in Chicago. But if you're worried, you might send a short radiogram to your banker."

"We have already been to the radio room," responds Anna. "They asked us to return in one hour, that they will try to help tonight, but several people are ahead of us."

"Maybe you should wait until we land in Hawaii. My information indicates it's simply rumors so far. Wouldn't it be best to await our arrival in Honolulu, so that you can telephone your advisors and speak with them directly?"

"I just don't know what to do," Ruth continues. "We're not investors, but all of our savings is in the banks, and there are stories of them shutting down. What if they do?"

"I'm only suggesting that there are so many reports, it may be helpful to hear from others. Besides, if your money is in a bank, the stock market shouldn't affect you. Perhaps someone has information that you find more factual. Look, just over there are the Clarks. They are both attorneys, too. Perhaps they can be helpful." He steps over to them, "Austin. Marjorie. Would you care to join us?"

"Did you hear what they are saying…" starts Anna.

"One hears so many things these days, Anna," Marjorie responds gently. "That seems to be part of the difficulty. Just what is troubling you?"

"It's the banks," exclaims Ruth. "We heard that they are closing the banks."

"Why, that isn't what we have heard, is it my dear?" she nods at her husband. "You received a wire this afternoon, did you not, from our banker?"

"Exactly, dear." Austin removes it from his inside jacket pocket. "From the Bank of Wilmington. It tells us that the newspapers are badly misinformed. Our government finance people assure them that the economy is strong. The bank assures us that our deposits are quite safe. The stock market fluctuations are simply aberrations. This is a great economy, so it will withstand a few changes."

"So, you see ladies," Marjorie continues, looking kindly at Ruth, "We are not worried just now. Let's all enjoy this cruise. Don't you think Honolulu is going to be exciting?"

As the Clarks move toward the steward, who has their cocktails waiting, Malone excuses himself and circles the room, looking for other signs of distress.

"*Signor* Duff," a quiet voice behind him. "May I interest you in an *aperitif*?" Count Sorvini moves toward him, striking in his fitted tuxedo and perfectly manicured gray hair.

"You may, *signor*," laughs Malone, accepting a crystal tumbler of his favorite whisky. "And how is your trip so far, Gio?"

"Very nice, my friend. Absolutely first-class. The dinner last night was splendid, if I may say so. The roasted veal was perfectly cooked, with those little potatoes and mushrooms -- and the then the fresh tropical fruits. Quite good. I went to the swimming bath today, as well. It was refreshing."

"The food is good, indeed," agrees Malone. "Of course, as a restaurateur you are a far better judge than I. As for the plunge, I must admit, I have not been there just yet."

"You will enjoy it, I assure you, Duff. For some reason it is called 'The Roman Plunge', though I have seen nothing like it anywhere in Rome." He pauses, then asks, "What word do you have from America? Any business news?"

"Are you referring to specific industries, or the markets in general?"

"Come, let us join Mr. Warren over there." Sorvini continues, "I hold no stock, if that is what you mean. So I gather only general information. You see, my restaurants in America and in Canada depend on wealthy people as our patrons. I must remain aware of their financial health. Ah, Mr. Warren, have you met Mr. Malone?"

"I have not," says the large man, taller than Malone and badly overweight. "Malone, is it? I received your business card in our suite. We were out when you visited."

"Call me Duff, if you would, Mr. Warren. And, yes, I'm sorry to have missed you. Is this your first cruise?"

"It is, and it will take time to learn the ropes, so to speak." He turns, his pink face sweating noticeably, "Sorvino. We were talking about the market before. I don't understand why you are not putting money into it. I can make some contacts for you."

When he was only eight, Chester Warren was bigger than the other boys, and whip-smart, knowing every over-the-fence shortcut in Brooklyn. He enjoyed taking things away from the smaller kids. He used to take marbles from the boys who gathered in front of Bolander's grocery store, competing for chewing gum. After he took their marbles, he made them hand over the gum and the pennies they played with. Then he squeezed their wrists hard and threatened to punch them, and he laughed as they ran off.

As he got older, this kind of bullying bored him, so he learned how to sneak onto the back of the horse-carts that went into the city, and he did the same thing to kids in other neighborhoods.

He especially liked to take money from "the dagos", the little black-haired kids who talked with funny accents, carefully avoiding their big brothers.

When Chester turned fourteen, he was as big as any college boy, with light brown hair and bright blue eyes, and a devilish smile that showed perfect teeth, despite his own bad hygiene. Big Chet is what they called him.

Big Chet continued to visit other neighborhoods, since he no longer had any fun with the frightened kids in his own. Now, he approached boys his age and bet them that he could get beer for them, with no difficulty. Even if the boys didn't want beer, he made them pool enough of their money to buy a few bottles, then went into the tavern and came back within minutes, beers in hand. He always kept the change, and confiscated half of the bottles for himself, then jumped onto the back of a passing cart to make his way home.

Once he arrived back in Brooklyn, he went to the old man who sold newspapers from a stand on the corner and traded three beers for a half-pint of whisky. Then he took the whisky home to his mom, who grabbed him and asked where he had been. She always smacked him if he was empty-handed, and she cursed and grabbed the bottles if it was beer. When he came in with a half-pint, she rumpled his hair and told him he was a good boy.

Chet studied hard at school. The nuns made sure that he did his homework, and kept him in check by challenging him to be their best student on every test, then praising his work. He was the top boy at arithmetic and spelling, and he even excelled at the catechisms, learning the creed and the commandments without a flaw. Seeing the power the nuns had, he always obeyed them, but he enjoyed making his classmates look bad.

Sister Beatrice Margaret was concerned with his way of pointing-out mistakes that other boys made, disliking his cocky smile as he interrupted with the correct answer. But the sisters knew what home was like for Chet, and they seldom corrected him.

His mother died when he was sixteen, and Chet was taken

in by his unmarried Uncle Seamus, a bartender who sometimes stayed out all night. Chet woke himself and dressed for school, putting chunks of old bread and cheese into a small sack for lunch, careful not to wake Seamus, when he was there, and the woman who was sometimes snoring next to him. After school, he worked in the bar's basement, sorting empty bottles for pickup, and hefting new inventory up to Seamus.

Chet never drank beer or whisky. His mother's habits angered him, and he was repulsed by people who had no self-control. He gambled, though, learning little tricks from bar patrons, and he utilized the tricks against the boys he met in the alleyways when work was slow. He angered them when he laughed openly after winning at dice. But no one challenged him, because he was big and he was easily provoked. Graduating at the head of the class of 1899 at St. John's High School, Chet was considered most likely to succeed. He was also considered a bully and the most despised boy in his class.

Seamus surprised his nephew by staking him to college. New York University was easy to get to on public transportation, so he could live in the apartment during his first two years. He was always good at numbers, so Seamus hired him to keep the books at the bar. Chet put his earnings away, and by the time he was a junior at NYU he got his own apartment. Uncle Seamus didn't care one way or the other, and Chet enjoyed the independence.

He was just beginning his senior year when he met Shirley. She was in his economics class, and their professor recognized each of them as his top students. The professor proposed them for jobs with an investment company called Bennett Finance. They offered intern positions to the better students, and often the interns chose to stay on.

Shirley was born in Glasgow, though her Scottish accent was all but gone after living in America for twelve years. She was a quiet girl, raised in the Bronx, and she admired Chet's diligence in school, and his confidence. It comforted her to know that Chet was capable on the busy New York streets, always knowing where he was headed, and how to get there. She liked his thrift, as well, and felt he would be a good provider. And Chet always made her feel special.

They were married in 1905, just one year after graduating, continuing at Bennett Financial, she as an accountant and he as an entry-level salesman. Chet learned to control his temper, and to use his barbed humor and sarcasm to rise above his peers in sales. Clients and bosses found Chet to be quick and amusing, a great story-teller. They saw no harm, or edge. To people above him, he was always deferential and flattering. To those below him, the other salesmen and secretaries, he was seen as boorish and offensive, and they avoided him as much as possible.

The salesmen, especially, were amazed at the way Chet moved up in the organization. As a sales manager, he continued to make them feel inferior, while pushing them hard to reach higher goals. As he rose, Chet made certain that more power was consolidated into his job, when other sales managers were moved or fired. While the people below him on the job ladder despised Chet, those above him saw Chet as a sharp, productive guy, who always came in under budget and ahead of goals. He got things done and showed them respect. This landed him the position as vice president of sales.

When Chet was named president of Bennett, he and Shirley knew they could afford a more comfortable apartment within walking distance of the office. They observed other executives and their wives, and learned to wear clothes like theirs, dine at the same restaurants, and speak the same kind of language. He even took to smoking an expensive pipe. They soon wore more stylish clothes at work, and accepted invitations to join the higher-ups at their clubs, though they rarely socialized outside of their company circle. Shirley dressed conservatively, in darker dresses and modest styles, and she continued to wear her hair long. As Chet advanced his body grew larger, and he seemed to fill the executive suite with his size and his bullying attitude.

When Chet was invited to join a special Pacific cruise just for millionaires, he was excited and flattered. "We deserve this, Shirl," he said. "We worked hard. Did everything they asked.

This means we're accepted. I wish those losers down in the sales department were still around to see this."

"Mr. Warren," Sorvini looks puzzled. "When you tell me that your investments are gaining sizable percentages every day, I have to wonder, does the price never go down?"

"Sure it does. But only after we sell," smiles Warren.

"You say 'we sell'," Sorvini continues. "Are you investing with someone else?"

"I am. One of those investment groups. Syndicates. Our banker put it together through a friend. When our expert tells us to buy, we get in when the stocks are low. When it goes up, he tells us when to sell. The expert's a Princeton man. Best in the business. The bank loans us the money, so we don't need more than ten per cent to get in. What do you think? Are you interested?"

"A few questions, first, to help me to understand. You are investing in these companies? Loaning them money to run their business?"

"Of course, we become stockholders."

"Do you have voting rights, to advise the board of directors? As stockholders?"

"Why, yes we do."

"So you know what they manufacture, or what they do? How well they are managed?"

"Our advisor does, actually. We just provide the money."

"When you and your investment group buy and sell so rapidly, how do you know which company you are supporting? How is it that you help advise them?"

"Come now, Sorvino. We can't possibly advise all of them. How could we know about their products, and how they make them? We simply go by the numbers. We sell when the stock is high, and buy when it is low. This is what yields the profits."

"And how, if you would tell me, is this different from

placing bets on a horse, or on a number?"

"But that's gambling, and gamblers take risks. We are talking investments here."

"That is just my point, Mr. Warren. I fail to see the difference."

"It is very different, Sorvino. We have a specialist who advises us. He studies the companies and gives us tips."

"I see, Mr. Warren. Thank you for explaining to me," says the Count, with obvious appreciation. "Most of my capital is tied up in my restaurants and with the purchase of land, so I believe I must decline. But, thank you for the invitation." He looks away and asks, "Duff, do you have some information for us this evening?"

"I do," Malone pauses, then says, "But it is quite conflicted. My contact provides only the headlines, and as you know, newspapers are sometimes not well-informed." He continues, as Sorvini nods in agreement. "One day the banks are healthy and thriving. The next, people are withdrawing their money. Truly, no one does seem to know the facts, certainly not the newspapers, so people often fear the worst."

"Fear of the unknown," Sorvini shrugs. "It is so easy to provoke fear. These negative statements, whether true or false, they carry the weight, as the Americans say."

"Don't you worry, Sorvino," asserts Warren, continuing to mispronounce his name as he moves toward the large bowl of shrimp. He turns back to add, "We know what we are doing. Those stocks will continue going up. Mark my words. America is the place to be right now. Automobiles. Skyscrapers. Electric toasters. Sales will continue. New products will be made."

Malone and the Count turn toward each other and share an understanding smile. Malone says quietly, "Let's stay on course, Gio. I believe we can provide the calming influence that people seem to need."

"Just so, Duff. Just so."

Chapter 18

To his colleagues, Werner Bergen is a modest wizard. He makes small miracles happen through quiet and peaceful action, always preceded by a good deal of clear thinking. He has traveled throughout the world, on steamships, trains and motorcars; ridden camels in the Egyptian desert, elephants in Madras, an ostrich in Queensland, and a water buffalo in Indo-China. When Bergen visits the western United States, he insists on riding horses, preferably a palomino. There are framed photos of him in American Express offices throughout the world, most of them perched upon some sort of animal, appearing very much at ease in his dapper suit and bow-tie. Notable, too, is his unruly shock of hair. What these sepia photos do not reveal is Bergen's once flaming-red mane, which is slowly fading to white.

If you first looked at Werner Bergen from the feet up, you would see handcrafted shoes, sharply shined, then neatly pressed slacks and well-fitted suit-coat of an expensive and conservative cut, a brightly colored bow-tie, and probably a vest. You would expect to see a neatly groomed, slightly eccentric corporate executive. If you started from the top, you might expect to find a professor in an old tweed jacket, or some sort of mad biologist, with fiery mane, worn longish and curling in all directions.

As a younger man, his red hair stood-out prominently at American Express headquarters, quite contrary to the image of conservative and well-groomed executives there. Only a man with charm, character and extraordinary talent could pull it off, to be his own man in a sea of matching suits and neckties. Bergen was all of these, with a warm smile to accompany the mischievous eyes of a man of good-humor and tolerance.

Today, Werner Bergen's legend is woven deeply into the fabric of American Express. He is seldom referred to as Werner, though that was his name as a boy in Germany, and it remained with him as he finished high school years in the Bronx. At Columbia

University he was called "Red", or "Bergen". He became "Bergen-san" in his sixth year as a cruise specialist, and his fourth working for American Express.

He joined the company shortly after his thirtieth birthday. As a small boy, he had been surrounded by ugly waves of partisanship and violence under Bismarck. At eleven, a long and traumatic steamship voyage brought him and his parents to Ellis Island, planting the seed that travel should be enjoyed rather than endured, and that peoples' small kindnesses often make the difference between a harsh experience and a positive one.

During his school years, Bergen earned highest marks in mathematics and science, but he loved history and the nuances of different languages. Later, he followed the writings of Goethe, Voltaire and Confucius, and was a dedicated reader of the American humorist and chronicler of frontier life, Mark Twain.

As a linguist, he was sought after by overseas travel companies and steamship lines, and joined North German Lloyd in New York. Four years later, Bergen was attracted to American Express, with its growth around the world and its respected cadre of managers. He felt they brought in good travel men, and they encouraged them to do their work without interference.

In 1925, when prohibition and wild parties were in full swing in America, Werner Bergen led a small group of American engineers to Tokyo and Yokohama, to observe the reconstruction efforts following the Great Kanto Earthquake of 1923, which had destroyed these cities and all the surrounding communities, shattering the lives of more than one hundred thousand Japanese. Even two years later, reconstruction was still in the early stages.

Bergen was a leader more than a guide. His unruly red hair marked him as unique among the black-haired Japanese, who came to call him *Bergen-san* and sometimes *Reddo*. He spoke the language of working class Japanese, as well as their elite, so his American clients were able to hold countless conversations with laborers, in addition to the wealthier business owners. From his own experience, Bergen understood the insecurity that comes with loss of one's home.

As he accompanied the Americans through Minato, Chuo, Ota and other damaged areas, he spoke quietly with the residents, who were methodically removing fallen wooden beams and shattered stones. When he translated questions from the engineers, about their methods of removal and salvage, he did it in a kindly way. When his Americans expressed surprise at the exceptional amount of material that was retrieved and reused, he translated this respectfully, omitting the Americans' occasional sharp comments about how much easier it would be to simply discard the old stuff and use new material and construction methods. Bergen sensed the desire of the Japanese to be efficient in their own way, choosing reuse of material over the American preference for speed and simplicity.

During a final meeting with their Japanese hosts, held in a spare and dignified inn in Nikko, a stark contrast to the destruction some sixty miles away, Bergen expressed the engineers' appreciation for the Japanese people they had met and interviewed. In fluent Japanese, he expressed words that meant tenacity, resourcefulness and respect, and he told them of the commitment from these engineers, of one hundred thousand American dollars toward their reconstruction effort. Then he translated into English, the Japanese leader's stunned words of appreciation for the Americans' generosity of knowledge and spirit. He told of their respect for the visitors' willingness to witness and understand the difficult period that the Japanese people were going through. Almost tearfully, Bergen expressed their hosts' overwhelming gratitude for the incredible, unexpected gift of money. At the end of his brief presentation, the Americans joined the Japanese in applauding the man they all now referred to as "Bergen-san".

CHAPTER 19

Malone saw the new Aloha Tower from several miles out, its ten stories gleaming high above the Honolulu palm trees. Easily the tallest building in Hawaii, Matson Lines built it as a landmark to welcome passengers to the islands.

He quickly spots his friend in the tan suit and Panama hat as the ship clears the harbor entrance. He knew Bergen would be there, to come aboard and greet them. As in Japan and ports around the world, Bergen-san knows all the port officials, so they will escort him aboard just as the ship pulls alongside the main pier, number nine, just before passengers disembark.

Malone remembers him and his wild hair, now gone to white. A small man with a luxuriant mustache, he is impeccably dressed, known always to wear a suit and vest -- dark tweed in the colder climates and light linens in the tropics -- and his bright bow tie. A devout bachelor, Bergen is always one to flirt with the ladies; and they seek him out, adopting him as their own special escort.

Invariably, he squires an admirer to a favorite garden, as if it were their own secret treasure. Or takes her to a quiet café at just the right time of day, a cappuccino or glass of port, positioned to see the sun rising over a small lake or watch it setting against a distant mountain range, beaming spectacular last rays onto one particular peak. To these discerning women, he is like someone they have always known, a favorite uncle with whom they are fully safe.

A man's-man, too, Malone recalls. Small and quick, his hands can find the solar plexus or the right spot to break a man's nose if he needs to. These skills had come in handy in Morocco, and more than once in Havana. But by choice he is a peaceful man, usually a peacemaker.

After the big ship is guided smoothly into the harbor, the tugs snug it safely against the pier. Malone hears music, and is delighted to see dozens of Hawaiian musicians visible along the wooden dock, surprised that they are dressed in dark suits and ties despite the eighty-degree temperature. They accompany hula dancers of all ages, wearing native grass skirts and colorful dresses.

Local greeters stand with fresh flower *leis* piled high, ready to be placed lovingly on the necks of incoming passengers in true Polynesian fashion. As the ship approaches, the calm harbor waters teem with outrigger canoes, paddled by bare-chested men wearing delicate blossoms and garlands of green leaves around their necks or crowning their heads, waving their paddles high between strokes, and smiling at the passengers who crowd the rails and wave eagerly back. The scent of flowers and the dark, tanned skin capture Malone's senses, and bring forgotten feelings.

He can't help but admire his passengers, crowding the rail, laughing and gesturing like crazy people. They have traveled the world, and they can buy anything they want. But there they are, waving like little children at the natives down there on the tiny boats, and tossing coins for the divers. Then he spots his friend at the top of the gangway, shaking hands with the duty officer in sharply-pressed dress whites, preparing to call the passengers ashore.

"Duff, old friend," waves Bergen doffing his tawny hat and reaching out his hand.

"Good to see you, Bergen-san," smiles Malone, "Quite a welcome you have here."

"It's the *aloha* spirit you are seeing. They greet every ship this way, and it is quite genuine. Far deeper than you realize. Just wait until we depart in four days! Leaving here is even more emotional." Looking him over, "Ready for some lunch?"

"You look quite fit, for a world traveler. Your treat?"

"It is, at the Royal Hawaiian. It is a fabulous new hotel. The food is fresh and wonderful, and it is served along the beach."

As they move toward the gangway, Malone hesitates and then smoothly steps around Bergen, touching the arm of a young lady, trim and attractive in a short pink dress and matching head-scarf. "Excuse me miss, are you looking for company?"

She glances up and breaks into a confused smile, “Why Mr. Malone. Of course. Are you going ashore now?” Then sees Bergen and nods to him. “If your friend doesn’t object?”

“Christy,” Malone begins, “This is my colleague, Werner Bergen. Werner, Miss Miller.”

“I’m Christy, Mr. Bergen, and I have the honor of working with Mr. Malone. I’m a ship’s nurse.”

“Friends call me Bergen-san,” he begins, “so please indulge me. And in what capacity does this healthy young man require a nurse, may I inquire?”

“What a remarkable question, Bergen-san. I often ask myself that,” she teases. Taking Bergen’s arm and moving smoothly down the gangway. “He tells me our relationship is strictly protocol. In case of a ship’s-emergency drill, or a sick client. But I have yet to grasp where dancing the foxtrot fits in.”

“Don’t listen to her, Bergen,” Malone smiles as he trails behind. “I believe she is exaggerating.”

They look up to see a sleek red-and-black LaSalle roadster parked nearby, with its convertible top lowered. “Our car awaits, but first I have a surprise. He pauses as two dark-skinned girls approach, twelve or thirteen years old, long black hair flowing in the warm breeze. Their dresses are colorful, and they carry strung flowers of pink, deep red, and soft white. They rush to Malone and stand on tiptoes to place the fragrant flowers over his head. Each of the girls puts a plump lei, filling his neck with vivid layers of orchids, ginger and pikake. Malone leans down, as they stretch their slim brown arms around him to kiss his cheeks and proclaim, “Aloha!” It is difficult to realize they are so young.

Knowing that Bergen had not expected two people, Malone quickly removes one delicate white lei and approaches Christy, deftly placing it over her head. Before he can withdraw, she says, “I believe they come with a kiss, too.” She looks softly into his eyes.

Blushing, he quickly touches her cheek with his lips and draws away.

"And now we have another surprise," says Bergen, "that few people get to see. Please, follow me. Don't worry about our cruise guests. My shore team will take good care of them." Bergen walks several paces up the pier, to the tower that they had seen from the ship. He enters at the base and leads across to an elevator, carefully including the two young Hawaiian girls before the cage is shut. "To the top, if you please," he says to the elderly Hawaiian with a full head of grey hair, who operates the elevator.

"My pleasure, sir," the man responds. He gives a grandfatherly wink to the young girls, and they giggle and cover their faces with their hands.

As they emerge from the elevator, the sunlight forces them to look away. As their eyes adjust, they cautiously follow Bergen to a corner of the platform that faces away from direct sunlight, overlooking buildings and wood-frame houses. Bergen gestures beyond, toward a distant range of blue-green mountains that are shrouded in mist. Christy walks to the rail and looks down at the milling crowd of passengers and greeters. Malone presses back against the tower building, clearly uncomfortable with the height.

"This is Honolulu, my friends, and we are atop its highest building, nearly two hundred feet tall," Bergen announces, both girls by his side. "Over there," he points toward the office buildings, in among the trees. "You will want to avoid downtown. This is a big city in many ways, and you are not to go there under any circumstances. See the traffic." He gestures toward a cluster of buildings down to the left side, with streets carrying automobiles past offices, and up toward the lush mountainside. "Just there," as he points to the closest ones, "are for companies and professional people. They are quite safe to visit in the daytime. But just over there, slightly to your left, where that trolley car is moving," he motions dismissively. "Those are where the sailors and the criminals hang out. Hotel Street is well known for ruffians and prostitutes. Whatever you do, do not go there nor allow our clients to be taken there."

"A bit like Havana or Marseilles, you might say," offers Malone.

"Just so." He acknowledges, "Now, if you look well beyond, up the mountain. It is called Nu'uanu. These islands were once ruled by a royal family, you know. Their rule ended just forty years ago, and their last queen, Lili'uokalani, died only twelve years ago. It was quite tragic. She and her family lived up there in summer, to get away from the heat. It is tranquil and quite spiritual. That is where the drivers will take our guests after they disembark." He moves to his right, to another corner that faces out along the coastline. "See there, that prominent mountain along the ocean, just beyond where the beach ends?"

"Yes, I see, Bergen. The shoreline is quite striking," says Christy. Malone watches from the entrance.

"That far peak is Mount Leahi. It is a dormant volcano crater, a favorite landmark for Waikiki visitors. Locals call it Leahi, which means 'brow of the tuna'. You will find that most references in Hawaii are about the sea and its many creatures. Westerners call it 'Diamondhead', because it is said that British sailors once thought they discovered diamonds on the crater's slopes. Though they had no value, simply worthless crystals claimed by greedy men, the name has held. Our guests can visit there, as well. The view is spectacular."

"And where is our hotel located, or can we see it from here?" asks Malone.

"Ah, yes. Same direction as Mount Leahi, but slightly closer to us." He waves his fingers toward himself, then points down to the right. "See there, the cluster of buildings just against the sea? Where those big white waves are breaking?"

"In amongst the palm trees and all that vegetation?" asks Malone, edging carefully onto the platform

"There are actually two hotels there. The newest is the pink one, the Royal Hawaiian. That is where we will stay. The white one nearby is the Moana, an older hotel that has been the mainstay for years. Quite a comfortable place. If you move your eyes further to the right, come this direction just a bit, you can see cottages along the beach."

"Those little structures?" asks Christy. "Near the larger buildings?"

"That is the *Halekulani* Hotel," responds Bergen. "Hale means 'house' and Halekulani means 'house befitting heaven'. It is quite charming, in a very traditional way."

"By 'traditional', I take it you mean 'South Seas' or 'primitive'?" asks Malone.

"That's it," laughs Bergen. "It is a bit primitive, a trait that I find very appealing. It is 'natural', you might say. Wouldn't you say so, girls?" He asks their two young hostesses.

"Yes, uncle," says the taller one. "But not primitive to me. Much nicer than my *hale*. It looks very much *Havai'i*, though," she says, pronouncing the word with a different sound.

Malone glances down at Christy and is surprised to see her watching him. She looks away as they walk to the elevator door, then descend to the lobby.

"Enough of this. We have work to do," grins the little man, waving his hat and thanking the two girls as they dash off. "This is just the beginning." He adds, "I will be the driver. Duff, you and Lady Christy please sit back in the touring seats. I'll amuse you on our way to Waikiki."

Bergen successfully navigates the twists and turns en route, then gasps, "My Lord, where did that come from?" as he swerves to miss a trolley car that appears on his left. "Sorry. I still can't get used to a tram on this remote island."

"Impressive reactions," grins Malone, slowly releasing Christy's shoulders from his protective grip, grazing the back of her neck. Pulling ahead of the trolley, Bergen turns right onto the next street.

They drive through a dense section of *ti* plants and low palm trees, and emerge into a spectacular clearing that is lined with towering palms along a carefully sculpted entryway of flowers -- vivid reds and pinks and bright yellows -- framed by large volcanic stones. "Incredible," admires Malone. "This feels like home."

"You mean South Africa?" asks Christy. "Is it like this beautiful place?"

"It is," he smiles. "Down in Natal, around Durban."

They approach a spectacular pink building, with high moorish arches and a prominent portico, featuring the name *Royal Hawaiian Hotel*, scripted like a giant signature just above the main entrance.

"The hotel opened two years ago," Bergen points out. "It is one of the world's finest, designed strictly for this cruise audience. It was filled with motion picture stars at the grand opening. They tell me that Valentino himself was here." Pointing at the picturesque driveway, he continues, "Shortly, our guests will arrive just there, in private motorcars with our best drivers. Our guides took them on a bit of a tour once they left the ship. You'll be surprised, I think," he looks over at Malone. "We often think the Europeans have the experience in tourism. But these Hawaiians have been welcoming visitors for decades, and they are among the best in the world at entertainment and sightseeing."

Bergen follows the narrow road that leads to the porte cochère, where the massive bell captain awaits in his creamy white uniform, festooned with two-inch black striping on his trousers. A handsome Hawaiian, his thick right arm is raised in greeting.

Two rows of dark-skinned bellmen line the driveway, impressive in their exotic cinnamon-colored uniforms and black Chinese skullcaps. The captain opens the front door with an enthusiastic, "Aloha, Mr. Bergen. How are you, today?"

"I'm fine, Moke. Just fine, thank you. These are my friends Christy and Duff. This is their first visit to the islands."

Moke accepts an armload of leis from one of the bellmen and gracefully places one over Christy's neck, accompanied by a powerful hug. "Aloha, Miss Christy. And welcome to our islands. This special plumeria lei, it is for you."

"We call those *frangipani* at home," adds Duff. "The aroma is spectacular."

"That it is," says Moke, with a mischievous smile, "and the basis of many famous love poems."

He repeats the presentation with Malone, including the hugs. Then for Bergen, Moke disappears for a moment and returns with a long strand of shiny green leaves, placing them lovingly around his neck and hugging him close, and then standing back, clasping his shoulders. "For you, my friend. This *maile*, is very special. Not flowering, only a little fragrant. Just plain and strong. Only for the *kupuna*. You should wear these proudly."

Bergen touches the plain green leaves, then places his hand on Moke's shoulder and says a quiet, "*Mahalo*, my friend."

As they walk through the gardens and toward the restaurant, Malone says, "Quite a chap. He is a handsome man, Mo-kay is it?"

"Well said, Duff," chuckles Bergen. "He was here for the grand opening and has been charming guests ever since. Before that, he used to be a beach-boy, much slimmer as a young man, teaching guests how to surf and swim. Very popular with the ladies, still. But he is the head greeter, now. He's a friend of Duke's -- and of mine -- and we will see them at the luau later this evening. He sings, and plays a deft ukulele, even with those large hands. And you'll be surprised, despite his size, he is quite an agile dancer."

As they walk through the lobby, Malone looks back to see Moke behind the wheel of their car, personally backing it into a prominent position, just left of the entry way. The open-arches transmit scents of jasmine and other floral delicacies blending with his plumeria lei, reminding him further of the sweet, sensual fragrances of home.

They share a quiet bamboo table near the sandy beach, beneath a banyan tree with sturdy branches spreading above them like a web. As they order drinks, Bergen continues with his quiet briefing, "Each of our guests has a private car and driver, and they will keep them throughout their stay here. They will be positioned at the hotel, on call day or night."

"And excursions," prompts Malone. "What are the

offerings?"

"Whatever they wish, except Hotel Street, of course. Our guests may call the front desk and refer to any of the tours that they see in their printed invitation. Each of them will have a personal note from me, advising that individual outings may be ordered, free of charge. It is included in their cruise fee. I have invited them to dinner here, as well, for a welcome luau. All other meals are to be taken independently, until our final banquet in the Grand Ballroom. They will receive no bill, but advise their name and room number when they arrive in the dining room. If they choose to dine in another restaurant outside the hotel, they simply pay for it on their own. American currency is used here."

"So all is arranged, and except for tonight we have no specific assignments," notes Malone. "Is it to be this way in every port?"

"Not quite, my friend. You do need to do a bit of work," Bergen chuckles, then becomes serious. "There are certain places, like our next port, Yokohama, and in each of our China stops, where strict control is maintained, and a group dinner is absolutely needed for every meal. Or at minimum, assigned seating in the hotel. In other ports, like Pago Pago, breakfast, and lodging are aboard the ship, with lunch or dinner taken independently on shore. Language can be a significant issue in most places we will visit, and people not knowing their way around. But Honolulu, or Waikiki at least, is quite self-contained. Drivers are knowledgeable and friendly, and nearly everyone you see speaks English."

"And the luu-a-u," starts Malone…

"Yes, the luau," Bergen smoothly corrects him and continues, "is all taken care of. If you -- and lady Christy, if you wish -- will help direct our guests to reserved tables at the front, after they receive another welcome lei from our hotel hosts, you may simply enjoy yourselves, and all else is in capable hands."

"Thanks for the invitation," Christy responds. "I wish I could join you two, but I'll be nearby. Captain Christian asked me to help host at his table."

"We'll be fine, Bergen," Malone interjects, with a noticeable edge to his voice.

Christy continues without acknowledging, "This is lovely, Bergen-san, absolutely lovely. You have thought of everything. But I must tell you, I'm overwhelmed. When I heard of the Hawaiian islands, I thought of little straw huts and primitive people. Everything here is lovely...but so modern."

"It is quite a contrast, I'd say. These elaborate hotels can mislead. There are many straw huts and modest shacks. At the same time, many of the people here are highly educated, sophisticated even, especially their hospitality industry, often graduating from American colleges. This is why you see many of them wearing suits and neckties, and stylish dresses, even in this heat. They don't want to be viewed as uneducated natives in primitive clothing. But they are fiercely proud of their Hawaiian heritage, and they wear suits to emphasize the point. The language and welcoming are foremost, though. You will see this at the luau."

Malone quietly watches the exchange, and sips his beer. "Tonight, then, Bergen, we host our own private Luau?"

"Not exactly private, Duff. It's for all the ship's passengers and staff, over four hundred people I should think, out on the beach. It is truly a group party, and everyone has been advised to dress casually. But we have our client tables right in front, where the entertainers can work their magic on our guests."

"And five o'clock. Is that a bit early?"

"Three hours difference, Duff. In San Francisco it will be eight o'clock already. No matter what our clocks tell us, stomachs will be rumbling by then." He adds, "Plus, they will have been out and about, and likely to be quite thirsty."

As Bergen predicted people are early, some fifteen minutes ahead of schedule. He and Malone join the hotel staff to present pungent flower leis and friendly embraces. At first tentative, Malone soon finds himself hugging the ladies with ease, after setting the blossoms onto their shoulders. They both end up with various shades of lipstick on their cheeks.

A large section of the beach has been carefully set aside for the luau, drawing guests toward lively music from musicians, three Hawaiian men with guitars and a ukulele, and two women, one with a standup bass, the other with ukulele. They stand comfortably on a small stage positioned beyond multiple bars. The luau was billed as a very casual event, so people are dressed for fun! Some are in beachwear for an evening swim. Others look ready to be marooned on a desert island, wearing dungarees and linen shirts, with colorful headscarves on many of the women -- and even some of the men. Shoes are left in a specially marked area near the entry, watched over by an attendant. A few guests, like the Warrens and Count Sorvini, wear slacks and light sportcoats, and appear hesitant when they are assisted in removing their shoes.

People immediately find their way to bars that are staged along the sand, and Malone watches for his clients, directing them to the tables reserved near the stage, next to Captain Christian and his special guests. The show begins early, with a handsome young musician explaining about the instruments and illustrating early island history with the help of young dancers, all of them young island women with long black hair and wearing coconut shell tops and palm-frond skirts. Malone admires the smooth tan skin of the dancers, and how the shells barely cover their swaying breasts.

"So, Mr. Cruise Director, how is your evening?" Duff is startled by a familiar voice, as Christy teases, "You seem to be preoccupied."

"Ah, yes," he looks down at her, "You have caught me out. I was admiring those lovely girls up there, dancing. Aren't they beautiful?"

Just then the dancers are joined by a dozen little girls, wearing the same costumes and moving their little hands and hips to the rhythmic beat.

"Now that is something I didn't expect," laughs Malone. "Those little girls are beautiful too, in quite another way. Charming."

She surprises him again by taking his arm and murmuring

something he can't quite hear, about someone's daughter. Then she removes her arm and continues gently, "So, Duff. Will you save me a dance later tonight?"

"Of course," he looks down, confused as she wipes her eyes and turns to go back to her table.

As the dance band slows the tempo and the saxophones glide through reassuring notes of "Always", Malone approaches. "Young lady, I believe this is our dance."

Finishing her sip of wine and setting the glass on the table, Christy stands and joins Malone on the dance floor. They are both quiet,

Enjoying the softness of her body, he asks, "Are you all right?"

"Yes. Now I'm all right." Moving in his arms, she changes the subject, "How did you decide to be a cruise director?"

"I often wonder that, myself. To explore the world, probably. Down at the southern end of Africa, I was curious about all the other cultures. And I believe I was looking for a bit of adventure." Shifting smoothly to the music, "How did you come to be a ship's nurse?"

"We must have similar interests," she responds quietly, "I wanted some of the adventure I heard about from my father, who was a sailor. And I want to learn about other people. Plus, I needed the money."

Then the moment changes, as the band switches tempo and Polynesian drums take over. They make their way back to the table just in time to hear good-natured cheers, as the hula dancers return and haul Captain Christian onto the stage, then roll-up his formal black trousers and tie a thatched hula skirt around his waist. Dancer that he is, the captain is adroit with his arms and quickly masters the hand gestures from the comely young hula teachers. But his downfall is the hip movements. He seems far more interested in their hands on his hips and enjoying their provocative outfits, than in actual movement. The drums cease and the captain smiles broadly as the little dancers escort him back to his table.

Now, fifty hula dancers take the stage -- all ages, from tiny little girls and boys, *na keiki* the announcer calls them, as well as women who seem well over eighty. All have changed costume and wear colorful dresses of a matching tapa pattern, smoothly dancing in unison.

Seated next to Christy, Bergen touches her arm and brings her over to where Malone stands quietly. He whispers to them both, "Just watch those older women. See how their expressions change, and watch their hands. The music begins, and they become regal, elegant. It always amazes me, how their faces and hands are transformed to those of young girls. Watch how they project. They are beautiful, and young again."

Malone watches Christy, who is clearly moved by Bergen's comments and absorbed in this special moment -- taking in the old and the young. Then she squeezes Bergen's hand and whispers a tearful, "Thank you."

Chapter 20

Malone senses the harsh buzz before actually hearing it. His hotel room is pitch black, and he gropes toward the sound. "Malone here."

"Mr. Malone? One moment please." Then, "This is Captain John Kimura of the Honolulu Police Department. I know it is the middle of the night, sir, but I need your help."

"Police, is it? What's happened? What time is it?"

"Three-thirty Mr. Malone, and two of your guests are here at the station."

"Two people? Tell me what has happened, mister…what is your name again?"

"Kimura, sir. Honolulu Police. Two of your clients are here, Mr. and Miss DuPris. They were found in a dangerous situation. They're safe, but lucky to be alive. If you will come down and vouch for them we can release them."

"I'm coming right away!"

Quickly dressed, Malone finds cars and drivers standing by just outside the hotel entrance, as Bergen had promised. Malone wakes the young man at the wheel, dozing in the dark front seat. "Son. Please. Do you know where the police station is, downtown?"

"Sure boss," he responds, straightening up and tightening his tie, immediately starting the engine. "Bishop Street. Been there plenty times."

"Quick as you can. We have two guests to pick up and take to the ship. I called ahead."

Ten minutes later they turn right, past darkened office buildings and dimly lit bars. Disheveled men in dungarees stand on the corner beneath the streetlight and smoke cigarettes, as they hunker near small clusters of barely-clad women, two of them waving to get his attention.

"Any interest, boss?"

A taut smile and a nod, "No thanks, driver. Another time, perhaps."

"Just kidding, boss. This a mighty bad place for girls. Even for locals like me." He giggles, "Cause sometimes they really be boys!"

"They asked for you, Mr. Malone," Kimura begins, setting his cigar stub on the dark-stained edge of the wooden desk. The stocky man looks tired in his wrinkled brown suit, dark necktie askew. "Before you speak with them, here's the situation. We picked them up over at the palace, and they're damned lucky. One of our street informants told us a small gang formed on Fort Street, near Hotel. That's a tough area, even for locals."

"We know of Hotel Street," Malone responds. "We warned them not to go there."

"Addicts don't listen, or they get a different message, Mr. Malone. Mr. DuPris and his sister were there late this evening, purchasing cocaine, and some men followed them. They proceeded a few blocks over past Bishop to the grassy area around Iolani Palace. That's where our police squad found them."

"Found them?" blurts Malone. "I thought you said they were safe."

"I mean that's where we located them, on the palace grounds. The thugs were headed their way. I know these men. They would have raped both of them, then sliced their throats and taken what was left of their stash. Our squad arrived first and nabbed them. Bums mostly, but one known killer."

"What were they doing on the palace grounds?"

"That's the awkward thing, Mr. Malone. I believe that Mr. DuPris is the brother of Miss DuPris?"

"Yes. That's right, brother and sister."

"They were on the ground, naked, Mr. Malone. They were in the act of copulation. They were obviously under the influence of drugs and could barely respond to our officers. We got them cleaned up and dressed, and have them here in the jail, in a private office. Would you please come down here and vouch for them. They insisted we call you, and no-one else."

"Christ, man. Screwing? That's intolerable," Malone scoffs. "What perverse..."

Kimura interrupts, "Not as unusual as you might think, Mr. Malone. We see worse around this district, when drugs are involved."

"All right, John. I understand," catching himself, he continues. "Thank you for briefing me, and for looking after them."

"You have a car outside?"

"I do, and I've called the *Malolo* and told the duty officer to expect us. We'll take them to their stateroom and assign medical staff." Malone shakes his head, "More than they deserve, damn them. Bloody arrogant kids, they are. Filthy rich and spoiled."

"They should be repentant for a few days, Mr. Malone. They came around a little, once we told them what happened. At first they didn't believe us, but this is a small station. They got a look at the thugs when we booked them, and were scared enough. When I told him they would have been raped and killed, they broke down and cried."

Chapter 21

Malone lies semi-awake, watching early sunlight spread across the garden, and listening to the surf splashing outside the open window. An unexpected memory of Arles flits through his mind, as the sweet garden scents wash over him, carrying memories of that passionate girl from Normandy. That was three years, and many nautical miles ago.

Clearing his mind, he pads over on bare feet and stands in his skivvies, looking out over the water and enjoying the fresh morning air. He is surprised to feel so good after the rough night. Vibrant yellow plumeria shine down below, attached to the tips of gray and barren stalks. The fragrant blossoms gleam with moisture and early sun, in vivid contrast with the stark darkness he experienced just a few hours earlier.

Malone scarcely slept after escorting Emile and Camille back to the ship. Fortunately, they tumbled into their suite easily enough, clearly shaken from the mess they'd been in. He was still angry when he got back to the hotel, unable to shut off the noises in his head. He must have dropped off to sleep, because he was awakened by the surf, and by his thoughts of Justine.

The smells, the sounds, the sun, he thinks. *And look at those breakers!* Slipping out of his shorts, he roots around in the dresser drawer for his swimsuit. Snatching a towel from the neat stack next to the bath, he steps outside and chooses what looks to be a path to the sandy beach. Though it is early, he sees three dark-skinned beach-boys, slim and fit, one of them sweeping and smoothing the sand with a long palm frond, and the other two setting up their surfboards for the guests.

Recognizing Mount Leahi in the distance, he decides to walk the shoreline in that direction, past the massive homes nearby, down the beach to the pristine sands beyond. The narrow beach is almost empty, with just a couple of bare-chested fishermen picking their way along offshore rocks, skillfully hauling in nets filled with a flopping silvery catch. Further out, dozens of men lie flat on their big boards, alternating strong brown arms as they paddle against the smaller whitecaps that break offshore. Three or four others hurtle toward shore, standing tall atop a big wave. As if choreographed, the surfers plunge into the foam in quick succession, heads popping-up many feet from where they fell, each swimming powerfully after elusive boards.

Still on the soft sand, Malone continues his trek toward the mountain, absorbing the welcome sun and feeling at peace. He knows he has another couple of hours before the breakfast meeting with Bergen.

He walks for ten or fifteen minutes, surprised to see a structure just above the beach, graceful arches and a sign proclaiming *War Memorial Natatorium,* leading to a huge saltwater swimming pool fed by the ocean. As he walks on, he is surprised again, by two familiar figures not far away: a shapely girl in bathing attire, and a small man in a tan business suit and hat. He easily recognizes Bergen, dapper even so early in the morning, in his linen suit and vest and the signature Panama hat. But Christy looks very much at ease in her dark swimming suit, displaying quite an attractive body. As he approaches, she is wrapping a towel around like a skirt. They are standing on the beach, looking back at a large section of land.

"Ahoy, you two!" he laughs, and they wave a response.

"Duff," exclaims Bergen, "What are you doing out here so early in the day?"

"I should ask you the same question!"

"Look at you, young man!" chides Christy. "I didn't know you even owned a swimming suit. You look quite fit."

He responds awkwardly, "Well, I couldn't sleep and ..."

"No need to be shy, Duff," she assures him with a knowing smile. "I grew up on the beach, and I'm comfortable around men without their clothes on. I am a nurse, after all."

"Well said, young lady," adds Bergen. "I haven't seen Duff

embarrassed before. It rather suits him."

"Enough, both of you. Now what are you doing this far from the hotel? It's quite a walk."

"Our driver brought us. Bergen-san told me about a beautiful little section of land on a cove, with a sandy beach."

Bergen adds, "This parcel has no name, but back there you walked along one of the local favorites, called *Sans Souci.* One of my Hawaiian friends looks after this land and has asked if I'm interested in living here. They have permission to build a house. The beach alone is wonderful, and the bit of a rise gives a full view of our surroundings. I've come here several times, and find it a peaceful spot. It could make for quite a nice home. You never know when I might want to retire."

"You, retire? Not in my lifetime," chuckles Malone. "But one could be tempted by this place."

"Just a thought, my friend." Turning to Christy, "Shall we give this fellow a ride, or would you prefer to walk him back?"

"There's plenty of time. If Duff doesn't mind, I'll escort him back to the hotel. I can explain the benefits of living near the ocean." Pointing toward the water, down to the left of the wide beach, "Besides, I want to show him the tide-pools down there. They make me remember when I was a little girl."

What an extraordinary girl. Malone strides to his room after escorting Christy back to the lobby. The day has gone quickly, and he must get to the ballroom for the final-night's event. *Say goodbye to the casual clothes. It's back to the tux!*

Formally attired and back on the job, Malone enters the main ballroom and stops abruptly. The staff must have carried every flower on the island into the room. Each table is filled with them, and the sweet aromas are palpable. He looks around the new ballroom. Glittering chandeliers, byzantine artwork across the ceiling beams, those arched windows -- it could be out of Constantinople.

Arriving guests scurry to the dance floor at the open end,

toward the elevated bandstand just beyond. A lively orchestra fills the room with "I Can't Believe That You're In Love With Me", with plenty of brass and a snappy beat. The energy reminds him of that last cruise to Rio. Warm. Plenty of suntanned bodies.

With the DuPris couple securely back aboard ship, Malone can concentrate on his clients, and he's determined to spend a bit of time with Christy, no matter what the captain has in mind. The walk along the beach was promising. *She's quite the ocean swimmer, and looks damned good in that little swimming suit. And comfortable around people. When we stopped to talk with the fishermen, she even had them laughing when she seized that little squid from their net and threatened me with it! She and Captain Christian may be attracted, but you never know.*

Sunset pours through the arched windows that are open to the sea. Malone recognizes the succulence of jasmine, coriander, and the faint scent of meats grilling outside. The soft Pacific air seems to refresh the dancers, who move gracefully across the spacious floor. The dance band, a fourteen piece group called the Johnny Noble Orchestra, is as good as any he has heard, and they know all the latest tunes.

He admires the women, in their thin silk gowns, or sporting shimmering tops and those short flapper skirts. Some of the men wear black tuxedos, as Malone does, while many more favor white dinner jackets and bow-ties. Among the dancers, he recognizes Gwen Gibson with one of the handsome beach-boys from earlier in the day, dressed formally, his dark hands sliding with familiarity across her bare skin, and lower. Her filmy dress and his muscular body move rhythmically to a gentle beat. Malone cannot escape the sensuality, and doesn't try.

Along the walls, bold murals depict bare Pacific natives in tropical settings. The powerful browns and greens and aqua blues are in perfect balance with the exotic natural surroundings. This could be what the Garden of Eden became.

Honored guests mingle at the head table, and Malone gathers his thoughts. He is pleased to see Alita and Lloyd chatting cordially with the evening's host, Hawaii's famed Olympic champion, Duke Kahanamoku. Bergen has described him well. He's a distinguished man. Very dashing. He's obviously comfortable in this public setting. Nearly forty and still athletic, he has been teaching Alita and Lloyd to use the surfboard, and he knows every one of our guests by name.

Malone recognizes that Kahanamoku is quite an astute businessman, too. He generously assigned his beach-boys to assist our passengers during the stay, especially the ladies. He saw them in their matching swimming uniforms. They were quite a hit.

As the dinner ceremonies begin, Kahanamoku welcomes the guests and asks everyone to stand for a blessing, beginning in the Hawaiian language. Then in English, he concludes, "These islands are a welcoming place. We are, all of us, part of a larger *ohana*, or family, brown skin and light. Let us be rich with love and kindness wherever we may travel. May the rest of your journey be safe."

The dinner is served on special silver and china, displaying the stylized 'M', since Matson is the hotel's owner. Malone is seated near Anna and Ruth, who are radiant together; and across from Austin and Marjorie Clark, who are eager to resume the topic of their *Italia* cruise, asking about the ship and ports of call en route to Rio. Malone is more concerned with Christy, seated over next to the captain, but he can't quite hear her. The only voice he can distinguish is that outspoken Warren, who is selling the virtues of his investment syndicate.

Gibson pays the driver and steps out of the spacious cab. He is impressed with the brightly-lit entrance, busy with well-groomed couples wearing light suits and stylish gowns. The Pacific Club is the address he was given, and he excuses himself as he passes between small groupings of people who chat comfortably as they stroll through the entrance.

"Mr. Knauss please. He's expecting me," he advises the maitre de', a tuxedo'd Hawaiian man of uncertain age, unsure if he should tip him a few dollars. He decides against it.

"Aloha, Mr. Gibson," the handsome man replies. "Mr. Knauss and his party are expecting you. Please follow me."

Gibson is surprised with such a greeting, and impressed by this gracious Hawaiian, who could easily be headman at the Waldorf. Following him to a corner table, Gibson is further surprised to see two people, not the solitary man he was expecting. One is stocky and rumpled, in a light linen suit; the other small and slim, in a black shirt, open at the collar and showing a gold chain. The slim man looks a bit like Valentino, with slick black hair and a thin mustache.

Without standing, the stocky man greets Gibson with a wave and gestures to the empty seat. "I'm Knauss, Waikele Land. This is Oveida, my assistant. You're Gibson, of course."

"I am Jason Gibson...yes," he says abruptly. "I thought we were meeting privately."

"Oveida is a good listener and will remember our conversation precisely. Does this bother you?"

"As a banker, no it does not *bother* me," Gibson replies with sarcasm. "But as someone who has been asked by a friend to raise a great deal of money for you, it does put me on my guard." Gibson knows that it bothers him a great deal, and he needs to be alert. He may cancel this loan idea.

Knauss glances at his assistant. "Mr. Oveida, would you please go in and ask Lopaka for a bottle of their best champagne? We would like a few moments alone."

Nodding, Oveida slips from his chair and strides toward the bar.

"Perhaps we should begin again, Mr. Gibson. I'm Carl Knauss, and I was told that you are willing to loan us a great deal of money. That is why we are here."

"And I, Mr. Knauss, was told that you wish to raise a great deal of money through investors, and *that* is why we are here."

"So, a small misunderstanding, it seems, with our mutual friend Thompson at Chumbley. Are you not in the loan business?"

"I am, and also I'm chairman of Worldwide Bank. You have heard of it?"

"Of course, Mr. Gibson, even out here in the tropics, we hear of important New York banks. Thompson said you were interested in loaning money toward our new venture in macadamia nuts."

"My bank is interested in sound investments, and I am interested in new opportunities to bring investors to worthy projects."

"So you are not here to loan us money? Just to find investors? How much time will this take, finding investors?"

"Only a matter of weeks, I should say. I'm sailing to San Francisco tomorrow, and expect to be back in New York by next Thursday."

Rubbing his face, Knauss looks toward the bar and nods. Oveida returns, followed by a waiter holding a silver tray with glasses and an ornate champagne bucket.

"Oveida, let us drink a toast to our friend, Mr. Gibson. I believe he will help us with our little project."

When the champagne is poured, he hands a glass to Gibson and continues, as Oveida reaches across to take a glass.

"To you, Jason Gibson. To your desire to help us with investors." With no attempt at cordiality, he adds, "May you also find a moment tomorrow to call your directors and find a way to loan us one million dollars. Immediately. Or there may be no need of investors."

Stunned, Gibson sips and sets his glass on the table, then rises from his chair. "If you will excuse me, I will not stay for dinner. I will carry your message to my board." Sliding his chair firmly beneath the table, he continues, "Rest assured, I will contact you tomorrow before I sail."

Gibson smiles grimly at the maitre de as he strides out the door, waving at a waiting taxi. "To the Royal Hawaiian hotel, please."

"I'm with the *Malolo* group, and would like to make a telephone call," he announces at the front desk, handing the young man a hand-written note. "Gibson, Jason Gibson. Please connect me with this number. Put the charges on my room account." He can hear rhythmic music coming from one of the ballrooms nearby, like drums and a chant, and piercing laughter. He keeps his head low, to avoid being seen.

Looking down, the desk clerk responds brightly, "Certainly Mr. Gibson. You and Mrs. Gibson are registered, of course. If you will take that telephone over there," pointing to a small table, "I will connect you."

"Something more private, please."

"Of course. Just go into that booth, and I can transfer the call over."

As he rides to his new ship, the SS *Cleveland*, Gibson is worried. Damn Thompson! Good thing I caught him tonight. He told them I would loan the money. He thought Knauss would reassure me. Knauss's attitude surprised him. Never thought he would be so arrogant. Never thought at all, damn him!

Waikele is fighting Dole and Del Monte, and can't win fairly. Knauss cut his costs by paying workers less, then cutting back. Just made a deal for macadamia trees near downtown, to raise capital, diversify. That's what the million is for.

Good thing the *Cleveland* is leaving tomorrow. He's a rough bastard. Glad to never see that Knauss again.

The taxi leaves him at the foot of Aloha Tower. The waterfront area is quiet and empty at this hour. He strides toward the wooden pier to take him to the *Cleveland.*

"Mr. Gibson," a low, unfamiliar voice from near the elevator. "It's Oveida. From the club."

"Ah, yes. Mr. Oveida," Gibson walks further.

"No hurry, Mr. Gibson. I'd like a progress report"

"I said I would call in the morning. Leave me alone."

"Your call from the hotel, was it helpful?"

"My call? What hotel?"

"Mr. Gibson. We have friends at the Royal Hawaiian. All over. Our workers have two or three jobs sometimes. They know what goes on here." He touches Gibson's arm gently, then grabs it tightly. "Come with me, Mr. Gibson."

"I can't. Let go of me."

"I carry a gun, Mr. Gibson. Would you like to see it?"

As the tugs ease the big ship away from the dock, Malone views downtown Honolulu and the sharp point of the distant Nu'uanu mountains through floating clouds of pale pink-and-red-and-blue streamers, providing a surreal link between the waving passengers who jam the rails, and their friends shouting alohas and bon voyages far below. Down on the water, agile outrigger canoes dart off the ship's beam, moving easily against its slight wake. Brown-skinned natives wave their own alohas and *a hui hou*s, while coin-divers entertain passengers tossing quarters, halves and even silver dollars into the sea. Off to starboard, regal paddlers wear the tall headdresses of their forbears, when kings, or na ali'i, ruled.

Unlike any port Malone has visited, Honolulu combines the joy of new friendships with the sadness of a departure. It's such a sensory place. Perfumes of pikake and plumeria in a young girl's hair, and the gentle tuberose in the gardens, and in the lovely leis. How special the textures and tastes of fresh pineapple and coconut, the sweet flavors of lilikoi and mango. And hugs! Everyone here offers a touch of the hand, an embrace. Bodies are enjoyed, displayed, shared. What a generous, loving place.

As he observes the debarkation, Malone recognizes several of the beach-boys at dockside, presenting massive leis to many of our women passengers before they board, accompanied by lengthy embraces. The women, many of them in tears, are the wives of husbands who appear to have returned to the ship early, or spent too much time in their rooms attending to their stock investments. *From the lingering touches, it's clear that I'm not the only one who finds it romantic.*

He feels the ship moving under its own power, disconnected from the tugs which trail further behind. His mood surprises him. Not sadness exactly, but wishing he could remain longer in these special islands. As Christy's smile invades his thoughts again, he watches the colorful flowers floating off the fantail, where passengers have tossed their leis into the sea in ritual tribute. Perhaps these blossoms will reach the shore.

CHAPTER 22

September 30, 1929
Departing Honolulu en route to Yokohama

Dear Mom and Dad and Mary,

We are leaving Hawaii tomorrow morning, and there are so many things to talk about. First, please give Mary a big hug from me. I miss her more and more each day.

I got your letter in Honolulu. Dad, you don't need to worry. I have learned some lessons about men. Mom, you would love Hawaii, with all the flowers and fragrances, and the colorful dresses. You would both love the beaches here. The hotel is marvelous, and right on the nicest beach I have ever seen. Bigger than ours in Long Beach, but I still prefer exploring the tide-pools with dad! I bet he and Mary are finding all kinds of new sea creatures. Speaking of tide-pools, we discovered one a mile or so from our hotel.

I told you about that Englishman, well he isn't English at all, he's from South Africa, and his name is Duff. He is the nicest man, but I don't think he has any idea about me. Well, he knows who I am, but he hardly talks to me. Did I tell you he is in charge of a very important group of millionaires? Just 20 of them, out of more than 300 on the ship. They depend on him for everything, and he has been just everywhere, and knows more about steamships than almost anyone.

I'm working hard, but we do have a little fun. Duff's friends are so nice to me. They have made me a part of their group, like one of the cruise leaders. One of them, an older man named Bergen, is such a gentleman, and everyone loves him, all around the world. He had flowers for me when I arrived, and danced with me at the Hawaiian party.

Speaking of dancing, I have a new friend, Captain Christian, the ship's captain. He is big and handsome and the best dancer!

Something more serious, we had a kind of accident in Hawaii, at least one couple did. They are young passengers, and very rich and flashy. They seem to be addicted to drugs, and as a nurse I am supposed to keep an eye on them. Duff and Dr. Stanley asked me if I would help them look after the couple, to keep them out of trouble. I told him I would try.

I have to go and will send letters to you from Japan. It will take a week or more to get there.

Take good care of yourselves. I miss you. I love you. Special love to Mary!

Christy

PS: People are talking about troubles with the stock market. It sounds important, but I don't know anything about it. You aren't part of the stock market are you?

CHAPTER 23

"I have to admire the man," Malone tells Bergen, as they sit quietly out on deck following the dinner show. "I had no idea he could be so amusing."

"Nor I. That Kirsch can dance, and sing a bit, too. His friend Toots is quite a singer herself."

"Notice how relaxed he seems," notes Malone. "Without that furry mustache, and with his hair slicked back, he is a better looking chap. A bit of a rugged face, this new look might just work for him in the talkies. You heard his comment during last night's show?"

"About brushing up on his horseback riding when he returns home?"

"That and the cowboy song he and Toots have put into the act. They look quite nice in their Stetson hats. Maybe he is destined for those talking cowboy movies he and I spoke about."

"His speaking voice, Duff. How did you describe it?"

"Like a man in need of a throat lozenge, I believe I said. But it is quite good when he sings. And it is just clear enough when he speaks. Just not like Ronald Colman, or some of the other leading men. A bit more like Louis Armstrong."

They wave at Kirsch as he and Toots stop for a break, motioning to join them. "Gin and tonic for the throat?"

"Thanks, Duff, but a beer is right for me. How about you, honey?"

"Champagne, if you please." Her smile brings admiration from the three men, as she sits close to Kirsch.

"It's a gift, we were saying, Aubrey. You both sing well together."

As Toots nods, slightly embarrassed by the attention,

Kirsch surprises them. “I almost quit singing, you know?”

“But why would you? You have a natural talent.”

“It would have been easy, Duff. Where I lived, out in the valley, the kids thought singing was for sissies. My best friend, Cobb, when we were sixteen, he embarrassed me at a school dance. I was singing with the band, ‘Melancholy Baby’ I think, and Cobb brought his girl right up next to the bandstand.” He is smiling, but his expression seems edgy. “I would sing a note, and she would interrupt me. Then I’d stop and make a sort of innocuous comment while the bandleader ran through the intro again. Then I’d start, and she interrupted again, something loud and making-fun of me. I almost gave it up after that.”

“But you didn’t.”

“No, Mr. Bergen, I didn’t. I wasn’t going to let them win, even though I felt a fool at the time.”

“And why didn’t you?”

“Have you ever been in front of a few hundred people, and had them listen to you? Listen closely? Then they stand up and applaud?”

Duff remembers the rugby finals in Johannesburg, and nods slightly, as Bergen watches.

“It’s a special feeling. You’re up there, singing a love song about a woman who left you, or a woman you want to meet, and you see people -- men and women in the front row -- nodding as you sing. Then standing and cheering when you’re done, ‘Well done’, ‘bravo’. You feel a special bond. Sometimes more than that, a power even. It’s exhilarating.” He pauses and realizes that he has dominated the conversation. “Sorry. I didn’t mean to get carried away. But that’s why I sing. I love the feeling when I really reach people.”

As they sit in a quiet corner outside the Veranda Café, Malone and Bergen wait for Christy to join them.

“So there you are Duff?” says a familiar voice. “We seem

to have missed our dance tonight, darling."

"Hello Anna, dear," Malone takes her hand. "Please join us. Care for a nightcap?"

"I do, you rascal. And I believe that Ruth will have a Tom Collins along with me. She's just coming along."

"Sorry to miss the dancing. How did you like Aubrey Kirsch and his associate?"

"First-rate, I'd say. She is quite a good-looker, and he seems very realistic in his cowboy costume."

As they order their drinks, Malone glances across the café, where Emile DuPris leans against Camille's shoulder. He excuses himself to walk over to speak with them, then sees Emile take his sister's hand and slip into the passageway, out of his line of vision. Malone follows behind, then turns back as they head toward the elevator.

"A bit odd," he notes to Bergen, as Anna speaks with the steward, then greets Ruth.

"What's going on with the DuPris couple?" Bergen asks quietly.

"I believe he was weeping. Not the sort of thing I would expect. They left for their room before I could offer assistance."

"I hope he is not back on the stuff already. He really is a difficult young man. And his personality changes constantly."

"What kind of stuff?" asks Anna.

"Just an incident in Hawaii, my dear," soothes Bergen. "a spot of trouble over in Chinatown."

"That sounds a bit reckless, if you ask me," she pauses as Ruth approaches. "Your drink is here," gesturing to the cocktail table next to her. "And here is an open seat. Now Duff, we heard more unsettling news out on deck. It was from one of the other passengers, not someone in our group, and we're just not sure what to do."

"What on earth did they say?"

"They seemed well informed and watch the ticker tape all the time at home. One of them said that we are heading for a big fall. He repeated what we heard earlier, that banks are about to close their doors because of investment loans. They are thinking of leaving the cruise just as soon as we reach Japan."

"You sounded so reassured by your attorney, when you spoke with her from Honolulu. At the same time, we should pay attention to changes." Malone continues, looking over at Ruth. "The two of you may want to contact your counsel again. Our shipboard news is so erratic, and every case is likely to be different. She will know about your own financial situation and your bank's." He adds, "May I suggest something? We can intercede a bit. Would you just jot down a brief radiogram message for your financial advisor? I'll personally deliver it to the radio officer and see that it's sent tonight."

"You are a sweet man, Duff," Anna exclaims, taking his hand. "We'll go and compose our message. Shall we find you here in thirty minutes or so?"

"Certainly, Anna. We'll be here."

"Duff, there you are." Gwen Gibson is pale and seems distressed. "I can't seem to find Jason anywhere."

"Can't find him? Did you look in one of the other cocktail areas? Or I could have him paged."

"That's just it. He wasn't in our suite when I boarded in Honolulu, but that's not unusual. He often prefers to be alone out on deck. I assumed he was there, or up here with you men. That's why I didn't say anything when we sailed. But now I see some of his clothes are missing, and a suitcase."

"That's odd. When did you see him last?"

"The morning we arrived in Hawaii. When I left with the others, he preferred to stay on the *Malolo* the whole time. Said something about using an office downtown to telephone the states. I didn't realize he knew people here."

"That was nearly four days ago. I'll get to the ship's officer and page him. He can't be far."

Bergen is with her when Malone returns, "It's been fifteen minutes, and he hasn't responded. I checked with the radio room and their log indicates he sent something at seven in the morning on Friday, the day after we arrived. Nothing since."

Gwen insists, "Well, we must turn around and go back. He must have missed the sailing."

A hesitant glance at Bergen, then to Gwen, "I spoke to the captain, and he says we can still communicate on the emergency channel, but he is unable to turn back. We've set course for Yokahama, and won't reach land for more than a week.

"This is impossible. Do you know how important he is? We can't just sail on while Jason is standing there at the pier. There must be something you can do."

"Gwen, please. The captain is fully aware, and he's doing all he can. We just need to know, for certain where he is. If you'll stay here with Bergen, the steward is bringing you a drink. I'll be back in ten minutes, and we'll have more to work with."

Christ!, thinks Malone, as he runs up the ladder toward the captain's quarters, two steps at a time. W*hy couldn't she say something before we left Honolulu?*

"No news, Malone," Captain Christian gestures toward the sofa. "Honolulu authorities have no word about Gibson. They will put out a bulletin and check the hospitals. They know he is an important banker."

"Captain," a steward approaches Christian. "There is a radiogram here for Mrs. Gibson. I'm afraid it was misplaced. We attempted delivery during the sailing, but we couldn't locate her. Then it was put in the wrong place."

"Carstairs, how could this happen?" Christian stares at the boy.

"I'm sorry, captain. No excuses."

Then he softens, "It's all right, son. I'm glad you found it and brought the message to me."

As the boy leaves, Christian hands the envelope to Malone. "Here. Let's see if this solves our little mystery."

Two figures emerge, slim and exhilarated as they glide out onto the dark fantail. They locate their "midnight corner", peering down at the luminescent churn of the ship's massive propellers.

"You know you're a splendid dancer, Emi. My favorite ever. Can't we just go back in and enjoy the band? I don't really like it here, so close to the railing.... Talk to me, Emi!"

Elbows on the salt-crusted rail, Emile is barely audible, "Not now, Cami. I'm all right."

"But you just stare and say nothing."

Emile reaches his arm around her thin waist, reaching downward and gently pulling her toward him. He rests his other hand on the safety line. "I see things out there, Cami. Sometimes it's just the sea. Sometimes another ship..."

"Are you still angry Emi?"

Impassive, he looks down at his sister and offers the hint of a smile. "No dearest. Not any more." He slowly runs his hand across her body, as his eyes return to sea, "They don't like us, but I don't care what they think."

"Emi, come, let's go back inside for one more dance. Another drink." She takes his hand in hers and leads him away from the edge, back toward the music.

It's obvious that Gwen is angry, with the message crumpled on the table. Bergen waves for Malone to sit, and to not speak.

"It's Jason, of course. That bastard."

Cautiously, Bergen asks, "Where is he?"

"Gone. He went back to New York while we were in Honolulu. Took a steamer that was headed for San Francisco. Said he had business to attend to."

"What do you want us to do?"

Looking over, she attempts a smile, "I'm sorry, Duff, Bergen. For being so rude. This has nothing to do with you. Just give me a moment and I'll be all right." She waves for another drink and continues slowly, "It is very complicated for Jason right now. At the bank. All of these trusts and loans, borrowing stocks and selling them again. People, close friends, want to borrow money. A few have lost a lot and they blame Jason." Her eyes fill again, "He always said it would come down to him."

"So what do you plan to do?"

"I plan to finish this drink and have another. Then I will go to my room and have a nice bath, sleep through the night, and enjoy the rest of this cruise."

"So you're not leaving us in Japan?"

"I wouldn't think of it. They say that Yokohama is lovely now. Then those other exotic ports. I plan to have the time of my life."

VIA RCA RADIOGRAM VIA RCA

OCTOBER 3 1929

TO DUFF MALONE

FROM MM ROBERTS

STOCK PRICES CRASH IN FRANTIC SELLING.

BANK, INSURANCE, INDUSTRIAL ISSUES FALL SHARPLY.

PROMINENT NEW YORK BANKER MISSING.

WHEAT PRICES DROP ON LIQUIDATION.

SEARS, ROEBUCK SALES GAIN.

NY TIMES QUOTES BRITISH CHANCELLOR SNOWDEN: US STOCK MARKET IS SPECULATIVE ORGY. VOLATILE LANGUAGE.

TOSCANINI GREETED BY VAST CARNEGIE HALL AUDIENCE.

CAPONE PLEA FAILS, JUDGE REFUSES RELEASE.

END

ROBERTS

Chapter 24

"So Gibson is missing." Malone leans back and places his tired feet onto the small deck table. The night is warm and the band barely audible. Malone and Bergen have found a private spot to fit the new pieces together after a long day. His hands are behind his head, propping it up in case there might be answers far up in the dark sky.

Bergen sits quiet and Malone continues.

"How does this affect us, would you say?" Looking over at his friend.

Speaking slowly, "Two things change now, Duff. First, how we need to look after Mrs. Gibson. Second, how his disappearance is interpreted by the others. Everything else is quite out of our control." He looks up, "Did I miss anything?"

"For now, those are the most important issues. We'll have to wait until tomorrow to see how Gwen reacts. She may just carry on and enjoy the trip, as she said. Either we arrange for her to return from Yokohama, or we help her to have a great time."

"Then there is Gibson's absence."

"Yes, there it is. It's going to panic some of them, who are already skittish. Leaving the ship. No word to his wife. Headline in the *Times*. It will only suggest that his bank has problems in this market plunge. And it could be the first of many that are closed."

"And what do you think his departure means, Duff?"

"I'm confused. I hardly knew him, but from Gwen's description he isn't the type to simply run away. He's an important man, and arrogant enough to think he can manage a crisis back at the bank. As for our passengers, I'm sure that many of them will want to get home. Unless we hear something different, they will be afraid their money is about to go under. And I think the further away we sail, the angrier they will get."

"That Snowden should be shot!" snarls Chester Warren, storming into the elevator cage, a massive cigar clamped in his fist. "And that damned Hoover, too. Why doesn't he do something?"

The moment the mesh doors folded open, Malone knew that the magic of Hawaii had vanished. Warren's hairy body is partially obscured by a blue silk robe and matching slippers, but Malone can see where his enraged skin is peeling from the serious sunburn acquired on Waikiki beach. He tries not to inhale the acrid cigar fumes as he watches Warren ball up the daily bulletin and fling it onto the floor.

"Swimming pool level!" he barks. "That Limey shit should keep his damned opinion to himself!" He looks at Malone and asks, "What do you think? Should you foreigners be interfering in our business?"

Malone ignores the tone, as he presses the button and calmly responds, "I saw Lord Snowden's quotation, too, Mr. Warren. A statement from the British leader is a bit out of place in an American newspaper."

"Damned right. President Hoover shouldn't allow it, either!"

"At the same time, yours is a powerful country and your actions affect the rest of the world. What if one of your banks were to close? Your market is down nearly fifteen points today. Just how are we to read these stock numbers?"

"Banks are a different story, Malone. As for stocks, it's transactions. Look at the transactions, man. Nothing out of the ordinary. Stock values may be down temporarily, as you say. Simply attracts more buyers. But does something under five million transactions seem like an orgy to you, when a normal day is three or four million?"

"You know your business better than I, that's certain, and I can't comment on all of the figures. But I'll certainly watch the transactions more closely. And by the way, is it not your congress that legislates your economy, not President Hoover?"

"What's that?" He glares, "Here's the stop for the plunge. Goodbye Malone."

Malone continues to the ballroom and finds Bergen sharing a small table with Gwen. She seems to be adjusting to the journey, and is compensating by drinking more cocktails.

Bergen begins, "Gwen just filled me in on a conversation with her husband shortly after we got to Hawaii."

"I spoke with Jason by telephone the first night I was at the Hawaii hotel. He was deeply worried about where the market is headed. He said it puts his bank at high risk."

"What can investors or depositors do?"

"That's just it," Gwen responds. "It's in the hands of investors. Jason insists it is out of his."

"What does he mean?"

"His bank has very little money to loan. The reserves are nearly gone. He said it is up to the investors in stocks. If they stay confident and leave their money in the markets and their deposits in the banks, we could just get through. But if they panic and sell, or withdraw their deposits, the banks are sunk. Then he said something about trusts."

"What about them?"

"That's what worries me. He wouldn't tell me. He just said not to discuss them with anyone. Keep them to myself. Of course I told him that I really couldn't talk about trusts anyway, because I don't understand them. Then he said something odd. About a pineapple company in Hawaii. It was related to a big loan."

"Did he say anything more about Hawaii? Any customers?"

"Nothing further. Besides, it's a New York bank. What could it have to do with Hawaii? There is something else. On my hotel bill, there was a telephone call to New York on our final night. For nearly thirty minutes, and it was while we were all at the banquet. I told them it couldn't be mine, so they removed it from the bill."

"Probably nothing. But let's store this away," suggests Malone. "Now, I just picked up a few thoughts from that Warren chap. Lord Snowden's public comment yesterday about our stock market really is inflammatory, but it doesn't quite match recent market figures. The number of transactions is up, but not abnormal. Even so, he thinks Snowden's remarks might cause panic. Add your husband's well-informed concerns, and it's obvious that something important is brewing."

"So what should we tell our people?" asks Bergen.

"We're a week away from our next port at Yokohama," sighs Malone, "so our only method of communication is still by ship's radiograms. Passengers can't really communicate with their banks this way, because the radio room has limited time and manpower. The radio officer couldn't possibly handle the large volume if people were to panic. That's why the ship's policy is against this kind of use."

Gwen interjects, "You could offer to assemble the financial orders yourselves, and use your influence to send them all to your Los Angeles contacts, but that would just create longer messages. And what if people change their minds, or send conflicting orders?

Timing is critical. They could blame you for missing the right stock price."

Nodding in agreement, Bergen looks at Malone. "If I read you correctly, we will help communicate to our passengers with daily bulletins. But we will not accept financial orders, nor recommend buying or selling."

"Agreed," Malone nods to Gwen and Bergen. Then he senses movement behind him and looks back at an approaching deck sailor, an unusual occurrence on this luxury ship.

"Mr. Malone," a young voice says.

"Yes, son," as he realizes he recognizes the sturdy boy from the hotel bar on the day after arrival there. "Paul isn't it? You're a deck sailor?"

"Yes, sir. Paul Timson. You bought me a beer at that beach bar." Looking around nervously, "Could we talk for a moment sir? I just have a question, but I should not be in here with passengers."

"Sure, son. Let's just go out on deck where we can talk." As they leave Malone asks, "What's this about, Paul?"

"It's some of us on the crew, sir. We hear the same news as the passengers, and we're worried about what we hear."

"What about it?"

"What's going on with the banks? That banker who ran away. What happens to us if our savings are gone? We're not like these millionaires, who have money stashed away. What if they shut down our ships and we don't have work?"

"I don't know, son. I wish I did. I think you and I are kind of in the same fix, though, because we both need to earn a living." They lean against the railing, as Malone gathers his thoughts.

"Sorry to bother you, Mr. Malone, but I didn't know anyone else up here who I could talk to."

"It's fine Paul. You're fine. I've just been concentrating on our passengers so much, it never occurred to me to think about those of you who actually operate the ship. I tell you what. I'll talk to people and try to figure out what's going on, and I'll tell you what I find out. We're due in Yokohama in a few days. I'll buy you a beer there, and we'll talk again."

"I knew you would help. Thanks!"

VIA RCA RADIOGRAM VIA RCA

OCTOBER 4, 1929

TO DUFF MALONE

FROM MM ROBERTS

WALL STREET JOURNAL REPEATS SNOWDEN QUOTE ABOUT ORGY OF SPECULATION & NY TIMES SAYS US TREASURY SECTY AGREES.

WEALTHY BANKER GIBSON STILL MISSING.

THE WORLD SAYS PUBLIC LIQUIDATION HITS LOW: MARKET SCARE ORDERS HALT TICKER FOR AN HOUR.

NASH MOTOR 9-MONTH EARNINGS UP.

30 PLANES READY FOR FORD CUP AIR COMPETITION.

SENATOR SAYS PROHIBITION AIDS HOOVER AS LARGE GRAPE GROWER.

ROBERTS

DOW CLOSED 325.1, DOWN 4.8 PTS & 1.45 PCT, 5.6M transactions

Chapter 25

Malone and Bergen meet in his stateroom for their morning briefing, where they review the recent radiogram from Roberts. "Here are my thoughts, Bergen. Tell me if I've missed something. I spoke with Captain Christian last night. He agrees that we need to get information out to everyone on the ship, not just our clients. We should hold a daily briefing for all of the *Malolo's* passengers, then distribute our briefing sheets to all aboard. That damned Warren demanded I take him to see the captain last night, ordering him to speed up the ship. *I don't care how much it costs!* Warren bellowed at him. *Just get us to a port!* He seemed mollified when the captain presented the facts. We are at peak speed, twenty-seven knots. There are no authorized ports on our route to Yokohama. And there are no port services available until daybreak on the day of arrival, three days from now. Warren went away for the time being, but we shall see him again soon."

Malone continues, "We're three days from Yokohama, and

when we get there, all hell will break loose. Without our help, all the passengers will have difficulty communicating back to America, not just our clients. We need to expand telephone assistance to every passenger, and tell them about it soon. The Commodore sent his approval last night. This, at very least, will give them a tangible plan as we sail on these next few days."

"It's the right decision, I'm sure, but only if our Japanese offices can find the personnel," Bergen cautions. "Here is what we are facing. The working assumptions are, first, that there will be few English-speaking people available dockside in Yokohama. Next, there will be a major rush to telephone the States, and there are few telephones. Then, telephone operators will not speak English. And finally, the markets will be closed for the day. It will be early Thursday morning in Yokohama, and people will be just starting their day. But in California, it will be two in the afternoon on Wednesday, the day before. All the way over in New York, it will be five o'clock Wednesday evening. Wednesday in America, but already Thursday morning here.

The plan we sent to our Tokyo office two days ago has been acknowledged, and I just added additional staff for the entire passenger complement. It will not be easy, because Japanese businesses are also overtaxed right now. But they will give it every effort."

"So," Malone continues, "It's time to share the plan and encourage these wealthy minds to work on solutions. We need to stem the wild speculation, for everyone's sake."

A storm warning is up and passengers have all been cautioned to take extra care. No-one is to be out on the lower decks, and limited movement is to be allowed indoors. Malone finds the dining room less than half filled at one o'clock. Although the chef created a safe luncheon menu for stormy weather -- clear soups, lean meats and plenty of white rice -- most passengers have chosen to remain in their suites.

The sky is black with storm-clouds, and the ocean is too

rough for socializing. As an old sailing man, he prefers to remain out on deck, craving fresh air and a handful of biscuits, along with a cold lager which tends to settle his stomach. He seems to fare better in storms than most passengers. Oddly, threatening seas never bother him the way heights do. And his early experience with drowning left him respectful of the sea, but not fearful.

He turns to see Bergen approach. "A seaman's picnic, I see," as he chuckles and snatches a biscuit. "I'll have some of the same myself in a minute. The ship's forecast is for rough waters until late, Duff. We really ought to be back indoors. If you agree we will circulate messages to our passengers about canceling the entertainment tonight. The captain has already advised the chef and the dance band."

"A good plan. It ought to be over in a few hours. And this ship is more than up to it. We should be in smooth waters by morning. I'll just go visit with Gio. I saw him earlier, and he asked me to stop in."

As he approaches Sorvini's suite, Malone hears violin music and women's laughter. The door is wide open, so he raps with his knuckles and peers into the room. Anna and Ruth stand at the bar with Alita and Lloyd, shifting in unison with the ships bumps and rolls. They are enjoying snacks and drinks, and singing along with the recorded music.

"Signor Duff! Come in. Come in. We are having a little party. Will you join us?"

"What fun. I'm impressed that you are all such good sailors."

"Pay no attention, is our motto," laughs Ruth. "We have plenty of supplies, and we are ready to party all night."

"You may have to if the forecast is true. I hate to tell you that the captain has cancelled all entertainment for tonight. With the help of our stewards, we can party in our suites, and the main dining room will have limited service, but the usual dinner dance is off."

"So then, Duff, we have no problems," assures the gentle

Italian. "Our impromptu celebration has already started, and all you need do is join us." Smiling knowingly, "We have a special allotment of red wine from Provence."

VIA RCA RADIOGRAM VIA RCA
URGENT...URGENT...URGENT

OCTOBER 6, 1929

TO MR. D MALONE AMERICAN EXPRESS

FROM J KIMURA HONOLULU POLICE DEPARTMENT

BANKER GIBSON'S BODY FOUND. SHOT AND KILLED NEAR PIERS.

HE MET W/ LOCAL INVESTORS.

SEPARATE MESSAGE SENT TO MRS. GIBSON WITH CONDOLENCES.

ASK MRS. GIBSON ABOUT KNOWN MEETINGS OR INVESTMENTS.

WILL CONTACT HIS BANK AFTER YOU RESPOND

END

KIMURA

URGENT. PLEASE RESPOND AS SOON AS POSSIBLE

Chapter 26

"Dammit, man. We're still out on this damned ocean! And I was sick as a dog all last night. Could hardly eat my lunch today." Chester Warren bellows across the table at Austin Clark.

"Warren!" chastises Clark. "Keep your voice down. It does nothing to help by shouting. Much like your barking about the stock market every day."

"Last night's storm was about as uncomfortable as the market reports."

"You managed to survive for another meal."

"I don't need to sit through this." Looking around, he realizes the silence his voice has caused, so Warren stands and gestures to his wife, "Come dear. The steward will bring something to our room."

"Must we, Chester?" she sighs, looking for the steward. "I just ordered a highball. And the dining room is awfully good."

"All right, but I refuse to sit here. We will take a table over in the lounge."

"Good riddance, I say," Clark shakes his head as the Warrens move away. "He is not a stupid man, but by God he is pig-headed. When we left San Francisco, he was the biggest advocate of the stock market. Felt everyone should invest. Even invited us to join his syndicate. Now he's squealing bloody murder."

"Hush, Austin. You'll get your blood up over nothing."

"I agree with you," adds Ruth. "Since exchanging messages with our attorney after we left Hawaii, I do feel safer. She believes that certain banks are truly at risk, but ours is not."

"Certain banks?" asks Gwen. "How would she know which banks?"

"It seems that some banks loaned a great deal of money to investors, and to farmers, but other banks did not. It could be as simple as that. As for us, we plan to enjoy this fabulous ship, and explore these new experiences."

"That's all I know, Gwen. Kimura says his body was found with a gunshot wound. I didn't know how else to tell you, except directly. His telegram is probably in your stateroom by now."

"But this is ridiculous. He's in New York. That's what Jason's message said. They must have found someone else in Hawaii."

"I hope so, and I will ask the police for more details. Your husband would be at the bank in Manhattan?"

"Yes, at the bank or staying in his club. They will locate him."

"Do you know anything about investors in Hawaii, or a meeting there? Sugar and pineapple are million dollar industries."

"I paid no attention to his business dealings. Although he did say something about a meeting in Honolulu. But he didn't share the details. Then there was that phone call charged to my room."

Yesterday's storm behind them, the main dining room is

once again filled. The band throbs with the tango beat of “It Had To Be You”, drawing smiling couples to the dance floor. Malone watches from his seat at the bar, his eyes on Emile and Camille, as they glide undeterred by the other couples. They turn and dip, their pale bodies close together, black and gold in tuxedo and silk, then swiftly reversing and moving together again. Their empty eyes stare past each other, well beyond the ballroom. Between dances they smoke cigarettes among the waiting couples, and appear nervous and abrupt. But when they dance, they look calm and surprisingly considerate of other dancers, yet very far away.

Since leaving Honolulu, the two have remained in their stateroom during the daytime, embarrassed or uninterested. Cocktails and dancing are their preferred state, arriving after ten every night and dancing until well past midnight, according to the bandleader. They leave a heavy tip for the band at the end of the evening, then cling together, skipping and fast-stepping their way up to their spacious suite, sometimes taking a quick turn around the fantail, high-kicking to the orchestra beat. Malone can’t tell if they have been back at the drugs, or if they are merely avoiding temptation. He realizes the third possibility, that they are in a state of withdrawal, surviving on liquor and the high they get from dancing.

Christy and Bergen return from the floor. “You seem a little down old man,” teases Bergen, in his gentle way. “You really ought to have a go.”

“You are a generous chap. How about it, Christy? May I?”

“If you can keep up, Duff. I believe this next one is a Charleston.”

“Let’s go, then.” Instead, Malone escorts her through the dance floor, then over near the bar. “I need to talk for a second.”

“If you say so, mister,” she smiles and winks. “It’s your three minutes.”

Ignoring her innuendo, he continues, “You see the DuPris over there on the corner of the floor?”

“I do.”

"Next time they sit for a drink, would you go over and talk with them?"

"Of course. Should I talk about anything specific?"

"You have experience with those on opium or cocaine, I believe?"

"I've studied it in nursing school," she responds slowly, "Are they using?"

Malone gestures, "I think they could be. I simply don't know. I don't want them to hurt themselves, or to get into more trouble. Will you get an impression by talking with them?"

Christy takes his hand. "You are a good soul. Looking after them, even if they are impossibly rude and spoiled. Yes, I can talk with them, size them up. I'll let you know what I think."

"Thanks. Now, if we can resume what we started back in Hawaii?" Malone leads her back onto the dance floor, as the vocalist begins a new tune, slower than the last. It's a bittersweet song, "She's Funny That Way".

Holding her lightly against his body, Malone finds Christy's arms up around his neck and her head against his chest, softly humming along.

"If I may, Malone," the unmistakable voice of Captain Christian startles him, saying something about a promised dance with Miss Miller and *may I cut in.*

"Ah, yes, captain," Christy whispers, as if awakening. She sees Malone nod and smile wanly as he walks off the floor.

Christy sets her breakfast plate at the empty spot. "Is this seat taken?" She looks over, "Want to talk about last night?"

"If you two would like to be alone,..." Bergen begins, eyebrows raised.

Christy touches his hand and assures, "Nothing like that. Something you're welcome to hear."

Malone begins, “I asked Christy to visit with our young DuPris friends at the dance last night. I wanted a professional opinion.” He looks at Christy, “What do you think?”

“They were pale and clammy,” she begins. “Also, very curt. I almost left them. Then, a moment later they seem friendly enough, speaking rapidly. And their eyes were unfocussed. Still taking something; or maybe they ran out and are just coming out of it.”

Looking over at Bergen, Malone suggests, “They’re moody, but they don’t seem overly anxious. Let’s assume they can take care of themselves while we are at sea, with some oversight from us. Christy can monitor their meals, to be sure they are eating. Then, when we reach Yokohama, let’s decide if we need to hospitalize them, or send them home. Yokohama offers alternatives. Once we are in Shanghai, though, it’s a different matter.”

Returning to his stateroom, Malone chooses to ride the lift. He accidentally pushes the button for the Roman Plunge, then taps his own deck. He waits as the cage-doors open, and before closing them again he hears laughter at the swimming pool. *A bit late for swimmers,* he thinks, halting the closing door, then stepping out.

As he rounds the dividing wall, he is surprised to see a stout dark-haired man in his undershirt and bare feet over by the pool, stripping off his tuxedo trousers and dropping them on a deck chair, laughing and moving toward an attractive woman already in the water, her dark hair soaked, and she is giggling.

“Here, Freddie, just jump in! Careful of the crystal!” she shrieks, guarding two champagne flutes from the impending splash. Then he swims over to her and they stand in the shallow end, raising the glasses and clinking them together, then embracing enthusiastically. They are both in their undergarments, obviously a bit drunk. Standing behind the tall plants, he feels protective, wanting to be certain they will not hurt themselves. Then he realizes that hurting themselves is the furthest thing from their minds. He is shamed at his lurking. She moves back, allowing his hand to rub her breast, and she grasps his underpants and pulls them down. Malone turns and strides to the elevator, remembering Lynette's softness all those years ago, aware of his body's reaction.

MALOLO DAILY REVIEW
At Sea
Tuesday, October 8, 1929
SS Malolo, Matson Lines

Day 16, Port of call: Yokohama, Japan

SHORE COMMUNICATIONS SCHEDULE

-- Telephone communications will be available upon arrival in port.
-- Shore excursions are delayed until 11AM.
-- Coaches will depart at 1130AM for all who wish to visit Yokohama, Tokyo and coastal cities.

TOKYO TOUR: *Those who choose the Tokyo tour will return and enjoy luxurious overnight accommodations at the Hotel New Grand in Yokohama.*

LOCAL TOURS: *Those who choose local tours will dine in style at the Hotel New Grand before returning to the ship following each evening's special receptions and dinners.*

Please be reminded that Yokohama time is 7 hours ahead of San Francisco:
8AM on Tuesday in Yokohama is 3PM on Monday in California.

****

Dow-Jones Final Figures for Friday, October 4 (New York, USA)
CLOSED 325.1, DOWN 4.8 PTS & -1.5%, 5.6M Transactions

JUST IN!
Dow-Jones Final Figures for Monday, October 7 (New York)
CLOSED 345.7, UP 21 PTS & +6.3%, 4.2M Transactions

Chapter 27

At seven in the morning, local time, the *Malolo* reaches Yokohama at last. For the past two days, the passengers have been tense, with heated discussions during meals. The cocktail lounge has been thick with smokers and drinkers until early morning hours. Yokohama is a three-night stopover, with a variety of shore excursions and special dining programs planned, despite the widespread discontent.

The tug guides the *Malolo* into port, past a hulking black vessel moored at the outermost buoy, flying a Norwegian flag. It is surrounded by small boats that will soon carry its passengers to shore. As Malone stands at his favorite thinking-place on the open deck, he considers his choices for this gray and rainy day. Bergen has his hands full with the shore excursions and the passenger communications plans. It is Malone's job to anticipate problems, and to overcome them.

He's prepared for a busy time of it. First, there is Gwen Gibson's telephone call to New York, and he needs to call to Kimura in Hawaii for an update. The biggest concern is the passengers. It's Tuesday in Japan, and last week's stock market figures were circulated two days ago, showing a loss of nearly five points, a noticeable drop of one-and-a-half percent. If Warren is right, it's significant that transactions are approaching six million. There will be new figures for Monday's market before passengers go ashore this morning, and people are definitely worried that the index will go down further.

Their attitudes add to the anxiety. Passengers are always confused after passing the international dateline, where they are suddenly plunged into the next day. It's human nature to resist change, and the dateline crossing had put travelers off these past few days, while they adjusted to tomorrow turning into today. The daily bulletin reminds everyone disembarking at eight o'clock on Tuesday morning in Japan, that the time corresponds with three o'clock Monday afternoon in San Francisco and six on Monday evening in New York. These times will be vitally important to people who are desperate to contact friends and brokers in America.

Malone reviewed the Yokohama procedures with all passengers during yesterday's briefings. Today's sightseeing excursions are delayed until late morning, so passengers can contact people in America. Now it is up to the temporary staff at the pier to carry out the plan, with help from Bergen and his team.

Bergen wired ahead for two-dozen English-speaking staff at pier-side, to accommodate passengers' demands for immediate telephone or telegram contact with the States. They could use more, but he knows that telephones will be limited and trained staff scarce. Bergen's people will translate for the agitated passengers, since long-distance operators will speak only Japanese. These assistants will be stationed in a small section of the pier offices, where a temporary bank of twenty or more telephones will be available.

With ordinary passengers, Bergen might anticipate an orderly and appreciative queue, where phone conversations would be short, out of consideration for others. With over three hundred millionaires, including worried traveling companions, there should be at least 150 important callers and the twenty telephone outlets will be quickly overwhelmed. None of these wealthy passengers is likely to accept a time limit.

The highly-privileged will want even greater attention than the merely wealthy, so Bergen arranged for additional assistance. His Japanese associates hired ten members of the American and British embassies, who have been brought in from Tokyo along with fifty paid students from U.S. and English colleges. Another dozen students will come from nearby Yokohama College. With embassy supervision, these students will meet disembarking passengers and escort them in hired cars, to nearby banks, hotels and business offices. Here, they will assist with overseas telephone calls and hand-written records.

Hoping that all arrangements have been successfully set up, Malone watches nervous passengers assemble on the departure deck in their dark suits and light raincoats, murmuring like restless cattle. The much-anticipated warm, clear weather has been displaced by dark overcast, with rain expected throughout the day.

Then he's surprised to see crew-members handing-out sheets of paper, and people beginning to shout!

"Look! The market is back up! It's up twenty-six points! Look!"

The ship's clerk rushes in with the newly printed briefing sheets, "Mr. Malone, these just came off the press from communications. Could it be over?"

"Let me see the numbers, son. Let's see what the shouting is about." As he reads, he allows a small smile. "This could be a turning point. Cross your fingers."

Bergen has gone ashore to brief his contacts. They, too, will be armed with the latest news reports from local radio broadcasts. Malone follows the passengers down the ramp, prepared to help with any questions.

"I say. Malone," booms Warren's unmistakable voice. "I can't be lining up there with all those people. Have you no special arrangements?"

"Why Mr. Warren," Malone responds. "Of course. I have a wheelchair just over there, and an attendant to help you to the car. See the sailor? The two of you can use that emergency ramp."

"A wheelchair you say? Like a damned invalid?"

"We are in a foreign port, in the rain, with nearly four hundred passengers ready to mutiny if they are not allowed off immediately. Would you prefer to confront them? Or will you make it easy on yourself, and accept the wheelchair?"

"I get you," Warren trudges to the chair and collapses into it.

The sailor covers him with a plaid shawl, hoists an umbrella over, and wheels him toward the quarterdeck, with a slight grin on his innocent face. Swiftly, he rolls Warren down to the pier, where a young girl in a tan mackintosh greets him and escorts them both to a waiting car, where Warren rises from the chair, slumps into the back seat, and is transported quietly away.

In the meantime, the main crowd is disembarking, unfurling umbrellas and streaming toward the telephone building. As expected, slower passengers prefer to move off with the waiting greeters and are placed in cars for private phone access.

Malone moves to join the stragglers, when he sees Christy beneath her dark umbrella.

"Not quite so festive as our Waikiki arrival," she begins brightly.

"Not nearly. But I'm encouraged by your smile. With all that's going on, I need a bit of energy."

Looking up, Christy takes his arm and says, "Those are

generous words. Shall we talk about it one of these days, when there isn't so much going on?"

Blushing slightly, Malone smiles, "I'm not sure what came over me."

Four hours later, Malone and Bergen sit in the ship's lounge, assessing the day's results.

"Our staff were splendid," Bergen begins. "And I told them so when we debriefed down below. I also told them, *If it hadn't been for the bloody passengers, it would have gone perfectly!* and they knew what I meant."

"Those young students were impressive." adds Malone. "They arrived with smiles and brimming with enthusiasm, and never lost their optimism. Even with hundreds of edgy passengers!"

"Quite a lesson for them," adds Bergen. "I told them that they had just seen human nature at its worst; people who are genuinely afraid of losing their life's savings. Most of the passengers were fine and reasonable. But the few spoiled ones took out their fears on our helpers."

"That was first-thing in the morning and our clients had just heard good news," reminds Malone. "Once the system was underway, how did it work?"

"My telephone supervisors report no flare-ups. We expected frustrations as calls were placed, with connection delays and poor sound in places. Overall, once the passengers reached their contacts -- solicitors, brokers, bankers, family -- reality took hold. Most were buoyed by the newspaper reports of stocks rising twenty points since Friday. This was such good news, they actually smiled at our helpers."

"So our clients feel better about the economy?" asks Malone.

"That's just it. The opinions are all over the place. Just now, the hopes are up. Some think the scare is over. I believe our passengers are fortunate to have just one or two headlines reach us each day. People in America must be getting bombarded with so much conflicting information, from radio, newspapers and street gossip, that they just don't know."

"That jibes," Malone nods.

"How so?"

"The number of transactions is back to normal, about four million on Monday. Chester Warren, despite all of his bullying, made a useful observation about gauging the transactions if we want a true read on things. When investors are confident in the direction, they take action, buying or selling. Right now, they are extremely confused, so they are taking no action. Trading is back down to normal."

"Next major topic: what about Mrs. Gibson? Did you get anything new from your police friend in Hawaii?"

"Gwen couldn't locate her husband in New York. She rang their attorney, and he had been worried too, for over a week. It seems that Gibson failed to make any of his normal phone calls."

"And what from Kimura?"

"He's certain it's Gibson they found. Appearance matches the old newspaper photos. His identity and money were undisturbed. Kimura thinks it's related to a big loan that may have fallen through, with a company called Waikele Land & Pineapple. It's a new Hawaii company with ties to the U.S. mainland. They're known to be over-extended for a new farming venture near downtown."

"I assume Gwen will leave us and go back to Hawaii, to verify his identity and settle her own concerns?"

"I think so, Bergen. She's not herself, and whatever conflicts they had, she's badly shaken."

"What do you think? Could it have been someone on the ship who did it?"

"Kimura hasn't suggested it, but we need to consider that one of our passengers might have killed him."

"Lord save us, if there isn't enough going on."

Chapter 28

"What are you doing?" Malone whispers, as he observes Bergen sliding his shoes off and setting them beneath a small bench near the front entry. They have knocked on the door of a newly built house.

Bergen looks up, then points at Malone's feet, "You need to do the same. It's a courtesy here in Japan, to remove our shoes before entering."

Quickly seated, Malone slips his shoes off and sets them next to Bergen's, then rises as a small and frail Japanese man approaches. He is dressed in a black western-style suit and black necktie.

Bergen smiles, and quietly greets their host. "Ariyoshi-san, how are you?" Bergen says gently, in the Kanto dialect that he knows Mr. Ariyoshi prefers to speak. Malone watches the old friends as they exchange bows and formal handshakes, then a lengthy embrace. It is obvious that their relationship has not changed over the years.

They found Mr. Ariyoshi's home with the help of a taxi driver who had known Yokohama well before the earthquake, and had kept a careful eye on the families who were returning as houses and apartments were rebuilt and became habitable.

"I was so sorry to learn of your family."

"Thank you Bergen-san, for your sorrow, and your good wishes. Gone. They are all gone, now, except my sister." He pauses and gestures toward the stairway. "I am fortunate to have my sister still alive, to share this new house."

"I hope that we will meet her, Ariyoshi-san. Perhaps before we return to our ship."

Unable to understand the exchange, Malone remains

in the background, allowing the old friends to converse before formal introductions. He admires the white orchids that rest in a simple black pot, sitting on the corner of a low ebony table near the window. Malone is surprised to see that the house is built in what he knows as a western style, with hardwood floors and blue pastel walls, and molded ceilings. The blue ceramic roof tiles are Asian, but the bold, square design is distinctly western. Mr. Ariyoshi had been an official with the chamber of commerce when Bergen led the American delegation, and is still a respected business owner. Now nearly seventy, he has retired from day-to-day work, and is writing a detailed documentation of the rebuilding process.

"And this is my dear friend, Duff Malone," he leads Mr. Ariyoshi toward Malone, who extends his hand and nods his head in reaction to their host's slight bow.

"My English is limited," said the smaller man, "but I try."

"Better than my Japanese, Mr. Ariyoshi. I am so pleased to meet you. You have a lovely home."

"If you wish, I will show it to you. Very new to me, but I already have a garden."

The three men walk to the hallway, where they are met by a young Japanese girl in western clothes, who skillfully carries a small tray containing moss green cups filled with fragrant tea. She smiles and nods as she precedes them to a door at the rear of the house. As she opens it, the sweet fragrance of flowers invades the room.

"Let us go and sit here for tea," he gestures to the doorway, and they pass through, locating chairs that look out on the colorful garden.

"What a serene place, Mr. Ariyoshi," Malone smiles. "It gives a special feeling."

"A tribute to my family, Mr. Malone. They are with me here in this garden."

"I can feel them, too," adds Bergen. "It is quite powerful."

"This is Yoriko-san. She is very helpful to me and my

sister," he nods at her as she quickly bows and enters the house, leaving the door open. "And Mr. Malone, where is your family? What part of America?"

Startled by the question, "I have no family, Mr. Ariyoshi. At least I am not married." Realizing he has not answered the questions, he continues, "I should say, my brother and mother live in South Africa."

Unconcerned with Malone's hesitation, he continues calmly, "Such a long way from here. I cannot imagine what it is like in Africa. So, you are not an American, though you live there now? And are you a South African?"

"I am, with a British passport since I was born in Scotland and moved there when I was very young."

"So, perhaps you are more of a citizen of the world?"

"Thoughtful of you to say that, Mr. Ariyoshi. Yes, I suppose I do feel a global affinity, more than to a single country."

"It seems so, from what Bergen-san has told me. So tell me, if you will, about one of your cities, down in South Africa."

"Our biggest cities are a bit like Yokohama, I would say, with shops and hotels, railways, automobiles, but a great deal of open space. And there are many mines there. Lots of mining machinery for gold and coal, and too much dust. It is quite different from Japan."

"What of lions and tigers, then?"

"The animals are there, out in the wild areas, the veldt, and people in smaller towns must be on their guard. But the animals do not like the big cities, as you can imagine." He nods toward Bergen, "Bergen-san has been there, and ridden an elephant I believe!"

"Ah, our friend Bergen," laughs Ariyoshi-san, showing his teeth in a smile. "He is known to ride even the wild animals. But we have no such animals here. Perhaps one day he will ride a dolphin."

Bergen lifts his cup in a small salute, the kind smile creasing his face, "That is my dream, actually. To one day swim among the dolphins. But not to ride one, my friend. To me, they are for swimming and dreaming, not for riding."

After a thoughtful pause, Malone asks, "May I ask about the rebuilding?"

"Certainly. What would you care to know?"

"If it is too sensitive, please let me know. I don't mean to pry."

"It has happened, and we must continue with our lives."

"I'm curious about the time which led up to rebuilding. How extensive was the damage? Was everyone affected?"

"All were affected, yes. Though certain homes were spared by the earthquake, the typhoon and tsunami were more thorough, destroying what the earthquake may have missed." Clenching his hands in his lap, he continues. "We lost nearly one hundred and fifty thousand people. It was a terrible time. Survivors were evacuated to places as far as Kobe. And looting. The fear of looting was truly terrible."

"Was the looting widespread?"

"That was the reason why it was so terrible. People feared looting, and there were many rumors, especially against the Koreans."

"What about the Koreans?"

"There has always been a feeling against outsiders here in Japan, and there were many Koreans working in our communities. Rumors spread that Koreans were looting our stores and homes. Groups of local people set out looking for them. Sometimes when they found them, they killed them. Okinawans, too, and other outsiders. We later realized that the looting was not what it seemed." Mr. Ariyoshi rubs his eyes with the backs of his hands, then continues. "Soon, we came to our senses. We stopped the violence against ourselves and our guests, and began the rebuilding. This is when I met Bergen-san."

Bergen places his hand atop the hand of Mr. Ariyoshi, calming him. "I did not know about the looting, and the vigilantes.

I do know that you and your community endured terrible losses, my friend. That is how I met you, with our engineers. I see you now, and am so proud of what you all have accomplished. Your courage. Your dedication. I wonder how our people in America might respond to a major tragedy."

VIA RCA RADIOGRAM VIA RCA

OCTOBER 12, 1929

TO DUFF MALONE

FROM MM ROBERTS

PRESIDENT HOOVER CONGRATULATES PRESIDENT CHIANG KAI-SHEK.

CUBS BEAT ATHLETICS FOR FIRST WORLD SERIES WIN.

STEEL AND UTILITIES STOCKS RISE.

WALL STREET BROKERS ADVISE TO BUY BONDS.

LEGISLATORS PROBE STOCK LOANS.

BANKER SHOT DEAD IN HAWAII, WORLDWIDE BANK CLOSED.

WIDESPREAD BANK RUMORS.

MASSIVE TEXAS OIL SPILL STILL FLOWING.

CHICAGO STORM, 16-FOOT WAVES ON LAKE MICHIGAN

ROBERTS

DOW CLOSED 352, UP 6 PTS & +1.7 PCT, 4M transactions

Chapter 29

"I should be in tears about Jason's death, but I'm not," Gwen says calmly from her perch on the examination table, as Christy checks her pulse. "He was such a difficult man. So damned selfish." Looking up, "I'm sorry for babbling. You have been such a dear to look after me."

"We're worried about you. Doctor wants us to be sure you're strong enough to travel on your own. The return voyage from Yokohama will not be quite as comfortable as the *Malolo.* As for Mr. Gibson, I don't know what to say. Except that I'm sorry for what happened, and what the shock has been. I've never been married, so I don't know how I might feel in your place."

"I should hope that you would have married someone you really cared for, and there would be a true sense of loss." Catching herself, "I'm not saying it right. I wouldn't wish that on you, of course. Losing a loved one. But the marrying part, I hope that's what you do." Smiling, "Someone you love. Maybe that handsome captain? He certainly has his eyes on you."

Christy looks away.

"I'm so sorry, I didn't mean to suggest..."

"No, Gwen. It isn't that, about Captain Christian. It's something else." She composes herself and continues, "The Captain is a nice man, and he's been very attentive. But he is also quite a serious man. Someone who likes to live in a certain, structured way."

"You're an observant girl, Christy. Good for you. I was afraid this seafaring courtship might be turning your head."

"It has turned my head, I admit. But not toward the captain. My parents told me enough about feeling attracted to a man, loving him, wanting to have his children. There's none of that with Captain Christian."

"But Duff Malone, on the other hand?" teases Gwen.

Again, Christy looks away and nods gently, "Of course, Duff Malone. If it were a perfect world, how could it not be? But sometimes our lives are more complicated. That's all I can say about it." Then forcing a soft laugh, "Besides, Duff can't seem to see it yet. He's so serious about his work, and worried about everyone else. We barely talk, except when our friend Bergen gets him to sit with us."

Watching carefully and wondering what complications Christy is avoiding, Gwen continues, "He does seem to always be busy, doesn't he? Planning for the next port, and making certain we are all happy. He is very good at it. And in his line of work, he must be a bit of an adventurer. But he's a dreamer too, I should say."

"Yes, all of those. And he is nice, but he just seems to be afraid to allow anyone to get too close."

Standing and straightening her travel slacks, Gwen takes her passport and documents from a matching beige purse, handing Christy a note. "I'd better hurry, to get over to my new ship. The driver is waiting at the pier. Here is my New York address and phone number. Call, or write to me, will you? I would like to know how you and your adventurer are getting along. I have a good feeling about you two." Leaning down and hugging Christy, "And if you ever want to share more about your complicated life with me, I'm pretty good with advice. Plus, I'd like to see you. Maybe even in Hawaii." She winks dramatically, "I would enjoy seeing one of those handsome beach-boys again."

"It is quite odd," says Bergen, as the *Malolo* edges its way out of the harbor under a glorious blue sky. "Our passengers seem to have completely ignored Yokohama. They should have been enchanted with this amazing place, to see its culture, its resurrection. What a sad and inspiring story. Yokohama was a much-anticipated stop for us before the earthquake, then the typhoon and giant tsunami, and now it is this beautiful new city once again."

Malone has seldom seen his friend so agitated. The usual laugh-lines around his eyes are dull, dark creases.

"The entire city was wiped out, and surrounding areas, and more than one hundred and fifty thousand people were killed or never accounted for. Can you imagine?" He rubs a hand through his rumpled hair. "And look at it now, just six years later, literally rebuilt from the rubble. But as people returned to the ship today, they spoke only about how the market is rising, and worrying about, will it last?"

Bergen's eyes acknowledge Lloyd Winston and Count Sorvini, who have brought their coffee over to the table. "I was just saying how our people should be delighted with their excursions into Yokohama. Every group I have ever accompanied has wanted to share stories about the colorful geisha attire and exotic silks, the flower gardens, tea ceremonies and the lovely little wrapped gifts. Especially with these past two days of sunshine." He shakes his head. "But so far, nothing but money-talk."

"I have always loved Yokohama," nods Lloyd, "We were devastated when the tragedy struck. But the resilience of these people is inspiring, after generations of storms and tidal waves. Their determination is quite a contrast to our own country at the moment. America's extreme capitalism has put us badly off our track."

"Extreme capitalism, Lloyd?" asks Malone.

Sorvini watches closely, his eyes following each, saying nothing.

"That's my term for the last decade or so. When everyone went wild after the war. And now people are fixated on money and borrowing. Gone crazy for big cars, big homes, big investments, and all these new electric gadgets. Is this what we have become? Defining ourselves by our wealth, and our things? The size of our houses? When Alita and I left for China, America was struggling to come to terms with job conditions of the working class, women's rights, diseases -- all sorts of moral and ethical questions, for the good of our country.

We supported President Wilson then, even if we disagreed with some of his measures. We were dealing with what was best for our people. If our president failed, we all did. Then the Great War happened, where first we supplied food and munitions. Brave Americans died helping our allies to halt the brutal expansions in Europe. As a country, we jumped in and fought for democracy."

He shakes his head slowly, "An heroic decision on our part, certainly, to side with the rights of people who were fighting Germany and throwing off the monarchies at the same time. These were actions on behalf of democracy, not capitalism. It was simply the right thing to do. Now many of our politicians make it sound like it was all about protecting capitalism, the right to make more money. But capitalism doesn't require democracy in order to flourish."

Sorvini's eyebrows rise, and his mouth twitches slightly, "You make an important point, you know. It was the right thing to do. For America, and for your many friends in Europe." He pauses and nods at Lloyd. "America helped the Italian people, for example, by bringing the bloody war to an end. We are not a democratic country by any means, yet we are also capitalists. Where I was raised, it was like prohibition in America is today, but for all of our laws. All the time, more laws that people ignored completely. Like capitalists, we bribed the police or the local officials in order to succeed in our lives. Not just business, but growing food, marrying, getting building permits, everything. If you do not believe in your country's leaders, you ignore their laws and find other ways to live. Though our government is militaristic now, with Mussolini the ruler, Italian people are quite different from their politicians. We are genuine capitalists for the most part. Italians have always believed in making money."

"You make an important distinction, Gio. Some in America think that capitalism is just another word for democracy," Lloyd responds. "But I disagree. There certainly is capitalism in totalitarian countries. A wise friend once told me that capitalism is the rich protecting the rich, and every man for himself; but democracy is all of us taking care of fellow citizens, for the common good. I like this second approach."

Sorvini lifts a hand and quietly adds, "We sometimes see Americans as a bit naive, if I may use the word. Living in New Jersey, I was aware of 'laws for this', 'laws for that', made by the politicians, and poor people had to follow those laws. But the people with money ignored what they did not like, and got to do what they want. Not much different from Italy. Capitalists, totalitarians, it is still the rich taking care of the rich. But America is a great country, not because of the capitalism. Many of us believe it is great because of the democracy. Voting. Speaking out. Things we cannot do in our countries."

Lloyd responds, "You have said it very well, Gio. I wish more Americans realized the distinction. Many do confuse capitalism with democracy, and we often use the words interchangeably. But often they are in direct conflict. In my opinion, America's major conflict is between capitalism and democracy. Greed and ideals.

The thought of free markets parallels the idea of our free vote, but they are not the same. Markets are not free if they are manipulated or controlled, so this is a misnomer. Democracy deals with our fundamental freedom as citizens, to be ruled fairly, and to improve our lives. That's what allows a man like Babe Ruth to move up, or George Washington Carver. We abide by laws, we vote for our leaders, and for their beliefs about how we wish to be governed, about how it must be best for all of us. We have a vote. And we have the rule of law."

Lloyd winces and shakes his head, chuckling at his friends, "I apologize for the lecture, but since I've gone this far, please indulge me this final point. Democracy is far larger than capitalism, which simply deals with selling and buying. And capitalists frequently use their influence to twist the laws to their own advantage, if they can. Capitalism is for the people who own and operate businesses, such as Henry Ford or Charles E. Mitchell. They risk their investments, and they benefit from the profits. But we need to remember that those profits are made with the help of workers who build the new cars and buildings so they can buy food and housing for their families. Owners and workers need each other. It's a covenant. Their work helps the worker survive, and it makes the owners richer. The covenant is to not let the gap become too great, between rich and poor, or the poor will rise up against them."

"I agree, Lloyd," Bergen's eyes are intense, clearly provoked by the conversation. "But the most important conflict between capitalism and democracy is not really with you or with me. I'm in the middle, and you are toward the top," startled by his admission, "and we can get along. It's with the people who run our government -- and those who run the unions I might add -- and those who influence them. As you have said, the craving for money seems to encourage people to cheat, to shave the rules. Politicians even change laws to make some forms of cheating legal. Big companies encourage people to buy things they can't afford, or don't need. That's why those new credit contracts are issued. All of this ensures that the money goes to the already wealthy, and not the lower classes. And it seems that union leaders often act like politicians, forgetting the workers' needs, and simply asking for more in order to win reelection and live like the wealthy. That's not democracy, it's capitalism."

Lloyd carries Bergen's point further. "Duff, would you or

Bergen go to war to defend your earnings? If someone said you cannot not earn your money from this cruise industry?"

"It wouldn't be necessary," responds Malone. "My employment is controlled by my company, by the bosses of my company. If they discharge me, I will find another job. So, no, I wouldn't go to war over my job."

"But if they fired you because someone else cheated, and discredited you -- or took credit for your work?"

"Of course not. I would find the bugger and pound him silly!"

"And so you might. But what if that liar could not be found, if he was too deeply hidden in the organization, by paperwork and personal connections? What if people lied about your work, or the value of an investment, or a company's worth? Because that is what capitalism can do, if it is not restrained or overseen by someone honest. Put it another way. What if your country's leaders said you had to go toil in a cornfield in Missouri, and that you would turn over all of your crops to the government, would you fight against that?"

"Of course I would. It happens in parts of Europe and Asia, Latin America," responds Bergen. "That's the difference between choice and no-choice."

"Would you fight the order that sends you to Missouri? Or physically attack the people who gave the order?"

"In our society, we get to decide for ourselves. I would fight the order in court."

"What if you had no courts, no democratic right to decide for yourself?"

"Then I would fight for democracy, against the king or tyrant who thinks he can order me around. We saw this in Prussia."

"Right again, Bergen. You would fight for democracy, but not necessarily for capitalism. Capitalism is a right we get, under the laws of our democracy."

Fully engaged by the topic, Malone asks, "So what's your

point about extreme capitalism?"

"It's that when money is the overriding goal, the main criterion for a man's worth, more important than his character, his ethical positions, the way he treats his wife and family. Just now, I believe we have reached an extreme stage. A very unhealthy one."

"And how about the way a man earns his money these days?" Malone interjects quietly.

"Point taken, Duff, if you refer to the stock market. If there is no labor involved, no product or investment of himself. People are investing in companies that produce things the investor often cares nothing about, caring only if the stock value goes up. And if there is an outside force that allows certain people to benefit from inside information, such as the syndicates? Or hide the money, like trusts? I find this to be a distortion of capitalism, a corruption. Today, we are seeing an extreme distortion. So much so, that even the privileged insiders are affected. For me, this is a fault of capitalism and not democracy. Plus, it is too much like gambling."

Chapter 30

October 4, 1929

Dearest Christy,

I hope this reaches you in Japan. Thank you for your letter from Hawaii. Mary is so precious. She and Pete spend every morning down at the beach, just the way you used to do. She misses you, and she tells us how much she loves you.

Your friends sound very nice, and they seem so willing to look after you. But what about that Captain Christian? Your father thinks he sounds unprofessional and a little fast, so be careful. Your South African sounds nice, possibly a little slow when it comes to noticing women, but probably harmless. We are confused about the couple and their drugs. Shouldn't the ship's doctor be looking after them? These millionaires sound like flashy people.

We are fine. I feel better now that the hottest weather is mostly gone. I still work at the hospital every day, and they are very understanding if I need to leave early some days, or need to bring Mary in with me. Your father has been hearing about problems with some of the steel companies. Sometimes deliveries are slow and they close the shipyard on some shifts. Something to do with transportation problems for the steel, I think.

We did love hearing about the flowers and lovely Hawaii visit. It sounds like a beautiful place. Is the weather always nice? Are you getting enough to eat? Your father is asking if you are taking care of yourself. I think we both know what he means.

We love you,

Mom and Dad

PS: We have been reading about the stock market in the papers too, and it sounds serious. We are not involved, so we don't really understand much about it.

October 10, 1929 *Yokohama en route to Shanghai*

Dearest Mom and Dad and Mary,

Yokohama was glorious. Such a dignified, gracious country. We had three sunny days, and our passengers were in a good mood, especially after seeing the stock market go back up on Monday. These millionaires are always looking at the stock prices, and missing almost everything else, except their cocktails.

Our first day in Japan, I joined a group for a private tour of a museum and some lovely public gardens, while Duff and Bergen visited one of Bergen's closest friends. Bergen-san is very famous in Yokohama.

Most of the city is new, and some of it looks American, like the Astor Hotel where we stayed. But all of the signs are in Japanese, and no-one else speaks English. A huge earthquake destroyed most of Yokohama a few years ago, and it is almost entirely rebuilt.

We even had a special tea ceremony in an old Japanese inn outside of town, which was not destroyed by the earthquake. We rode there in a private motorcar, if you can believe it, even over here in Japan. They drive on the left side of the road!

The next day, we all went together to an elegant new hotel for a special Japanese dinner, then we all danced to a western orchestra. Very fancy.

Mary would love the gardens here. They are so carefully designed and cared for, like little paintings filled with the brightest possible colors. The food is unusual, but Bergen-san always finds us something we can recognize. I would love to bring Mary here!

Dad, I have never seen so many ships in a single harbor. I recognized some of the flags, from Denmark and England, of course. But flags from many other places I did not know. Most of them were anchored far from shore and had to use little boats to bring in their passengers. The Malolo *must have paid lots of money to come all the way in to the piers. Our passengers were very impressed.*

Something strange happened after we left Hawaii. Gwen Gibson, a new friend of mine, told us that her husband, a famous banker, was not aboard ship. He left us in Honolulu without anyone knowing it! She was very upset and worried.

Tomorrow morning we sail for Shanghai, and I am sort of concerned. It sounds like a mysterious city. Mr. Bergen said that he would show me some of his favorite places, including artwork that is thousands of years old. He is such a dear man. He promised to take me on a rickshaw, too. It could be exciting!

I'm told that we will not post any mail from Shanghai, but I will write you again from Hong Kong. Their postal service is supposed to be quite dependable. Maybe I will receive a letter from you in Hong Kong.

I love you! Please give big hugs to Mary!

Christy

Chapter 31

"Good news," asserts Chester Warren, eyes shining at his two companions. "The decline has stopped, and the market is up over six percent. Now is the time to hold on and to cut costs."

Austin Clark responds, patting his jacket pocket and then his slacks, until he locates an after-dinner cigar, "Are you talking about government costs, or corporate?"

"All of it. We can't continue this high-living, where even the workingman can afford to invest."

"Are you saying we are in financial trouble?"

"Of course not. It's just time to tighten our belts for a few months. It will help the market straighten out."

From his left, a new voice is heard. "So you're saying that Henry Ford should lay workers off?" says Jonathan Lemmon, a banker who is not a part of the American Express contingent, taking the empty seat across from Warren.

"Exactly, Lemmon! And so should Standard Oil, National Bank and the U.S. Government."

"What about farmers?"

"What do you mean, farmers?"

"Who will buy their crops, if people are laid off?" Lemmon frowns.

"They can sell them to the wealthy. There's plenty of us left. Or sell them overseas. Or in Canada."

Clark adds, "Cutting people from banks and the government? You're talking about educated people. What would we do with highly educated poor-people? They could eventually align with the masses and there could be violence."

"Let them clean buildings, or streets. Repair machinery. They'll find something. How about another war?"

"That war remark isn't funny," Lemmon trades glances with Clark, then asks, "You are saying that businessmen should fire workers, as a way of helping the economy? What does that have to do with the price of stocks? Or banks closing?"

Wincing as if he were addressing small children, Warren says, "Improve the efficiency by cutting costs. Improve the value of a company, because of increased net profits. The bottom line. The government should work the same way. When companies do better, then stocks do better, and loans become stronger."

Lemmon asks, "Do business owners have no responsibility to employ workers? My mathematics tells me that increasing sales has a greater influence on the bottom line than does cutting expenses. If people are not employed, how can they purchase cars or houses, or dine in restaurants, or even exist?"

"Owners have no obligation. It's as simple as that."

Clark puffs his cigar and asks, "Should the government find a way to protect banks from failing? Like an insurance policy?"

"Hell no," blurts Warren. "A good bank is well run, and it will survive. A bad one isn't, and it deserves to fail."

"Isn't that a bit cold, Warren?"

"Cold is what happens when you get fired, or when your parents die." He adjusts his black tie and looks up at Clark, "These financial things are strictly business. And I was serious about a war."

"You were gone overnight, Gio. I hope you enjoyed your time in Yokohama," Malone sets his whisky glass on the bar.

"It was good, Duff. A nice visit. Not as exciting as Arles," chuckling, "but very nice."

Tickled by the unexpected reminder, "No spontaneous parties, you mean?" Then, serious, "Do you mind if I ask how you liked Yokohama? We are wondering why our passengers seemed so indifferent to Japan."

"Not at all, Duff. I am most interested in Japan, and particularly in Japanese dining."

"So you did not take one of our excursions?"

"Actually, I did, into Tokyo. It was quite interesting, but then I left the tour when it reached the Imperial Hotel. I went by rail to visit certain restaurants in Shinjuku and Akasaka. I returned by private car."

"You explored, then, as you did in France? Did you feel safe?"

"Of course, Duff. Japan is quite a civilized place, perhaps the most civilized I have ever seen. And as you know, those of us in the restaurant business tend to look after one another."

"One day I would enjoy the time to really explore a country, get to know it as I used to in Egypt and Kenya."

"And Arles, my friend? You, too, were exploring a bit."

Duff smiles again at the reminder of how their friendship formed, and of Justine. "Of course I remember Arles, Gio. But time was so brief there. Far too brief."

"You will find the time, Duff, I am sure of it." Sorvini looks him over, "You are an inquisitive sort of man, and people like you. You will see Japan and much of the world, in your new life."

"New life, Gio?"

"You are on a new path, I think. We are a bit similar, Duff, though your background is more complicated than most, coming from South Africa. It is a country that Americans find quite mysterious, or do not know at all. This suggests an adventurous spirit, coming to America, and you seem to want to see what is on the other side of things. At the same time, you wish to please people far more than I do," He swirls the clear liquid in his glass and says, "This cruise is a beginning for you, I think. Just a beginning."

Setting down his glass again, Malone stands and pats his friend's shoulder. "I'm not certain what you mean, nor why you have said it. But I like the thoughts."

"Ah, Duff, here are Mr. and Mrs. Clark. I have been meaning to speak with them. He went to university in Boston, I believe. We're thinking of opening a restaurant there."

VIA RCA RADIOGRAM VIA RCA

MONDAY OCTOBER 14 1929

TO DUFF MALONE

FROM MM ROBERTS

TODAY'S NY TIMES:

COMMERCE DEPARTMENT DENIES SEVERE DEPRESSION IMPENDING.

CITES MISTAKEN FED RESERVE BOARD REPORT.

GOLD INFLOW AND CREDIT POLICIES HOLD DOWN U.S. INTEREST RATES.

AT&T SETS RECORD FOR 9-MONTH NET.

WHEAT PRICES DROP AS LEADERS SELL.

AUSTRIAN BANK CLOSES.

CUBA BEING ELECTRIFIED. U.S. HAS 90% OF EQUIPMENT CONTRACTS.

ATHLETICS DEFEAT CUBS IN WORLD SERIES.

LARGEST SHIP EVER BUILT IN U.S., SS PENNSYLVANIA, COMPLETES MAIDEN TRIP.

AIRLINES CARRIED 14,784 PASSENGERS IN SEPTEMBER.

END

ROBERTS

New York Market Figures for Monday, October 14

DOW CLOSED 350.97, DOWN 1.7 PTS & -.5%, 5.5M Transactions

Chapter 32

"It's a harsh city," Bergen begins, leaning forward in the straight-backed chair, glancing over at Malone. Each holds the printed itinerary sheet that Bergen has prepared. Despite the humidity, he looks comfortable in his white linen suit and lively red plaid bow-tie. "The Chinese are often abrupt, and their language sounds rough and aggressive, as German sometimes does, and Russian. They spit a lot in Shanghai, even the women. And you'll see them pissing against a building. Even the women."

Before Malone can ask why such a godforsaken place is on their itinerary, he continues, "It's also an exotic city, often called the 'Paris of the East', and with good reason. Like Paris, Shanghai is a crossroads for many cultures, seething with merchants and politicians from all nations. The big countries live within the

International Settlement, keeping them safe from the Chinese warlords, and from masses of uneducated peasants who come from the countryside, looking for work. Foreign warships stand in the harbor, ready to protect their trade interests. The British influence is longstanding, as is the Russian. The Americans are here, along with French, Italian, German and every other so-called civilized country.

Shanghai holds priceless artifacts and jewels, silks, and breathtaking works of art that are thousands of years old. You can hear incredible music, eat complex and delicate foods, watch ancient forms of dance. But Shanghai is also harsh, conflicted and wide-open. The stench of open sewers and sights of people defecating at the side of the road are startling. There are opium dens, rough bars and brothels, and dangerous thieves moving through the streets." Looking tired from his preparations, he pauses, "As always, it is our job to show our guests the best of these cultures, and shield them from the very worst."

Malone reads through the sightseeing tours, to understand his assignments. Once they tie-up at the pier, passengers will have questions about the tours they have requested.

Bergen continues, "We spend three nights in Shanghai. This afternoon, we offer shopping excursions in closely monitored groups, using motorcars. Tonight, fifty passengers -- including all of our clients -- will dine, celebrate, and stay overnight at the Astor House Hotel. It is quite elegant. Night clothes, razors, French perfumes and other personal amenities will be provided in each hotel room. All others will attend elegant Chinese banquets near the hotel, which will run until near midnight. Immediately after, they will be brought back to the ship. It is important to control our movements in this place." He pauses in case Malone has a question. "The next day, the same patterns, with a different group of fifty staying at the hotel. Everyone else returns to the ship, without exception."

Malone asks, "Shall we be positioned on the ship, or ashore?"

"Ashore during the day, until about 4 o'clock. The ship's

duty officer will oversee our people through the night, and he will know where to reach us if something happens. As always, at the end of every day I will verify each excursion's actual return time with the tour company, account for each and every passenger, and receive any incident reports."

"What about telephone communications to America? People will be eager to call for news. And I need to contact Roberts in Los Angeles."

Bergen responds quickly, "Very difficult in Shanghai. The telephone system is nearly impossible, and our influence here is severely limited. I will get over to the embassy on Huangpu Road when we arrive, and explore methods for overseas communications. And I can try to get through to Roberts. Embassy staff will provide bundles of the latest American newspapers, which are likely to be a month old, and some from Britain that are a bit newer. Those will be brought aboard and papers placed in individual staterooms later today. Even old news may be better than no news."

"Meantime," Malone adds, "we distribute today's briefing sheet, with updated stock market prices and any other recent information. This morning our people will read of a market that is only slightly down, but with five and a half million transactions -- about one million more than normal. Something seems to be stirring."

"One final item," Bergen reminds. "We have a special itinerary for the DuPris couple. We assigned Mr. Newton, a very capable guide, along with an experienced Chinese driver. Their orders are to spare no expense, but to keep them away from the International Settlement, especially the French Concession. We want them far from those opium dens. We have them scheduled for museums, galleries and elegant clothing shops, with stops at two of the finest restaurants in the city. Plenty of champagne, but no free time."

The dusty Humber touring car moves away from dockside, with Camille and Emile nestled into the spacious rear seat. "You there. What is your name again?" demands Emile.

"Newton, sir. Please call me Newton," placing two fingers on his hat-brim, in an informal salute, continuing in a soothing voice, "and this is our driver, Mr. Chung.

"Well, Newton. What have you planned for us? Is there anything worth seeing here? It looks shabby and the stench is disgusting!"

"We have an interesting itinerary, I believe, Mr. DuPris, Miss DuPris. Shanghai is quite an ancient city, with many cultures. We know of certain shops that specialize in ivory, silk, fine antique artwork."

"Good God! Don't look out the window Cami, that's a body floating there, in among the turds!"

"Emi, stop looking then. We're in China, so nothing should surprise you. Quit grousing and let's leave things to them," she mutters, placing an ivory holder between her lips, cigarette glowing.

"Fine, then. Drive on." He flicks his hand and glances into the distance. "By the way, ah, Newton. You must stop at a bank or something. We need money."

"Sir," he responds carefully, "I will be pleased to handle any transactions, add them to your account. No additional charges or fees. Simply a courtesy."

"Dammit, man, I said I wish to exchange money." He wipes his forehead in agitation, as Camille shakes her head briefly. He continues more slowly, "We wish to negotiate for ourselves with these merchants."

"As you wish, Mr. DuPris. We will stop en route."

Once the currency is traded, Emile seems to calm and they tease Newton. "Are you Chinese, may I ask?"

"No sir. A British citizen, from Yorkshire.

"Ah, my mistake. You are a short chap, and I know the Chinese are a short people."

"As you say, Mr. DuPris." Newton glances at Chung, with a small wink.

"So, Mr. Newton. Do you know what Americans like to do?"

"A bit, Mr. DuPris. I believe that some Americans wish to see the art museums, and others the shops." Watching closely, he continues, "Some of the younger men prefer to find a local pub, or cocktail establishment, and have some drinks."

"That sounds better, Newton. Take us to one of those."

"Emi! You told me I would see shops," Camille injects.

"There are shops on the way, miss."

Newton remains alert in the front passenger seat as the couple reclines together in the rear. Thinking he has heard a question, something about a prickly pear, Newton turns toward the couple, then looks forward again as he realizes the youngsters are simply exchanging gibberish.

He watches carefully through the windscreen as the bulky automobile edges slowly through the crowded and bumpy street. Chung leans forward to better gauge the tiny spaces between his front bumper and the approaching buildings, careful to maintain enough movement to prevent the crowd from collapsing in on them. He brakes quickly to avoid hitting a small man carrying a live pig. After a time he stops before a spare wooden structure that is fronted with broad tables filled with stunning materials of deep reds, pinks and royal blues, rolls of silks and cottons. Camille gasps, "Emi, this is just what I want."

"We will shop here," Emile proclaims, remaining seated as Newton steps swiftly out and opens the rear door for him. Exiting, Emile turns to offer his hand, as his sister slides swiftly across.

"We may be here an hour or so. Wait for us," he orders, as they stride toward the shop arm-in-arm.

While Newton and Chung wait, they watch peasants struggle past, with occasional Anglos stopping and sorting through the merchandise. Newton nods at a friend, also waiting with his car and driver. "I'll just be over with Mr. Eustice there, Mr. Chung. If you will stay with the car, I will keep an eye out."

Chung acknowledges with a brief smile and returns to the driver's seat, removing a dark cigarette and leaving the door ajar.

As time passes, Newton looks at his pocket watch and walks over to Chung. "Forty minutes now. I shall just have a look." Then he walks into the shop.

Quickly he returns and tells Chung, "Find me a telephone, man. They've gone!"

It's past six o'clock, Malone exhales in frustration. I haven't heard from Bergen since three when Newton told him that they entered a small silk-shop. The shopkeepers said a young couple left through the back, out to a small alley, a sort of bazaar. Any number of possible escape routes.

Malone agreed when Bergen preferred not to work through the Shanghai police. They are known to be corrupt. Instead, Malone asked Lloyd for help with some of his old friends at the British embassy. This British network offers a better chance of success when looking for wealthy young caucasians speaking English.

They leave contact information at the radio room, and are driven to meet Bergen at the Astor House. His long friendship with the general manager, a German ex-pat, gives access to a functioning telephone, and a room if they should decide to stay the night. It is far too late to telephone Los Angeles, so Roberts' update will have to wait.

Malone nods to Bergen, "We know where they disappeared, and they will be nowhere near that place by now. What did our man Newton indicate, exactly, about what they said to each other? "

"He said there was a great deal of serious whispering, and when they spoke aloud, he didn't believe much of anything they actually said. They played mocking, sing-song word games -- something about a 'prickly pear' -- obviously trying to put him off, and they were most successful at that." He adds, "They did flash a good bit of money, American dollars of course. And at their request, he took them to an exchange to obtain Chinese currency for shopping, but they also got British pounds. Newton lost them in the shop."

"They are spoiled, and will want comfort along with their narcotics," Malone thinks aloud. "The plainclothesmen should first ask at the fancier clubs, obviously where English is spoken. If those are not successful, they should try the ones where the wealthy Chinese gather. Leave the rougher places until last."

"It's a good start," Bergen agrees. "But if they disappear into this city, no-one will ever know it. At best, we will find them before they reach the opium. Or, they might succeed and return to the ship in a stupor. Even that could be fatal, depending on the quality of the drugs. Indo-China opium is still coming into Shanghai, and so is the Arabic stuff.

"Come inside Cami, walk slowly and look at the silks," Emile whispers as he closes the thin bamboo door, leaving Newton and Chung outside. "They will speak English in there, I'm sure of it."

"Why would they?"

"Newton brought us here so we could negotiate. They must." Leading his sister by the hand, Emile slides through the small doorway, into a room crowded with rainbow colors. Beside a small wooden table, placed just inside the open rear entry, sits an old Chinese man who watches them without greeting.

"English. You there, do you speak English?"

A small smile appears behind grey wisps of beard, then waves weakly as if he cannot understand.

Flashing a wad of British pounds, Emile says one word, likely understood in many languages, "Opium!"

The smile disappears and the man stands carefully, struggling on brittle legs, as he makes his way out the back.

"Emi," should we trust him?"

"No worry, Cami. He wants the money. He knows Newton brought us. He'll help."

Camille lifts a thin bit of violet material when Emile says, "He's back. Quick Cami, he's asking us to follow."

Taking her hand, they step onto the narrow wooden board that covers dirt and garbage in a narrow alleyway. "Careful Emi. Not so fast."

The alley is short and Emile sees the dirty automobile with a Chinese sitting behind the wheel, the shopkeeper standing at the open rear door. Handing him a clump of bills, Emile slides into the car and pulls Camille behind. Smiling now, the shopkeeper closes the door, turns and steps back onto the wooden walkway.

"Where are we going?" Emile demands, as they creep along the crowded dirt road.

"It's like living in an ant-hill," chides Camille.

"Driver, I asked..."

The driver holds up his hand in acknowledgement, then reaches back with an open palm.

"He wants you to fill it."

"I know, Cami. I know what he wants." Emile places two bills in the hand, and it quickly closes around them.

"I thought we were lost," Camille pouts, slowly stepping from the car, locating a dry spot of dirt to stand on. "That man never said a word to us."

They follow behind the European in the dark suit, who had greeted them in French-tainted English and asked them to come inside the walls, through the heavy door that closed tightly behind them.

"Do you have a name?" asks Emile.

"No, sir. Follow me please."

They walk down a narrow corridor, "It looks like a hotel."

"Shh, Cami. I don't think we should talk yet."

The European stands before a door that is slightly ajar, looking expectant.

"Here you are," Emile hands him several bills. "Is this enough?"

The man raises two fingers, and Emile slaps two more into his hand. The European quickly departs.

They enter a room lit by a single candle and smelling of old smoke. It is large as hotel rooms go, with dark padded surfaces placed low against each wall, like wide shelves. Frayed blankets lie in loose piles. In the center, on the low table where the candle sits, is a round tray containing two metal objects topped with dirty glass cylinders. Next to them are long tubes, soiled and stained. Next to the table sits an oversized lounge chair. On it are two silk garments, badly worn.

Lifting them, Camille shudders, "Robes, Emil. They're not even clean."

"It won't matter soon, Cami. We have this room and we shall soon be dreaming beautiful dreams."

"What about all those other beds?"

"Those are for other times, when lots of people rent the room."

"Must we take off our clothes this time?"

"Remember our agreement? We always remove our clothes."

"But is it safe?"

"I paid the man. He will keep us safe." Emile strips off his suitcoat, then trousers and underwear, as the European returns with the pipes.

"Now you," as Emile wraps the old robe around him.

"Opium first," she insists.

The man approaches the tray and drops a tablet into each

pipe bowl, striking a match to ignite the lamp oil to vaporize the tablets. Then he leaves.

Soon Emile lifts the dark tube and inhales. "Not ready yet."

Moments later, Camille lifts hers and inhales deeply. Then again. Closing her eyes, she slowly removes her jacket and blouse, then her silk undergarments, laying them all at the end of the lounge.

The candle provides dim light, flickering through heavy smoke, and the room is full of men. Camille and Emile lie sleeping, as if on center stage. Sprawling along the walls are a dozen men, partially covered by their robes. Sucking on the tubes, they watch the sleeping couple, like unruly creatures measuring their prey. Comatose, and naked beneath their open robes, the two pasty Americans are the object of great interest.

The European brings a new customer, a small man dressed in western suit and tie. The men close the door and locate an empty cushion, where the European drops the paraphernalia and leaves the room. The little man places his clothes on the bench and wraps his robe loosely around his freckled body. He edges over to Camille, taking her pink nipple beneath his forefinger and thumb, then touches his lips, looking triumphantly around the room. Some of the groggy men laugh, and a muffled word is said. The new man smiles and rubs her stomach, then down between her legs. More laughter. When the European reappears in the doorway, the little man removes his hand and scurries back to his place.

The European leaves again and a thin, bearded figure rises from his cot, approaching Emile, who lies with his mouth agape. The little man starts to rub Emile's stomach, imitating the other man and smiling around the room. Then the door slams opens, and two men in suits stride through, pushing the little man aside.

"Wang-chen was right," says the bigger one. "This is them."

Having given up hope, Malone and Bergen decide to accept the general manager's dinner invitation. Karl Wasser and Bergen are old friends from the hotelier's early days in Zurich then Berlin, and he has become the most respected hotel man in Shanghai. Seated in Wasser's private dining room, they are startled to hear the buzzing telephone.

"For you, Bergen-san."

Bergen takes the receiver and listens, giving no indication of the news. Then he smiles and motions to Malone with his hand, indicating he wants pen and paper. "They are alive?" Bergen repeats, so that all can hear. "Good job, man. Where are they now, and what is their condition?"

Malone raises his hand, indicating he is ready to write.

"They were found at a club in the French Concession, and they're comatose. Location too complicated to describe," Bergen waves for Malone to stop, repeating, "You're taking them to the ship. Likely to be there in one hour. We will see you there. Thanks!"

Malone gathers their belongings and walks to the lobby, heading to the entrance where a car and driver are waiting.

Bergen follows, as Wasser walks them to the port-cochere, "My apologies, Karl. Thank you for your hospitality. I know you understand. Damn them, anyway! Thank God they are safe."

VIA RCA RADIOGRAM VIA RCA

THURS OCTOBER 17 1929

TO DUFF MALONE

FROM MM ROBERTS

LEADING ECONOMIST SEES STOCKS PERMANENTLY HIGH.

INCREASED EARNINGS JUSTIFY RISE, PRAISES TRUSTS.

BANKER'S KILLER CAPTURED IN HAWAII.

RCA DECLARES DIVIDEND OF 7% FOR PREFERRED STOCKS.

$30 MILLION DEAL FOR NEW YORK CENTRAL & PENNSYLVANIA RAILROAD

$13 MILLION PROFITS FOR POWER & LIGHT AND FEDERAL WATER UTILITIES.

21,602 PEOPLE JAILED IN YEAR FOR DRY-LAW VIOLATIONS.

END

ROBERTS

New York Market Figures for Thursday, October 17

DOW CLOSED 336.1, DOWN 11.1 PTS & -3.2%, 8.2M Transactions

CHAPTER 33

"They're thoughtless," sighs Christy, still in nurse's whites after her morning shift. "Spoiled rotten. No cares for the trouble they caused."

"Are they responding?" asks Malone.

"Slowly, but yes, they're coming out of it. Dr. Stanley looked in on them ten minutes ago."

"Why on earth do they put themselves in such danger? First Hawaii and now here? You would think they might learn."

"They were groggy, but they did talk some. Emile says they have no idea what happened. Just a few puffs and they must have passed out. He went on about their childhood, babbled in French some of the time." Christy adds, "They seemed to be confessing, or confiding, and I don't know why. Except for my nurse's uniform."

"Angels of mercy, and all that."

"Yes, all that. Especially when people are medicated. They often see us as sort of saints."

"What is it about where they grew up. You said something about Philadelphia?" Malone asks.

"Not so much where, as how. Of course, they are brother and sister. Their parents were older when they were born two years apart. Mother nearly forty when she had Emile. Even as infants, their parents were not around much. They traveled, and left the kids with an *au pair*, who was with them for years."

"So she provided stability for them, as their parents did not?"

"That's the terrible part. The au pair was a vile woman. Emile said she molested them as tiny children, and it continued until they were in their teens. Touching them both. Making them touch each other. Disgusting things. This was discovered by a tutor when Emile was fourteen, and she was fired."

"Fired, you say? Not arrested?"

"No. The parents didn't want the shame, or the complication. The kids don't know, precisely. But it helps explain how anti-social they are. Keeping to themselves. Some sort of pact."

"Emile told you all that?"

"Between the two of them, it came out. They seemed to want someone to know why they are so attached to each other."

"And it helps clarify that scene in Honolulu, at the palace."

"That and the drugs. You know, Duff," Christy shakes her head, "Who could blame them for not trusting anyone? They were left a lot of money, but nobody to look after them, for comfort or guidance. I'll be glad to get away from Shanghai. Those kids will be, too."

He nods, "I only hope that this talk of financial crisis doesn't panic them. The money protects them, keeps them in their fantasy. We can shield them from it for a while, but if it's in the stock market, they must know their money is at risk."

"I wish I could figure it out," Malone mutters as he looks again at the day's announcements, then at the stock numbers. "The market is down eleven points, stock trading is all the way up to eight million -- double the normal -- and some respected economist says things are good!"

Bergen responds, "It just doesn't make sense, does it? Either the newspapers are colluding with the bankers, or they aren't reading the same numbers we are."

Duff interrupts, "Did you see this about catching Gibson's killer? Maybe something in here about it."

Bergen spreads the radiograms across Malone's dressing table, as they sort through the stack of messages. They hear passengers laugh and chat outside his window, as the *Malolo* passes out of the Yangtze and back into the China Sea.

"Here it is. From Kimura. 'Arrested Knauss from Waikele company, and his security man, Oveida, who was killer. No resistance, and complete confession. Gibson reneged on loan deal. Waikele is bankrupt. Mrs. Gibson to arrive this week. Kimura.' "

"Not much of a mystery it seems," observes Duff. "I expected it to involve some sort of robbery, or gambling."

"Sounds like there is more to it, though. He mentions a loan deal that fell through. I wonder how Gwen will handle it." Bergen turns back to his financial messages. "Will you look at these? Total conflict. Each story carries a different message. We received a half-dozen wires in just the past two days."

Malone reads them aloud, "This one says, 'Scare Orders Halt Ticker For an Hour in Feverish Day.' Then this article, 'Brokerage Houses Are Optimistic on the Recovery. Thirty-five largest wire houses of NY Stock Exchange met today. Conclude recent selling induced by hysteria. None knew anything disturbing to general market.'"

Bergen observes, "You notice it is the brokers who are optimistic, and think the public is just panicking. They want people to buy their way out of trouble. Obviously, they have a great deal to gain, whether buying or selling. Then it is the financial analysts and bankers who provide these conflicting facts, and they say 'Don't buy. Leave your money in the bank.' "

Malone nods, "And don't forget the politicians. It seems to be their job to calm the citizens, by telling them that everything is all right, and investors should all hold-on and do nothing. What a mess it is. Perhaps I should ask the Commodore for some guidance, before we carry on?"

"It's Thursday night in New York, Duff. Why not send off a message for him to see on Friday morning?"

Malone and Christy watch the dance floor. Something doesn't seem right with Emile and Camille. Their dancing is skilled, but slightly reckless, more flamboyant. They bump several people, without apology. Now Camille pulls Emile toward the exit, animated.

"I'll just follow a moment," Malone nods toward the couple. "Shall I escort you over to Bergen?"

"No, Duff. I'm fine. You go ahead."

The youngsters have headed aft, and Malone sees them darting down the port side ladder. *Going to the fantail.* Malone slows his pace, assuming they will be repeating their dance routine. *The music is quite clear down here, despite the sound of the engines,* he thinks as he sees them twirling around toward the rear safety lines. He can feel the salty spray from a crossing breeze.

"Emi," squeals Camille, "that was too high. Don't swing me so high back here. It's slippery!"

A rapid drumbeat adds to the tension, in an uptempo version of "Chinatown My Chinatown", with a cool, high clarinet solo. Malone sees where Emile is guiding them, and he darts from the shadows, rushing toward the dancers who are still over twenty feet away.

Unaware of Malone or the moisture and intent on the

rhythmic dance, Emile carries his sister through another determined arc toward the back edge of the fantail, building momentum as they twirl. Nearly upon them, Malone slips on a slick spot and falls into a slide, gliding toward the safety lines behind the dancers. He tries to roll as he slides, grabbing for Emile's leg, just touching his shoe. Malone knows he is running out of room, as he slides closer to the edge, desperately trying to grab the stanchion, or a cleat or something on the deck. He missed Emile but must save himself from slipping into the sea.

The ship's momentum pulls him toward a pole that secures the safety lines, and he grabs it, thrashing his left leg toward a bigger one to halt his slide. A searing pain in his ankle jars him, but he can't let go or he will roll off the back edge of the ship. So he holds on tight, his ankle numb, unable to move.

Just then Christy reaches him, with Bergen and the ship's duty officer right behind. "Don't move, Duff. Just lie there. We have help coming."

"Get them! Our dancers! Where are they?"

"Gone, Duff," she chokes back a sob. "You tried. You nearly had him, but he was already tossing her into the sea," Christy weeps openly. "Then he jumped in after her. It was terrible." She buries her face in his neck, holding tight, then releasing him as the officer moves Malone away from the edge.

Malone's ankle throbs as they move him, then more pain as they set him against the bulkhead. "Try not to move, sir," the officer soothes. "It seems to be be broken."

Malone eases himself up in bed, unable to move his leg. It is tightly wrapped, with a huge bag of ice set against the ankle. Christy and Bergen sit quietly, seeming to be in shock.

"So there you two are," Malone smiles weakly. "Tell me what happened. I thought I had them."

"You nearly did, Duff," Christy confirms softly. "They were determined, both of them. Emile twirled her toward the railing, then up and over. You nearly reached them, then you hit that slick spot. I couldn't believe it." Her eyes fill, as she continues, "That's the part I can't believe. She didn't say a word. Looked as if she was expecting it. Then he jumped over himself. I was so close. I think I saw him smile." She covers her face with her hands.

"They gave you pain medication," says Bergen. "To help you sleep. It could be broken, or a bad bruise. They said you would be on crutches for a few weeks."

They sit in a favorite corner of the Veranda Lounge, recounting events of the day before. Twenty hours out of Shanghai, the heat and humidity have dissipated, and the atmosphere is somber. Malone sits at an angle, his ankle elevated on the chair across from him. The assessment is a bad bruise from hitting the stanchion, but not a break. His crutches lie beneath the table, stowed to prevent the waiter from tripping.

Captain Christian approaches, nodding to Bergen and touching Christy's shoulder, then standing next to Malone. "May I have a word?"

"Of course, Captain, what is it?"

"It's about the accident, your young couple. Mr. and Miss DuPris. First, I'm glad you are safe. They say it was quite a close call. Five people saw them go out out on the fantail, having a dance, the way they always seem to do. They saw what you tried to do to save them." He smiles a grim smile, "One of the passengers said, at the beginning it seemed beautiful really. He hoisted her in a slow spin, like in a dance contest or a ballet. Then they saw you rush toward them, as he picked her up and over. They couldn't believe their eyes. Of course, we hit the alarm and circled back." He sighs and leans on the round table, "Protocols were all in place. Time and position noted. But the darkness. The water temperature. We did all we could to spot them. But if they didn't want to be rescued..." He stands to leave. "Quite a shock." Then he turns and walks away.

Malone thinks about what the captain has said. The slow realization, the finality. *They are asleep now. I remember the acceptance of just slipping under. I hope it was peaceful.*

It is six in the morning, and the waiters are busy setting tables for the breakfast service, anticipating early diners. They smooth the white linen and carefully set matching napkins at the left of each place. They refresh the silver coffee urn on the table, the one where the three of them had sat through the night. Looking weary, Bergen and Malone glance up as Christy returns holding a note.

"What is that, my dear," says Malone, nearly whispering.

"What did you say?" Christy replies swiftly, clearly exhausted, but startled by his endearment.

"What is that in your hand?"

"Oh, yes, the note," she touches his hand as she gives him the small scrap of blue paper. "It seems to be a poem. A very strange one. What does it mean?"

Malone reads aloud,

To all who sail on in this hollow world!
Here we go round the prickly pear
Prickly pear prickly pear
Here we go round the prickly pear
At five o'clock in the morning.

Between the idea
And the reality
Between the motion
And the act
Falls the Shadow
(and the dance)
Ta, Ta
Emile et Camille

"T.S. Eliot," says Bergen.

"What?" asks Christy.

"It is from a poem by T.S. Eliot. Called The Hollow Men, quite powerful. And very depressing. The youngsters must have added the bit in the beginning, and about the dance there at the end."

"I also found this," Christy hands a wadded paper ball to Malone, who unfolds it carefully.

"A telegram. From their attorney. It says their bank is shut, that their allowance is gone. It sends the attorney's regrets."

"Poor, troubled souls," says Malone, standing and looking down into Christy's moist eyes. They reach toward one another in a soft hug and she begins to cry.

"It's all over the ship, man," Austin Clark addresses Malone while the waiters deftly clear their breakfast dishes. Malone is visiting at each table, struggling on his crutches to carry a quiet message about the DuPris. Clark continues, shaking his head, "That strange couple. They went into the sea?"

"I'm afraid so, Austin. They seemed determined to go through with it. No crying-out. No fear."

"Any word from their family? What could have caused it?"

"There is no family. No-one except their solicitor. There were plenty of likely causes, but there will be an inquiry."

"Must be this damned stock market. Everyone says so. There is such pressure."

"We know it is possible, but they had so many emotional issues. And you knew about the incidents?"

"We did. Everyone knew. Those reckless young people! But the stocks, and their savings. Could it have been too much for them? Truth be told, I'm concerned enough, myself, that Marjorie and I must get off at the next port."

"What's that, Austin? I thought that you felt that your holdings were secure."

"When we thought it was just the investors who were in trouble, the speculators, we were secure. But now, with Gibson's death and Worldwide Bank closing, there could be more. We are not sure about our own bank, but we suspect they may have gotten into the investment schemes. We need to get back where we can actually talk with them or move our money. We need your help with travel plans."

"Our next port is Hong Kong tomorrow," Malone advises. "and then nothing until Pago Pago in two weeks, then another fifteen days to California. There will be ships within days from Hong Kong, going direct to Los Angeles or San Francisco. Shall I wire our staff to book you something?"

"You can do that?"

"Of course. We have colleagues there who can transfer your things and arrange overnight lodging, or transport you over to the ship, depending on the schedule."

"Get us out soon, would you?"

Moving over to the Sharpmans, Malone is startled to hear, "Absolutely, they committed suicide. If there wasn't a note, one will be found shortly." Looking up Dr. Sharpman continues, "It completes a familiar pattern, Duff. Please, sit down. We are so sorry about your ankle," nodding to the empty chair. "I was just telling Raisa, the narcotics and liquor, compounded with obvious depression and erratic behavior. Those children did not give themselves a chance."

Raisa quietly places her hand on her husband's. "You remember our nephew, don't you?" Patting it, as she addresses Malone, "Philip was a kind boy, and quiet for the most part. But when he had his spells, he was very difficult. We were fortunate. He found someone, and he found something he was good at. He is a carpenter now, in Roanoke."

"Your story has a happy ending, then," says Malone, with a small smile. "I'm very glad. This one is full of mixed emotions. They were never kind, and they seemed drawn to the most difficult situations."

"Part of the pattern, as I said. Troubled people often feel more comfortable with losing situations. They feel that they are not worthy of winning, and it takes a great deal of courage to break the pattern. There was certainly nothing you could do or say."

"Your thoughts help to make some sense of it, Richard, and yours Raisa." He rises to leave. "Thank you."

As he moves toward the salon where Chester and Shirley Warren are dining in their usual isolation, she is uncharacteristically vocal with her husband. "Chet, I know they were spoiled. And they had no discipline. But did you ever try to talk to them, to hear anything about them?" She is direct, but not harsh.

"Malone," Warren interjects, looking up. "Please join us. We were discussing those two wayward kids."

"There you go, Chet," interrupts Shirley. "I'm sorry, but I object to the word 'wayward'. I spoke with her twice. He left her alone for a few moments, just sitting there. She was confused about many things, and needed help."

"Did she listen?" he asks.

"She wanted to talk, not listen. She said something about feeling bound, bound together or something. 'We are bound together, and will end together.' She said something like that."

"Foolish talk from a foolish girl, that's all."

"She wasn't being foolish, Mr. Warren," Malone corrects. "I believe Mrs. Warren has a good understanding of what she was saying."

"What do you mean, Malone, 'A good understanding'?"

"I mean that they were truly bound together, first as children living as only-friends. No-one else around them, except a stern guardian. They trusted no-one else -- dancing, sleeping, living. They shared a joint allowance. They could not seem to break away, or to be away from each other."

She looks at Malone for a moment, "Mr. Malone, thank you for telling us. Chet and I, each of us, we grew up as only-children, quite alone it seems. We know nothing of those two. But we thought things, suggested things about them. No-one approved of their, ah, troubles." She looks over at Chet and, surprisingly, takes his hands in hers.

Though she seems a serious woman, there is obviously a softer side. Malone adds, "They did bring so many things down on themselves. But they had such a small world, consisting only of themselves. I agree with your observations. And I'm glad you were able to listen to her. To allow her that moment, at least, of human contact."

"Enough, Malone," Warren interrupts, then slows, "and thank you for what you just said to Marjorie." He pats her hand. "I… just thank you."

Recognizing the importance of their moment together, Malone excuses himself and struggles across the lounge to where the Anna and Ruth are seated. "May I sit a moment?"

"Of course. As long as you like. Is it true about those poor children? Is that how you hurt yourself?"

"It is, Ruth. So you know what happened?"

"We do, Duff. They were so troubled. Still, it is hard to believe."

Anna adds, "It makes you feel fortunate."

"Fortunate, Anna?"

"When you are different from other people, as they were, you make choices. They chose to avoid reality, to live on the edge, exaggerate the difference. Look how they dressed, and how rebellious. They chose to be totally different, freaks almost."

"We're considered different, too," adds Ruth. "You know this, Duff."

"No different from any of my friends" he grins, gently grasping her wrist. "Smart, stylish, interesting."

"Just like a man," Ruth looks at Anna, shaking her head and smiling. "We carry around this serious secret, and he doesn't even notice."

"Because we are lovers, Duff. Not sisters."

"I know that, of course," he smiles. "But I'm not sure what I'm supposed to say. I see you as my friends, and you give me energy with your smiles and your thoughts, and your genuine affection."

"You see, Ruth, all this pretending? It doesn't even matter!"

"Actually it does, dear," Ruth takes her hand, her eyes glazing. "Not to Duff, obviously. We were talking about being different from these other passengers. You and I choose to fit in, to be sisters as far as others are concerned, when we would really like to be ourselves. To dance together, and hold hands the way people in love do. Our worldly friend Duff wouldn't mind, because he's a bit different, too. But all those others. No, to them we need to be sisters."

Malone approaches Alita and Lloyd, who stand alone, quietly looking out to sea. They look up as they hear him approach, "May I interrupt?"

Lloyd moves aside to allow space, "Of course, my friend."

"How are you doing, Duff?" asks Alita. "It looks painful."

"I'm doing better with these crutches," he smiles over at her. "Christy is not herself just yet, but I believe the others are coming around."

"Tragic business," says Lloyd, as Alita excuses herself. Soon they see her walk with Christy through the port-side doorway, arm-in-arm, into the open air.

"There is a finality, isn't there Lloyd? So unexpected and quick?"

"Finality, yes. But unreal, too. Something about the enormity of the sea taking in two tiny people. You are at sea so often. Do you not fear the ocean? The size, the power of those waves, the constant threat that something could go wrong?"

Nodding his head slightly, "I respect the sea more than

fear it. Strangely, I never liked swimming as a boy, as I found I was not so good at it. It seems foolish, really, for me to spend so much of my life out on the water. But I trust this ship, and I know the ocean is powerful in the absolute. Larger than life. You look at those enormous swells. Endless. Infinite, like mountain peaks, or clouds, or deserts. But I respect and trust the enormity, and accept what it brings. If this ship went down tomorrow, I would try to save myself and others, of course. But if all else failed, I would accept it. I have no choice."

"Just as those two young people had to know what they were doing. They may not have liked their destination, but they respected it. Needed it. From all I have heard from the observers, they did not fear it. Not even a cry." He takes Malone by the arm and motions to the steward, "Come, let's join the ladies and get them a drink. We can share a peaceful thought, then pull things together."

Chapter 34

Malone's first impression of Hong Kong begins well outside of port, as they pass barren islands at the mouth of Victoria Harbour, through a seething mass of boats and people and floating debris. Thousands of odd-shaped vessels, large ones that look quite seaworthy and smaller ones that seem little more than rafts. They sail in all directions, steadily moving people, animals and parcels between somewhere and somewhere else. Angled sails that look like parchment, capturing the gentle wind in delicate pastel folds. So much like Malone's sketchy image of China. Gentle blue and soft rose, pink and tea-green. Thousands of them, busy, moving, shifting, staying out of harm's way.

Kowloon comes into view off to port, then Hong Kong Island to starboard. He observes the hulking ferries that slog between the two urban centers. "How do they do it, Bergen? How do they not all crash into one another?"

"Controlled chaos," he laughs. "They know these waters, and they know how to come just close enough to warn the other chap off. Look at them! They are master sailors."

"We're in for it, aren't we?"

"Yes, Duff, we are definitely in for it for a few hours. The British constabulary are respected in Hong Kong, and they are dead serious. They see much smuggling and violence in this harbor. Nothing surprises them."

As they approach the pier, Malone looks north toward the forested mountain ridge that lies behind Kowloon, like a dense green wall. To the south, the hills of Hong Kong island provide an equally rugged fringe.

Malone watches the police waiting to board, as the crew swiftly fix the lines and set the gangways. Captain Christian has already announced that all passengers must remain for a short time, until the investigation is complete. He leaves Bergen to negotiate with them, to allow him ashore so that he can oversee the land arrangements with his Hong Kong colleagues. Malone struggles up the outward stairs to assist the captain with any questions about the DuPris couple.

"You say they are Americans? All your passengers are Americans?" he hears the stocky Englishman in his dark uniform, a local policeman.

The captain responds patiently, "They are. They are special guests of my company. All from America."

"And was there any trouble on board?"

"On the contrary. Everyone was quite cordial. Except for the stock market information, this was an elaborate and very successful pleasure cruise."

"The stock market?"

"This is a special group of passengers, commander. Everyone on board is a millionaire. That is, they were when they were invited, and when we left San Francisco. But many of them are afraid they won't be tomorrow. They keep a sharp eye on the daily bulletins about their investments."

"And this couple who were lost?"

"We know they received a telegram from their financial man, advising they had lost all their savings. We believe they couldn't face it, being destitute. They jumped to their deaths."

"Seems a bit extreme. We know about financial worries here, but to kill themselves?"

"There were drug problems, as well. They acted irrational throughout the cruise. Most recently, three days ago in Shanghai, we rescued them from an opium den. Bad drugs nearly did them in. Since then they stayed entirely to themselves. Until the last night, when they came back for a late dance. We're certain they took their own lives. Mr. Malone here, our cruise director, tried to save them."

"How is that?"

"As I reported earlier, I followed them," Malone replies. "I could see them going for the fantail and followed...."

"Excuse me, Mr. Malone," nods the policeman. "You need not go on. Your story corroborates what we heard from others and read in your own statement. No need to put you through it again. If you will just complete the paperwork, captain, for our records, your people are free to go ashore. That is, if you have no dangerous passengers."

"No-one dangerous. But I must tell you, at least half our passengers will be leaving us here and booking immediate returns to America. They are that worried about their money."

"Even here in Hong Kong, the British mainly, some say we are headed for a crash, and we aren't sure what to make of it."

"Nor do we, commander, I assure you."

"The Commodore authorized extra shore staff to meet with all passengers when we go ashore, Duff, not just our clients. We're to help everyone who wants it. Matson transferred payments over to Dollar Lines, to assure return accommodations on direct cruises."

Malone nods back at Bergen, "How many are leaving, do we have a count?"

"More than a hundred. Among our group, we are losing the Sharpmans, the Clarks and the Warrens. From the entire ship, we have booked fifty people aboard the *President Monroe*, leaving in two days direct to Los Angeles. Another hundred or so will depart the next day on the *President Harrison* to San Francisco. The hundred and forty-four passengers who decided to stay with us on the *Malolo* are booked for the next three nights at the new Peninsular Hotel, right near the harbor. They'll be very comfortable."

"They will need comforting, I'm afraid. This morning's news from America is worse." Malone sets the local British newspaper on the table, with the headline: *Worldwide Bank in NY Fails. Depositors Panic.* "Gibson's bank, has closed its doors. When he was shot, their customers panicked and withdrew their savings.

They shut down, but not in time to save the bank. Stock brokers are optimistic, of course, but the market says just the opposite. It's down nineteen points, over five percent, with the number of transactions nearly doubling."

"Clark spoke with his financial man," Bergen responds. "There was some sort of meeting of the brokerage houses over the weekend. They say the increased selling comes from public hysteria, and not from anything wrong in the stock markets. They say it will right itself, if only people will listen and stay calm. If they hold onto their stocks and leave their money in the banks, things will settle."

"That is the frustration, isn't it?" Malone responds, exasperated. "It's impossible to decide who to believe. The British newspapers in Hong Kong have been filled with information, all of it conflicting. It must be far more confusing in New York, with all the newspapers and magazines, and the radio commentators."

"People seem to believe the worst possible news," sighs Bergen. "It's safer, I suppose. If you act on the worst, you may stay safe if it actually comes true. If you act only on the good news, you could be badly surprised." He shakes his head, "How are we to know the real facts? Must they be numbers, like the daily figures from the stock market?"

"Lord save us," smiles Malone, "if we accept stock market numbers as facts. They are so fickle...all over the map, up one day and down the next. Always with a different excuse. No, I believe those stock numbers are simply opinions. Listening to people like Warren and Clark, market numbers are reactions to what certain investors believe, based on the conflicting headlines, or their financial advisors. Some numbers are even contrived, the result of distortions created by syndicates, to make investors believe the stocks are worth more than they really are."

"Buying at a higher level than they are worth, the way Warren described it?"

"And then selling to investors who believe the value will increase even more, not realizing that they are overvalued.

When the stock goes back down, because the value was inflated, syndicates decide whether to buy back at the lower price -- making automatic profits and getting the stock back. Or they leave those alone and go after other holdings."

Bergen responds, "But once the market posts its numbers, don't they become facts? They certainly act like facts, because those numbers determine if someone made money, or lost it."

CHAPTER 35

October 16
Dearest Christy,

We enjoyed your letter from Japan. It sounds so beautiful, and Mary laughed about all the music and parties. Your dad said the gardens and colors you described remind him of his visits in the navy, when he was allowed to go ashore and explore little neighborhoods. Thank you for brightening our day.

We hope you receive this in Hong Kong before the ship leaves. We must tell you that everyone here is now aware of the stock market problems, and we are all worried greatly. The investors are pressuring companies to fire people in order to save money. My job at the hospital seems safe for now, but your dad is worried. Government contracts are cutting back and they are shifting him to daytime hours, because they closed down the night shift. We can still make ends meet, so don't worry. We just thought you should know about it.

We hope this finds you happy and filled with new stories to tell us when you have time to write. We always appreciate your news.

We love you and Mary sends special loves,
Mom and Dad

October 22
Dearest Mom and Dad and Mary,

Thank you for your letter, and I am so sorry about dad's job. His seniority there must mean something, and everyone loves him (How could they not!). I hope things don't change too fast, because I feel very helpless all the way over here.

There is so much happening over here now, I don't know where to start. I'm fine, but there has been some terrible news.

First, these millionaires are in a panic because of the stock market. Two of them killed themselves when we left Shanghai. They just jumped overboard! I was the one who found a note in their room, and a telegram telling them that they were broke. They are the couple my age who had drug problems in Hawaii. I am so sad for them. I spent time with them as the ship's nurse, and I never liked them. They were so selfish. But no-one should end their own lives. Then that famous banker, Jason Gibson, was found shot in Hawaii. My friend Gwen, his wife, had left us in Yokohama to go back there and help find him, but we read that he was dead. I am very sad for her. His bank was shut down, and this has really panicked our passengers.

Half of the passengers demanded to leave the ship in Hong Kong because of the banks and the stock market. Duff and his people helped them all get faster ships back to the States. They had to get home as soon as possible. Duff worked so hard to help everyone!

Some passengers have stayed on board for the rest of the cruise. Most of my friends did, because they seem to be safe. Two girls, Anna and Ruth, are wonderful. They are so positive and caring for everyone. Count Sorvini, did I mention him? He is an interesting little man from Italy, but lives in America now. Alita and Lloyd are diplomats, and they have sort of adopted me. Another hundred passengers who are not Duff's clients have stayed with the Malolo. *They count on him for help. Then there are Bergen and Duff, of course. And a famous movie actor, Aubrey Kirsch. Quite an interesting group of people.*

Finally, I'm not sure how else to say it, I'm in love! I really am. I'm sorry to be so far away and you can't even meet him. Dad especially, so he wouldn't worry. I haven't forgotten that I'm a mother. I know that he might not understand. But I think he will.

I wish you could meet Duff. This will sound crazy, but right now he doesn't know how I feel about him. He is so confused that he thinks Captain Christian and I are a couple, and he gets a little jealous at times. Bergen-san and I agreed to straighten Duff out when we reach Samoa. There is just too much going on with the passengers and the stock markets until we get there. Bergen suggested that we should wait. He told me that Pago Pago is a special place. There is an aura or something that gives the spirit a better chance. I think he was serious. I hope I can wait until then to tell Duff. I just know he will love Mary.

I'm sorry to load all of this news into one letter, and please don't worry about me. I knew it was important for you to know, and that I can handle it. I'm telling you all this because we won't receive any mail until the ship reaches San Francisco on November 20. A lot is likely to happen between now and then.

I will telephone when I reach San Francisco. I love you, and will ask Bergen to help me say a prayer for you and your jobs. He will understand why I'm turning to him for help.

Special love to Mary,
Christy

"A lot is likely to happen! I'll say! And most of it is not good."

"There is nothing you can do, Pete. Look at the postmark. They are almost in Pago Pago. In another few days she will have told him."

"It's so damned frustrating, love. I wish she had never taken that job on the ship."

"She's an adult now, and a stubborn one, just like you and me. Once she makes up her mind, there is no changing it until she runs into her own conflicts."

"But she's such a little girl sometimes, and men are crazy around her. Look what happened in San Francisco."

"That's not fair, and you know it. Look, Pete. She's our girl, and we need to trust her. When she leaves Samoa there is nowhere else for trouble to happen."

"That's just it, love. I will try to trust her, but most of the problems she told us about happened on board ship. Think of it, she will spend almost two weeks with a man, on a luxury ship, after telling him she loves him. That looks to me like a fancy honeymoon! For most things I trust her, but nobody is that strong."

"Still, we can't do anything about it." Doris takes Pete's face in her hands and kisses him on the nose.

"You are impossible, love. You know how that makes me laugh when you do that."

"I do, my own love. Christy is our daughter, she is a smart and responsible girl. If she thinks it's the right thing to do, then we just have to trust her."

VIA RCA RADIOGRAM VIA RCA

THURSDAY OCTOBER 24 1929

TO DUFF MALONE

FROM MM ROBERTS

PRICE OF STOCKS CRASH IN HEAVY LIQUIDATION.

HUGE SELLING WAVE CREATES NEAR PANIC.

TREASURY OFFICIALS BLAME SPECULATION.

TREASURY FAVORS $200 MILLION CUT IN FED TAXES.

CONSTRUCTION DROPS 57 PER CENT IN NY STATE.

PENN RAILROAD PLACES RECORD ORDER FOR NEW RAILS.

END

ROBERTS

New York Market Figures for Thursday, October 24

DOW CLOSED 299.5, DOWN 6.4 PTS & 2.1%, 12.9M Transactions

Chapter 36

It is deathly quiet as the *Malolo* glides from Victoria Harbour just before noon on October twenty-fifth, easing its way through the busy sampans and junks. With only one hundred and forty-four passengers on a ship designed for more than six hundred, the mood is eerie. Malone walks through passageways and promenades that are spotless, but nearly empty, and the main dining room is unoccupied. On the pool deck, he observes a handful of people lagging at the swimming pool, guzzling gin fizzes and sidecars, a few of them drinking straight whisky. These remaining passengers, while they have chosen to stay the course, are anything but festive.

The observation decks are empty and the giant ballroom is deathly quiet. Stewards and dining staff stand mute, shifting from foot to foot, unsure of their roles. The pianist delivers a random succession of familiar show-tunes, trying to lighten the atmosphere. It is lunchtime and passengers are not at their usual tables, nor chatting amiably at the buffet. They are simply not here. Instead, they remain in their suites, or sit in the lounge next door, or out on deck ordering more cocktails.

"Lloyd, what do you suggest?" asks Malone, as they look through the large port-side windows, sizing up the passengers. "You saw today's bulletin?"

"I saw it, Duff, and I'm stunned. How could they even process so many stock sales? Almost thirteen million. My God. What is happening to our country?"

"Everyone is trying to sell. Too many for them to process. In two days the market has fallen more than thirty-three points. Who knows where it will stop?"

"Strange, isn't it? Three hundred people started our trip as certified millionaires. Most of us are about to go bust, even these remaining few. What do you suppose they will do? Alita and I should be all right. Our money isn't in banks or stocks, and we aren't afraid to work for a living. And you can find work, certainly. You're young and your industry is resilient. But what will they do? What can they do?"

"Some of them are strong," nods Malone, "That's pretty clear. Ruth and Anna, the count, even Aubrey Kirsch. They know how to work. I'm just as worried about everyone else, the people who haven't invested. What will happen to their money, or their jobs?"

"There is so much we don't know. It is damned frustrating."

Standing near them, they overhear Captain Christian, who has waved the head steward over. "Frederick, will you ask the chef to delay luncheon service for thirty more minutes. We will work with our guests to be seated by two o'clock. Please extend my serious apologies, and my gratitude."

Looking anxious, but obviously relieved by the captain's personal apology to the chef, the steward walks swiftly through the serving doors, taking his assistant with him for moral support.

He suggests to Malone, "Let us do what we can to bring our people into lunch. I'll instruct the wine steward to uncork another thirty bottles above the normal allotment. It may help steady some nerves, or at least tranquilize them."

"Thank you, captain, then while they nap we can work on some sort of miracle this afternoon, in anticipation of the dinner chimes."

Malone's mind is far away, as he becomes aware of a question from Bergen.

"What is our plan now, Duff? It is the Winstons, Sorvini, the Swanton sisters, Kirsch and Miss Beeson remaining on board with us. What is our role now?"

"Much the same, I should say. A lot will depend on how the passengers are dealing with the changing financial news. We have all become friends, so we'll respond as friends do. But we need to be professionals, too. Be there when something is needed, or if they want to talk. Let them be, when they prefer to be alone."

"Shall we continue with the stock reports?"

"At this stage, yes. We need to keep everyone on the ship informed. We also need to know the situation that faces us as we get closer to America. I'll ask Roberts to provide any reports."

"Good idea. It's hard to imagine what we will face back in America."

"Some of them may think the country will be the same when we get back, but there could be riots. We may find violent people on the streets of San Francisco. Our passengers are upset and some are afraid, but at least they are civil with each other. Can you imagine what people may be like, confronting harsh realities? Out of work? Out of money? We need to prepare ourselves for a different kind of world. We don't want to frighten our guests, but just help them to be prepared when we arrive. I wish we could just skip Pago Pago and go directly home."

"I agree, but we both know why it isn't that easy. Matson has mail contracts, cargo to deliver or pick-up, international filings that regulate ship's movement. The captain's hands are tied to the current schedule. We must make the best of Pago Pago."

As they approach Pago Pago, most of the men are back in their lightweight shirts and tropical slacks. Flapper attire slowly returns during dinner -- short skirts, skimpy tops, headscarves -- with an increased noise level, and everyone aboard is drinking heavily.

When they left Hong Kong, many of the men had taken to wearing dark suits and neckties, as if they were going to their offices or a funeral. For a day or so they sat around the little deck tables and held edgy conversations about tightening belts, selling their houses, and canceling major purchases.

It didn't last long, and now they have moved to the opposite extreme. While some of the wives continue to wear formal outfits, many more are dressing casually, reverting to the comfort of lounging trousers and revealing tops. There is loopy laughter, and the band is frequently asked to play the Charleston. It sounds as if the crowd has decided to enjoy the rest of the cruise. After dark, no-one goes near the fantail.

Tonight, *Aubrey & Toots*, as they now bill themselves, dress in matching tuxedos, singing catchy tunes and showing deft footwork in an innovative tap-dance routine. They end the set with "Makin' Whoopee", and the audience laughs knowingly, as they tease with suggestive words about philandering ... and paying the consequences.

Malone observes from across the table, catching Kirsch's eye and waving them over to join the group.

"Fine show, you two," says Bergen, pulling out two chairs.

"We just want to give our audience a bit of a distraction. You know, make them laugh a little, and remove of some of the scowls we have been seeing."

"We're glad you remained with the cruise."

"Thanks, Duff, but we pretty well had to," taking Toots's hand. "We need the work, and we are making new friends. Besides, my astrologist never wired me back, so we kept away from the stock market and we can't have lost much. My real money's in a small bank that seems to have stayed away from the risky investment business."

"Tell them, hon," laughs Toots, taking his arm.

"We caught a break, I think. A producer sent me a wire in Hong Kong. Offered me a secondary part in his new talkie. It's a western, and I'm to be the pal of Whip McCord, he's the star. I play the guitar and do some trick riding. We start shooting in November, out in the desert."

"Great news," Malone exclaims.

"Well, it's thanks to you. You said something about doing what I like, instead of what other people tell me. I'm a horseman, born to it. So I put out some inquiries and this is what came back."

VIA RCA RADIOGRAM VIA RCA

WEDNESDAY OCTOBER 30 1929

TO DUFF MALONE AMERICAN EXPRESS SS MALOLO

FROM MM ROBERTS AMERICAN EXPRESS SAN FRANCISCO

STOCKS COLLAPSE IN 16 MILLION SHARE DAY.

EXCHANGE TO CLOSE FOR 2 DAYS

END

ROBERTS

240 Issues Lose $15,894,818,894 in Month

New York Market Figures for Wednesday, October 30

DOW CLOSED 230.1, DOWN 30.6 PT & - 11.7% 16.4M Transactions

CHAPTER 37

"It's over. It has to be. Here is the latest from Roberts," Malone says, as Bergen joins him in his stateroom. "The worst news so far. Sixteen million sold. This is four times a normal trading day."

"What do you suggest we tell them, Duff?" he asks quietly.

"There's more," Malone adds. "The Commodore sent a detailed wire to help us understand the severity. Panic set in yesterday in New York, and nearly every investor tried to sell their holdings at once. It shut the market down for a time. Big companies like General Motors and the Rockefeller family made a public show of buying stocks, so others would follow. The markets did rally briefly, but then closed at this low."

"We must tell the remaining passengers."

"That's taking place now. It's in this morning's daily bulletin. The frustrations are likely to increase as we cross back into the American time zone in five days, then sail on to Pago Pago."

"Mr. Malone," announces the small man in a smartly

fitted tuxedo. "I am Jonathan Lemmon. I represent the remaining passengers on the *Malolo*."

Startled by the formality of his tone, Malone looks across at Bergen and Christy, then places his napkin aside and stands, gesturing toward the lounge.

Lemmon follows and continues, "Several of us have met since departing from Hong Kong, and we want you to discontinue your briefing sheets, immediately."

Entering the lounge, he turns and responds. "Of course, Mr. Lemmon. If this is what you wish. May I ask why?"

"Too distressing, Malone." He raises his hands and his face relaxes, "It isn't you. The stock market news is simply too distressing for us, and impossible to deal with out here. Today's news was the worst so far. But there is nothing that we can do." Looking down at his feet, "For three more weeks on this ship, there is absolutely nothing we can do to change our circumstances. And so we will spend no more time or emotions on it. We will enjoy these last days, and will face what we must, when we must."

"I believe I understand. There are to be no more updates from me. At the same time," Malone extends his hand, "will you please tell me when there is something that you do want. Any sort of services, or special arrangements."

"One thing we discussed, in our group, we do wish to request," grasping Malone's hand, "is a memorable party when we cross the dateline, this one last time. Something that none of us will ever forget."

"You can count on it, Mr. Lemmon. One that we will never forget."

As they cross the dateline, three men in a donkey costume weave onto the dance floor as the band plays "Show Me The Way To Go Home", champagne bottles hanging out from under the drunken animal's flanks like green testicles. Unable to agree on a direction, the men inside jostle and bump before collapsing in a pile. Malone watches the stewards approach and patiently unstack them, assisting them off the floor to the safety of their tables, no longer a donkey, just tipsy men in soiled white dinner jackets.

It has been a long night, filled with forced laughter. Malone shakes his head as he leans against the far bulkhead. *I must get out of here,* he chides himself. *I have done what I can. I need to sort things out.* He had watched the raucous crowd, safe in their colorful costumes, carrying out the fantasies that every crowd has when it crosses the dateline. Like any important feeling, when gaiety is forced, it doesn't work. The laughter seemed louder than usual, the music faster, and the conversations exaggerated. His own dismay with Captain Christian and Christy seems exaggerated, too, distorted by this unreal setting. He sees them enter the ballroom after a short break outside, and slips away before they see him.

As he walks to his stateroom, Malone realizes what he is doing is petty. He has chosen to detach himself, to avoid a confrontation. Though it is his choice, he feels isolated and alone, with the kinds of hurt feelings that he has carried with him since childhood. *You are such a prig,* he tells himself. *Such a righteous prig!*

"There you are, my friend," he hears Lloyd's calming voice. "Alita and I took Bergen for a stroll. My God, that music was loud! But when we returned, no sign of you."

"It was too much for me, as well," Malone smiles, realizing how much he enjoys Lloyd's company.

"How about a bit of a sit-down after all that frivolity? Here, I'll just bring this with us," grasping a bottle of cognac.

They locate two soft lounges on the main deck, and sit comfortably. Jackets and ties off, they swelter in the warm air that dampens their shirts and saps their energy. It is nearly one in the morning, Samoa time, and they are due to reach Pago Pago by daybreak.

"Do you still maintain," asks Lloyd, his feet propped against the railing, "that investing seems a lot like gambling?"

"That's an odd topic for this time of night, Lloyd, and a

familiar one. Why? Do you have some new ideas?"

With a good-natured smile and a mischievous look in his eyes, Lloyd continues. "I've been giving it a great deal of thought since our earlier conversation. Neither of us has anything pressing at the moment. Though we're mostly in agreement, why not talk about it some more?" He pats Malone's shoulder and continues, "You know, don't you, that the stock market is full of controls? That corporations must meet specific standards, and maintain documents to support their financial claims? So must the investment people."

Malone nods. "That may be, but it's not only the companies and the brokers that I worry about. It's the investors! Some are people like me, who may not know all that much about a company's structure -- or their financial statements. But we are asked to accept certain claims from our brokers or friends, and then to invest based on this limited knowledge. We are the gamblers.

He continues, "Then some investors work with professionals like our missing banker, the late Mr. Gibson. He loaned money to people like me. He also invested his own -- large sums, according to his wife. And he talked about trusts that hid their investments, and syndicates that influenced stock prices. This seems a lot like the odds that favor the gambling establishment."

"But, Duff, let's look at it another way. Some say that we learn from the big investors, indirectly, when stocks go up or down. Their research tells them when to jump in, and when they do we see it -- or our brokers do -- and we jump in, too. They benefit a few dollars more per transaction because they sell off early; but can't we benefit, also, when our investment goes up? Then we can pull out just as it begins to go down."

Malone asks, "But is this not a corruption of the system, on a fundamental level? Does this not give them indirect control over millions of investors, people like me who might follow their actions, but lag behind them?"

"Then that is why you must research the company you invest in."

"I know I should research first, but that isn't my line of

work. I'm a travel man, not an economist." He smiles to lighten the comment, "Blast it. When I speak with a banker about investing, he seems offended that I don't know as much as he does about the companies that are offered as stocks. It's like a baseball fan who loves his team, and doesn't understand why I don't know all about it and love it just as much as he does. To avoid embarrassment, I don't speak with him any more. What I do is choose not to invest. I put mine into the bank as savings. Buy property. Or place it in a vault in my home, if I have a vault."

"Do I take it that you equate investing with gambling, because neither one is clear to you?"

"That's it in part, though I understand how the game works, like landing on the right number in roulette, or holding the best cards. And I can see the pay-offs from stocks, like dividends. But in neither case do I see how the pay-off is calculated or merited. What did I do to earn it?"

"That's it, isn't it? You do come back to that," he slaps the rattan table with his hand, celebrating his point. "You didn't turn a spade in the earth, or create a fine art object, so you feel you didn't earn the money! Is that it?"

"I would say more yes than no, Lloyd. You're approaching my concerns. And with the way the stock values were going up when we left San Francisco, I truly feel the money is not earned. Not by me, and not by those syndicates or trusts. Plus, they're earning too much of it. That's why I feel it is like gambling. It's not a reasonable thing, especially if it's the result of manipulation."

"So you believe the theories about manipulating the market?"

"Of course. Don't you?"

Lloyd hesitates, then goes on, "It's possible, but I truly hope not. Those financiers keep a close eye on each other, and there are strict laws."

Malone responds carefully, "Perhaps it is the ethics of it all that concerns me. Democracies seem to work, only if people are honest, or laws are enforced. You were in the war, were you not?"

"I was, in a sense," Lloyd responds. "when I served in China as special envoy."

"As a foreigner, I can tell you that I respect America and it's heroism in the war. Saved Europe, I believe. Maybe the world. From all I read, President Wilson is a highly ethical man."

"He is an idealistic man," clarifies Lloyd, "and ethical. But the business of politics is often a difficult place for an idealist, especially if he is ethical too. There is constant conflict between democratic ideals and business needs. As we discussed, democracy and capitalism are two very different philosophies."

Malone concurs, "You Americans are justifiably proud of your democracy and your role in the World War. But the war ended in 1918, and it is as if your country left its ethical standards behind. This current focus on money and investments, on business growth, and on establishing prohibition, then ignoring it -- this is quite an opposite phenomenon. It may be that all people in a democracy have the right to express their opinions, or to invest. But the success of their investment seems under the control of wealthy capitalists."

"Now you are taking my earlier argument, and I am in complete agreement." Chuckling to himself, Lloyd adds, "With this talk about ethics, we both sound like we are advocating Christianity, instead of capitalism or democracy."

"You know, Lloyd. There is another major flaw to my arguments."

He laughs, "A flaw? And you are willing to admit it?"

"I am. It's that I don't really care about money."

"That's it? That's your flaw?"

"Well, it seems to be. As I look at your points, which really are more in agreement with mine than disagreement, and from what others have said, it's pretty clear that I don't hold the same interest in money. I care about my work, and about the quality of what I do, but I have never asked what it is worth. When I moved from South Africa to New York, I didn't ask them what I would earn, though they told me later and I was quite amazed."

"You moved half way around the world and didn't know what your salary would be?"

"I did. I knew I wanted the job and the challenges, and I trusted they would pay me a fair wage."

"Don't you worry about what you might do if the economy continues to break down?"

"I don't like the prospect, the pain it will inflict on people who are already struggling, but I trust I will find work, will get along."

"This does explain a lot, I must say," Lloyd shakes his head, still smiling. "I took you for quite a worldly fellow, and here you are, an idealist and a dreamer."

Chapter 38

Malone isn't troubled for himself. He's always found a way to survive. He is seriously troubled for people he knows and cares about. What of his brother Sandy and his family? How will it affect his friend Hamid in Cairo if wealthy people lose all their money and stop traveling? What about the steamship companies? How can they survive? What about this little port of Pago Pago? Can they get by without the occasional shipload of tourists, bringing money into their bars and cafes, and buying local crafts?

Then he realizes that these people are the most likely to survive a financial crisis. Hamid is a worker and he knows how to get along in his crowded city. While the cruise companies will cut back on their schedules or reposition their ships, and very likely stop building ships for a while, this protects only investors and management. What of the crew members who provide the services and operate the ships. Can they learn other trades? Or take their savings from the U.S. and live a less extravagant life somewhere overseas? As for people here in Samoa, they will survive. Bergen says they live from the sea, fishing and harvesting from the oyster beds. They have chickens and pigs. And they grow sugar cane and rice, and have forests filled with avocados and bananas.

If things fall apart, it's these sophisticated people, the higher-ups, who seem unable to take care of themselves. The investment fellow, Warren. He will be lost without the routine of his work, and the prestige. He came up the hard way, and so did she. But he has gotten arrogant and sloppy. Can they remember how to work hard? Can he learn how to clean an office or repair an automobile? Is he willing to? What about Gwen? What about Toots? Those two seem like realists and hard workers, with enough humility to find other jobs.

Gio will surely survive, maybe even thrive, with his knowledge of how rugged individualists operate. He's a kind chap, mostly. But I'm sure he can be ruthless when it comes to survival.

As they complete the slight turn to port and glide toward the pier, he views a plain village in the distance. Things are not so different here in Pago Pago, thinks Duff, from many other parts of the world. Quite different from America, but similar to villages in the rougher places he has visited in Africa or South America. Pago is likely to be like small villages along the Indian ocean, with dirt roads and wooden sidewalks forming rudimentary towns, containing little shops and an old bar or two, with cracked front windows and benches out in front for drunks to sleep things off.

From the bay, he sees a scattering of palm trees around a tiny clearing that contains the village, and what appears to be a gathering of huts at the water's edge.

They ride into town on a bumpy cart, and Bergen points out thatched-roof homes, called *fales*, strategically constructed across the road from the bay. Instead of solid foundations they are perched atop posts that allow air or water to flow beneath. Further along is the town Malone saw earlier. It has a primitive shop and an old bar, already open for business at mid-morning. A white sand beach shines in the distance, framed by tall palms and overseen by huge oval rocks standing quietly in the off-shore waters. They looked like giant haystacks when Malone saw them from the sea. To his left, he sees steep green cliffs, very different from the gradual slopes that lead down to the beaches in Honolulu or Durban. The sheer peaks and rough vegetation remind him of rugged Caribbean islands like St. Lucia or Martinique. Pago is familiar, yet quite different. He is intrigued by this island.

Half of the passengers will be out on excursions, motoring to the other side to see the blow holes at Leone Bay, and to visit thatched-hut villages. Others will remain aboard ship during the stay, ignoring what they consider an obscure port of call, determined to drink away the remaining time.

Against his will, Malone promised Bergen he would join him and Christy for a drink in the village with some of the ship's crew and a small group of local English and American ex-patriots. His own internal competition with Captain Christian irritates him. Malone suspects that this party could mark an end to his own interest in her. It feels as if she is about to make some sort of announcement. The captain is likely to be there himself.

Bergen walks ahead, explaining that he has to meet someone at the bar, while Malone lags behind, wandering off the main street to investigate the village. Then he slowly makes his way down the dusty road toward the bar, passing scruffy plots of land and a shuttered general store that must have been washed away from some recent storm. He's in no hurry to find out what's next.

The uneven strands of tiny seashells hang down in swaying rows that act as a door to the old bar. They clack noisily as he pushes through, and he's surprised at the darkness. Malone hears a familiar old song blaring from what must be a victrola. He first heard that magical voice back at Jeppe School, singing "Vesti le Gubba" from "Pagliacci". Coach Scott had been a serious collector of opera recordings. Here in this obscure bar, the familiar sound of Caruso throws him off guard.

Bergen and Christy stand at the end of the bamboo bar, chatting and looking every bit the hosts, talking and laughing. *Why don't I just turn around and get out of here?* Bergen is in his tropical suit and vest, ignoring the moist heat. He looks like an English gentleman.

As he sees Christy, Malone nods, then hesitates when he finds her eyes fixed on his. In her thin blue top and trim tan trousers, she looks like the heroine in a Valentino desert movie, or Amelia Earhart's pretty sister. Something seems different. "A beer please," he manages, as he nods to the sunbaked bartender.

Christy leans toward the old man and smiles boldly, "Would you mind asking that gentleman who just came in to come over and sit by me?"

The bartender winks and says, "You heard the young lady, son. I'll just put this beer over here." And places it next to her.

Unamused, Malone moves down the bar and takes his place on one of the bamboo stools. "Is this better?" asks Malone, tersely.

"What's wrong with you, Duff? I was just teasing. You look upset."

"Something is going on, and I'm not in on it," Malone begins, agitated and speaking louder than intended.

Before she can respond, Bergen edges over, cautioning Christy. "Hold on, Duff. Just give us a few minutes. We want to show you something. Just bring your beer …no …no…don't pour it in the glass. Bring the bottle."

Malone feels Christy take his left arm, snugging it up against her body and turning him toward Bergen, who takes his right arm as they push through the shells. She carries his beer and they climb into a dilapidated wooden cart, with a mule patiently waiting in front of it. Bergen strides around to the left, while Christy pushes Malone into the center and sits next to him.

Like an experienced driver, Bergen sits tall and flops the reins. The mule cooperates by struggling down the dirt road. A wide beach is visible in the distance, rimmed with palm trees, and he assumes they are headed there.

"Where are you taking me?" he asks nervously, and swigs his beer. "I don't think I like this."

"Just stick with us," assures Bergen. "You'll be glad you did."

Christy squeezes his hand and adds lightly, "Go with your instincts, Duff. Trust us," as she leans against him gently. "Just down the road, and then we can get out," she smiles in a secretive way.

Passing the few townspeople, large men and women in colorful garb who laugh and wave as they pass, they are soon outside of town. They sit back to let the mule take them along the bumpy road, then Malone sees a clearing with a small embankment leading down to a beach. As they step off the cart, he sinks onto soft white sand and observes heavy stones grouped together to the right side, separated by rows of downed palm trees, placed end to end, that look like benches; then another circle inside that's made of smaller, charred stones. Obviously a place for cooking and sitting, since a fire isn't likely to be needed for heat in this tropical place.

They brush themselves off, Christy offering a hand of support to Malone. Bergen tethers the mule to a nearby bush and waves them onto the beach.

Bergen startles them by instructing, "Leave your shoes and socks here. Much better to walk in bare feet. But look out for sharp stones."

Now barefoot, Christy takes the middle, with Malone on one hand and Bergen the other. They shuffle back toward town in the warm white sand, their hands palm-against-palm, swinging their arms like three school chums. The sun is high and bright, and the water is shimmering. As they walk on, Malone looks to his right at his two companions, working up his courage.

After a few minutes, he announces, "All right, this is about enough! The setting is lovely, but I have something to say."

"Shhh," whispers Christy. "Just walk for a bit. Please."

The surf rolls over their feet and gently splashes their legs, but they continue along the beach. The warm water is soothing, and Malone feels his anger calming. As they approach a rise in the sand, then step down into the shallows of a small lagoon, they see dark bodies moving on the beach ahead.

"Look!" gasps Christy. A half-dozen large creatures are moving off of the sand, and entering the slapping surf. All except for one, which must have gotten flipped onto its back. "Sea turtles."

As they approach, the lone turtle's legs are flailing and chopping the air, and its head is bobbing and gasping. "We have to help," Christy cries. "Look how helpless it is."

"Of course we do," Malone moves quietly over to the struggling creature. "Bergen, would you come give a hand to this edge? It must be three feet across."

They grunt and lift, flipping the turtle onto its feet, and watch as it lumbers into the ocean froth and disappears, then they rinse their hands in the salty water.

"Thank you for helping," sobs Christy. "I'm sorry I'm

upset. Thank you for setting it free."

Bergen wraps an arm around her, careful not to drip sea water on her clean clothes. "It's all right, my dear. You were right to be concerned. It's fine now. Let's walk on and calm down."

Malone sees how comforting Bergen is, as she takes their hands again in silence. The three of them continue down the beach, with no more sea creatures in sight.

As they walk further, Malone looks over at Bergen, intending to say something about turning back, only to realize that he has gone. Looking down at Christy, he asks, "Where…"

"It's just the two of us, Duff. Bergen left us a moment ago. Let's just walk."

Hearing nothing further, he senses that nothing else need be said, so he goes on with his hand still holding hers. As they walk she adjusts them, gently entwining her fingers into his and holding tighter. He no longer feels like a schoolchild or a chum.

They continue in silence, then he stops, finally adding things up. Malone turns toward Christy and looks down at her, into the blue, knowing eyes. They kiss quietly, and draw apart to see if the moment is real. They wrap their arms around each other, holding tightly, and kiss a long, deep kiss.

CHAPTER 39

Malone sees their shoes as they make their way back up the beach. He has no intention of releasing her hand.

"This is where we started, I'm sure of it...," he begins.

"It's fine, Duff. Bergen went into town for a bit. He'll come back for us."

"But the party. Don't you..."

She laughs softly, "Stop managing things for a while. He knows what he's doing. He'll come back in due time. Let's just sit here. Tell me what happened back there with the turtles. Why was I so emotional? And why did it take you so long to figure things out"

"I'll start with the turtles. I was emotional, too," Malone begins quietly. "Turtles can suffocate, you know. It happens."

"So you have done that before? I was so surprised, so worried for them."

"When I went ashore in Mexico, I saw rough men who used to flip them onto their backs in front of the tourists, to make money. They were local vagrants who bummed money however they could. They would flip them onto their backs where they would start to suffocate, from their intestines crushing their lungs. The men laughed and told people they were being tenderized while they died, and they would taste better. Said they were setting them up for slaughter." Malone withdraws his hand and places them together in front of him.

"The soft-hearted tourists would offer to buy the turtles, and the men would laugh and charge them 'one gringo dollar'. When the tourists paid them, the vagrants would flip them upright and run off, as the poor turtles staggered back into the water." Malone looks deep into the water and continues quietly, "I saw the same kind of men in Naples and Marseilles, preying on children, not turtles. The kids would be at the waterfront, taking money and food in exchange for going into the park with them."

"What did they do with the children?" Christy asks.

"Unspeakable things, that starving people are willing to do for money. But when I saw them, they did nothing," Malone says quietly. "Each time, I gave the kids money, more than they ever expected, and told them to buy food. To go home. Then I threatened the men with their lives."

Reaching over, she touches his face. "I watched you tonight. I saw you react. There was more than just the turtle in your thoughts. I didn't know about you and creatures struggling for life, but I'm not surprised."

Malone draws her to him and they kiss again, with tears moistening their lips.

"I thought you were in love with the captain," Malone whispers.

"The captain? What are you taking about? I'm in love with you, don't you see it? That's why we set this all up!" She holds his eyes with hers. "Erik Christian is my friend, and he's a wonderful dancer. But I'm certainly not in love with him. He's a friend. But you're special. I'm in love with you, and I thought it was time you knew it."

"But what took you so damned long? I was so upset. I was about to tell you to leave me alone... but then I couldn't decide what to say."

"Bergen and I were afraid I had waited too long, and that's why we hurried you out of the bar. It was clear we'd upset you. But aboard ship, with the passengers panicking and what happened with those kids, the dancers. We just couldn't get your attention."

"And it's not just the captain! You are such a flirt!" Malone continues, with a gentle tone.

"I guess I am a bit of a flirt." She laughs, "But what about you? You are, too!"

"Me? I don't dance and jolly it up with people the way you do, flashing those blue eyes and pretty legs."

"Yes, Duff, you are quite a serious sort of man, but I do see the way you look at me, and treat me so kindly. That's a form of flirting. And how you look at women!"

"What do you mean, look at women?"

"Just that. Do you think we aren't aware of how you admire us, our bodies, when you are talking with us? Is that not a form of flirting?"

"I do admire a beautiful body. I admit that. And these new outfits are quite revealing, with nothing underneath. But have I ever offended you, or embarrassed someone?"

"Of course not. We love it, at least I do. Toots and Gwen do, too. But your watchful way is seen as a form of flirtation."

A voice breaks in from the road, "So you two have found each other?" asks Bergen casually. "I'd say, it's about time."

Malone catches his breath and says, "So this is your surprise? You knew all along that I felt…That is, you were aware.."

"Yes, Duff, we were aware," she interrupts. "We just weren't sure how to get your attention. As you said, you are such a proper sort."

Bergen adds, "I tell you, Duff. If I had half a chance, I would sweep this lady off her feet and marry her in an instant! But I don't have a chance, my friend. For some reason she prefers a younger man."

"I do adore Bergen," laughs Christy, looking up into Malone's eyes. "And I love to dance with the captain, and laugh and meet his fascinating friends. But I have feelings for you that are very different. You are so unlike everyone else that I know. Sometimes you seem distant and so damned arrogant that I could scream. Other times, you are the kindest man. Your eyes tear up when you hear about people who are troubled or grieving. And you often miss some of the small things going on around you.

You just gaze out in the distance, and I think you are so far away from me and everyone else. Or want to be. And then you tell me something sweet and personal, and I want to cry. You care about giving people a chance to succeed. You worry about the shape of the world, and all of its shortcomings. And you sometimes lose track of the time or forget to bring your wallet with you, so Bergen has to pay for dinner, or for your laundry. So I have made up my mind, Duff. That even though you act like a shoe-clerk some of the time, I love you."

"Hello, you three!" comes a familiar voice from the sandy crest. Ruth leads Anna by the hand, as they make their way down to the soft beach, lifting their loose tunics to free their legs.

"Where were you?" asks Bergen.

"We found a lovely little lagoon down the way, just over there," Anna points beyond the palms. "There are cottages that we booked for the day. We've been sitting with a bottle of wine and talking, then we decided to explore and here we are."

"This is such a lovely place," adds Ruth gently. "Spiritual, even."

Christy nods, "Spiritual. Yes it is. A place where people can share secret thoughts." She glances at Duff.

Watching Anna and Ruth, Duff senses a kind of tranquility he had not seen before.

"We think we would like to return here," says Anna. "but just to visit. It would be difficult to live this far away from New York."

Ruth adds, "But it has made us think. We want a peaceful place, and we love Anna's parents' cabin, up in the Poconos. They no longer use it. Maybe we could make a home out of it."

"We don't know precisely what we'll face when we get home, any more than anyone else does," says Anna. "but it's a place we love, and it is the right time for us."

The rough fern brushes against his arm, deep green and slightly moist. After following the narrow trail through the dense foliage, they emerge into sunlight and stop short. "My God, it's beautiful," he says.

Christy nods, "The sunlight! It's like honey through the trees."

She steadies herself against him, and he's aware of the electricity. Of the touch of her hand and nearness of her body, and the aroma of her hair. He sees the beauty around them, but is deeply aware of her.

"The water, it's so clear!" she gasps. You can see the stones at the bottom. And look at the little silver fish swimming past."

"They're beautiful, and very deep down I think. Bigger than they look. So are the stones."

"And up there, do you see the halo around the palms?"

"Think it's an omen? It's magical."

"There's the little cottage."

They approach a primitive structure, with its heavily thatched roof. "What did you tell Bergen?" Duff asks, as he ducks his head and follows Christy through the entry, viewing the simple room, a single, spotless space, with window openings letting in the sunlight and fresh air. A deep red flower sits comfortably in a water glass on the tiny dresser.

"I asked him to arrange a picnic basket for us, here at the lagoon."

"And he said?"

"He told me to look for the cottage, patted my hand and said, 'take care'."

Duff spots the worn basket. Opening it, he laughs, "That Bergen thinks of everything. A lovely bottle of wine to accompany quite a little feast! Look at that fresh bread and fruit! Even a corkscrew tied-up with a ribbon, attached to these wine glasses." Impulsively, he takes Christy's hand, "Shall we explore our little paradise? Let's go sit by the lagoon with our wine. Perhaps it's where Anna and Ruth were sorting out their future." He leads her down the wooden steps toward the water.

"Sun bursting through the trees and flowers. All the greens

and golds!" she turns in a circle, to take it all in. "And see those huge trees with craggy roots hanging down from the tops. Like an ancient world."

"It's lovely, and so peaceful -- as if we're the only people who have ever been here."

"Like Adam and Eve?" She teases, "Is there an apple in the picnic basket?"

"You know what I mean," he laughs. "You have to give me a little license here. I just found out I'm in love, you know, and it tends to cloud my judgment."

"It's all right, Duff. Exaggerate all you like." She looks around, "Let's go sit over on that rock, there by the water."

Duff kisses her gently, and holds her. "I never imagined a moment as beautiful as this."

They sit quietly, circling their feet in the pond.

"How lucky we are, Duff." She looks away and wipes her eyes. He must not have seen her, because when she turns back, Malone is reaching down into the clear water and touching her foot, playfully. She steadies herself, "Duff, there is something I need to tell you."

At the same time, he looks at her, startled and blurts, "Christy. Look at the sun! I totally forgot." Quickly, he reaches for the lunch basket and begins cleaning up.

"Duff, what's our hurry? We aren't due back on the ship until seven."

"I forgot all about my appointment. I'm to meet with a local man. Strict orders from New York."

"How could you have a meeting on this remote island?"

"It's difficult to explain. But I know it's a serious matter. It's about my future."

Christy frowns, "Am I not about your future? I was about to tell you something important."

"I want to hear everything you have to tell me," touching

her cheek, he adds, "Can it wait until we're back on the ship? When I got this assignment, the Commodore directed me to meet with a man here in Pago Pago. He's to brief me on plans for new aircraft for carrying passengers. Far bigger than Lindbergh's. To take people all over the world."

Knowing the moment had passed, she reluctantly joins his line of thought, "Dad told me about airplanes, and I know about Amelia Earhart and Charles Lindbergh. What's this about?"

"Before I left New York, the Commodore told me to consider leaving the cruise business and take a job with an airline company, probably in Hawaii."

"It sounds strange to me, Duff, and a little mysterious... and it's clear that my thoughts will have to wait."

CHAPTER 40

Duff stands on the dock and watches the small boat motor away, smiling weakly while Christy waves again. With the ship sailing in two hours, he will have just enough time for a short conversation in town. *Maybe we should just stay!* He wishes silently, unwilling to awaken fully from this dream.

Retracing his earlier steps, Duff pushes through the seashell curtain and enters the bar, locating what looks to be a local man sitting alone at a small table. The stranger is weathered, with a scruffy beard and a khaki hat with one side of the brim tied up like a desert soldier. Seeing a small wave of the hand, Malone walks toward him, reaching out.

"Martin Bradley?" he asks.

"The same," he replies, in a clear and pleasant voice with a sharp Australian accent. "Call me Wings. And you must be Duff Malone."

"That I am. The Commodore told me I would be pleased to meet you."

"Walt is a kind man, and an old friend. Please, sit."

"He didn't tell me much, I'm afraid. But he did say you would have something important to discuss."

"I do, Duff." He raises two fingers at the bartender, who nods and pries the caps from two brown beer bottles, setting them on the bar.

Malone gets up and grabs them, bringing them back and handing one to Bradley.

"I'll make this brief, Duff. I know you need to get back to the ship. I'm an engineer, aeronautics. I also know a bit about marine engineering, ships, small boats, those kinds of things. I have an idea that the Commodore is aware of, and I think he believes in it as much as I do. It's a passenger airplane." He smiles, "Want to hear more?"

"Of course."

"It's a flying boat, literally. We know people are experimenting with large aircraft that can carry passengers. You know, like those planes that fly the mail around America, speeding up the delivery of letters? Only these carry people, enough of them to make the flights profitable enough to compete with trains and maybe ships."

"Go on!" exclaims Malone. "An airplane that can carry that many passengers? How many did you say?"

"These planes will carry fifteen, twenty, maybe. Fifty passengers, eventually."

"I have heard of the mail planes, that fly from small clearings and empty roadways. They are even launching them from ships over in Europe, when they are near enough to shore. And they're building airports for them, like that new one about to open in Honolulu."

"Mail delivery is a driving force, Duff, for consistent revenue. Military, too, as a new weapon carrier, and for troops. And this plane takes it another step, as a flying boat, carrying passengers in addition to mail. It can lift off from a lake or the ocean, and it can land there. You get someplace in hours, not days the way it is with steamships. There could be retractable wheels, too, to fly from places that have no bodies of water. The Russians are experimenting with it. And the Germans, Brits, French. Lindbergh and Earhart have made it appealing to the public, and we need to develop the aircraft."

"Why so secretive, Wings? And why are you sharing this with me?"

"It's more than a dream, Duff. Pago is where I choose to live, but I'm in regular contact with the States. This is a remote place and I can get my design work done here without anyone looking over my shoulder. Last time I was in New York, I met with the Commodore, together with an interested American named Juan Trippe. He has operated mail planes in the Caribbean, and passenger flights around New York, and he has created a company called Pan American Airways. He envisions this passenger airplane as a clipper ship in the air, transporting people from coast cities to places like Bermuda, Cuba, Hawaii, even as far as here, or China. The Commodore discussed your background with Trippe. He's assembling a dynamic team, and they want you to help establish the flights out into the Pacific, from Honolulu, once we have the engineering perfected."

"The Commodore is going to fire me from American Express?"

"That isn't what I said, Duff. I assure you." Bradley smiles gently. "Walt sees big opportunities for this airline travel, competing with steamships and trains. Everyone is concentrating on speed and cost. Planes will be faster and cheaper. The first ones are at least three years off, before they will be in commercial use. They will hold twenty passengers and crew, and fly over a hundred and fifty miles an hour. Go as far as Asia and Africa, eventually. And he wants you to lead the office in Hawaii. Trippe has agreed, and American Express will be your first customer."

"I'm shocked," Malone admits. "It sounds so promising, as if this financial crisis is not happening. I wasn't prepared for such an idea."

"Take your time, Duff, and think about it. Nothing has happened yet, but it will. I'm aware of the stock market, and know that people in America are in for a very bad time of it. But regardless of what the economy is doing now, it will recover eventually. And somebody has to plan for the future. The engineering exists. People will want to travel abroad, all over the world, faster than they have ever done before. First, we have to create the planes, map out the organization, and negotiate landing rights in foreign countries. The last part will be your first job. When you reach San Francisco, I suspect the Commodore will confirm all of this."

Leaving the bar, Malone struggles with colliding emotions. Although he's exhausted and painfully in love, he feels the surge he used to feel before the big rugby matches, or when he accepted the job in New York. He remembers being stunned, unready. He also remembers how honored he felt, how he wanted to make his coach proud. As he struggles, Duff silently makes his way down the uneven road toward the dock, where the small boat awaits to ferry him back to the *Malolo.*

Chapter 41

As the ship pulls out of this tiny port that few had wished to visit, gliding past Whale Rock and through Niuloa and Breakers Point, Malone is still struggling to sort things out. He has difficulty thinking of anything except Christy, and he feels drugged. He wants to be with her now, to breathe in the scent of her hair, to touch her. He hated running off like that.

But here he is, back on the forecastle as they leave another port of call, planning for the final leg of the journey. The passengers still need his attention. The market continues to collapse. And it's another twelve days before they reach San Francisco.

There are decisions to make about this new airline idea. Wings says that the travel business is heading toward airplanes, but how could they replace these luxury liners? He can imagine flying from Hawaii to San Francisco, and arriving the same day. Good for a professional man, perhaps. But where is the space, or comfort? Why would you trade shipboard elegance for time? His passengers could have used this kind of speed to get back home from Hong Kong, but that's an exception. Is this what life will be like? Speed and price more important than comfort?

If he accepts the Pan American offer, it will mean another big move, off to the Hawaiian Islands. He'd be traveling throughout the Pacific. Australia, probably, and Japan. *And Christy! Whatever am I thinking? She's an adventurer, but could she really live in Hawaii? What would she do? Could she put up with my travels?*

As he leans against the familiar gray capstan, he watches another vessel off in the distance, steaming on a steady westward course. *It's a good omen,* he thinks. *I'll work with what I know, and deal with the uncharted when it appears.*

Dinner is long over and Christy had been silent, except for pleasantries with other passengers. She seems withdrawn, and after a perfunctory dance he walks with her to a remote table where they can be alone.

"I've told you I'm sorry about running off like that. You were about to tell me something important this afternoon," Duff reminds her as they sit in the warm air.

"It's important, but I'm not sure I'm up to it right now, Duff. Let's just talk a while."

"This has been a wonderful day." He searches for the right words. "Please believe me. This has been the happiest day of my life, because of you. I didn't want it to end."

She takes his hand, squeezing it gently, "Don't fret, Duff. I know you had an assignment, and that's what you do. I just need to get used to it." The small turns at the corners of Christy's mouth signal that she is relaxing. "It's been a glorious day for me, too. And I know you wouldn't have run off if you had a choice."

"You looked so serious, and I wanted time to listen carefully."

"I know. I know," she soothes. "I'll come back to it. First, tell me about your important meeting back there."

He closes his eyes to recapture the gist of his conversation with Martin Bradley. "Mr. Bradley -- that is, Wings -- is an engineer. He is designing a large airplane that can land on water, and take off again with a load of passengers, twenty people or more. And it will fly long distances, eventually from New York to London. From San Francisco to Hawaii. It can get people there in a single day, not three or four days, the way the ships do now." His eyes are bright as he continues, "With refueling stops, these Flying Clippers could transport passengers to Japan or Hong Kong, or over to Africa."

As Malone talks, he frees his hand, gesturing erratically, his voice rising and looking out in the distance, as if peering out toward Tokyo or Paris from high in the air.

"I can see how exciting this is, Duff. But what did he want from you?"

"That's just it, Christy. He didn't want anything, except for me to think about the new job."

"The one you mentioned when I was leaving?"

"In Honolulu. He said that a new airline is forming. A man with an unusual name, Juan Trippe, wants to hire me."

"And why would you go with someone you know nothing about?"

"But I know about Trippe from the Commodore. And Wings told me the Commodore was going to advise me to accept this new job. That American Express expects to be his biggest customer."

"So you would consider moving to Hawaii for this?" she asks, calmly.

"I would," he reacts, then catches himself, "but only if it's something that you would want to do."

"And if I had complications?"

"Complications? I think they would pay me enough, you wouldn't need to work. You could be home. We could have a family there," pausing to complete his wish, "couldn't we?"

The edges of her mouth moves again, a sad smile this time. "Now it's my turn, Duff. This brings us to my serious point."

"Go on," he places his hands over hers.

"Duff, there is no other way to say this. You mentioned having a family. I already have a child, a little girl." She stops to watch his expression.

His eyes and mouth relax and he gently says, "Tell me more, love."

"I have a daughter, Mary. She's two years old now, and lives with mom and dad down in Long Beach. She loves them very much." She blinks away sudden emotion, and continues. "I was in my third year at St. Luke's, and I met this intern. He was from Stanford and we met at a dance up in San Francisco. He said he would marry me when he finished his internship. Then one day I found out he was gone to an assignment in Maryland. I never heard from him again. And I was pregnant."

"How did you get through it? School? The pregnancy? Life?"

"Mom and dad are wonderful. They're special. I dropped out for one term and stayed with them at home. Mary was born in January, and I went back to school in September. It wasn't easy on them, or on me -- or on Mary. But we made it work, and I got my nurse's degree."

"And her father? Does he know about Mary?"

"No," she pauses, "I couldn't bring myself to tell him. He didn't care about me. He didn't deserve this baby."

"And what about this cruise?" he asks gently. "With a baby, couldn't you stay home with her?"

"This was an unexpected assignment, and I need the extra income. I do plan to work down near Long Beach, the hospital where my mom works. But this job was offered at double the money. So here I am."

Duff touches her cheek, "I'm glad you told me. Glad you're here."

"You're glad?"

"Of course. I love you. Anyone who is part of you, I will love. And you are quite a woman. Now, will you tell me more about Mary? Is she smart and lovely, like her mother?"

"Smarter and very beautiful. She's a fun, energetic girl. And she loves her grandparents!"

"I can't wait to meet her. I don't know much about children, but I know I'll love her."

Christy is silent again, gathering her thoughts. Then in a whisper, "You surprise me, you know?"

"And how is that?"

"In a good way. Of the many reactions I thought about, this is one I never considered. You're an understanding man, Duff." She looks at him with clear eyes, then sits back and continues in a stronger voice, "As an understanding man, I'm going to make another suggestion that may surprise you."

"And what is that, love?"

"I want to stay with you tonight. Is this too bold?"

He nods and says quietly, "Not at all. It's what I want, too. For the rest of our journey."

Chapter 42

They lie on his bed, with covers off and the open porthole providing early morning air. On his back, Malone's arm engulfs Christy's slim body, drawing her against him. His hand rests on her back, touching her with the tips of his fingers. "Are your eyes still open, love?"

"Wide open."

"You are amazing, you know. I feel quite safe with you."

"Why amazing? You are safe with me."

"It's just me. My own fears, I guess. I'm incredibly happy now for the first time, maybe ever. And worried that something might come along and spoil it! I want to protect you."

"I love that you want to protect me," she puts her hand onto his chest and he covers it with his, "but don't overdo it! I like doing things for myself, too. And don't worry, love. I'm here. I'm not going anywhere."

"We'll have to find a balance, it seems. Last night you asked me what I love, what I really care about. I've been lying here thinking about it, and may have an answer. First, I love how open you are, how direct. That you and I lie here without our clothes, and there is no pretense. No covering up."

"But that's the way I am. We agree we're in love. We have made love. Openly. Willingly," she slaps him playfully on his stomach. "So what is there to hide? I say what I mean, and I believe that you do, too."

Once again, he draws her to him and laughs, "That is another thing I love, the willing part. But it sometimes requires a bit of a break. So I'll tell you what else I was thinking about."

"I promise to listen, but don't wait too long. You were telling me what else you love."

"I think I'm like you in some ways. I love my work.

Visiting new places, meeting people, learning about new cultures. Doing the best job that I can for people."

"And you care nothing about money," she teases. "That's pretty evident. Although everyone else on this cruise says that money is the most important thing."

"Oh, I think there are at least two or three of us aboard who don't think that. Money is important to some. People like that Chester Warren, and most of our passengers. But I'm heartened by people like Alita and Lloyd, Gio, Anna and Ruth. They have plenty of money, but they're decent, thoughtful people. They care about others. And Bergen, of course."

"I also see that they are closer to you than other passengers. Kindred spirits, as you might say?"

"They have become good friends."

"And what about your family? I never hear you talk about them."

Looking beyond her, he blinks hard and responds in a voice that she hasn't heard before, "Family. You're quite right, I don't speak of them much."

She remains silent, unsure of what to say, until he continues, sounding more like himself. "For a time I was very angry. In school, in my work, I used to pick things apart, find all the flaws. Then I realized that we all have choices about our attitudes. I prefer to be positive, not dwell on the negative things. I choose to concentrate on how to make things better. To help people get along. My family are not part of this picture. My true family is my friends. South Africa is no longer part of my life. Not simply because of how far away they are, but they're part of the unpleasant past. While I do care about my brother and his life, we no longer know each other. It's been too many years. My father died long ago, and I didn't ever know him. As for my mother, when I knew her I grew to hate her. I won't go into the reasons. Now, I simply have no feelings for her."

She leans her head against his chest. "I'm so sorry I asked. I'm sorry you are so hurt." She remains still, against his body. He feels her tears roll down his side.

"I'll be fine. You make me fine. I came to terms a long time ago, that these feelings are not there. That's why friendships mean so much."

She strengthens their grip. "I can feel your love. I really can. I feel sparks when you touch me! And I'm happy when you are around me. I just worry about you." Sitting up, she laughs, "Do you hear that? Now I'm saying how much I want you to be safe! We sound like a couple of parents here, instead of lovers." She leans over and looks at him gently, "And so we are, my love. Are we not? I want you to meet my Mary. She will love you, too."

"See how positive we both are?" Malone chuckles, "Who's going to be the realist in this relationship?"

"You leave that to me. You provide the dreams, and I will make sure we reach them. Now come back here."

Chapter 43

The sea is calm, the weather warm and humid. If tonight is any measure, the final leg of the journey promises to be the most subdued yet. Even the dinner music is muted, with the greying, usually-upbeat pianist quietly humming to himself as he plays “Bye-Bye Blackbird” in a minor key, then slides into a wistful version of “Stardust”.

“Why is it, Duff, that everyone appears so tired, but you seem very happy?” asks Gio, in a gentle tease.

“I think you know more than you let on.”

“This is true. I would be a very mediocre Italian if I did not recognize when two people are in love.” He pats Duff’s hand, “And where is lady Christy this evening?”

“She’s in her room writing to her parents, telling them about our plans. She should be here shortly.” Pausing, “I’m surprised I never asked you, have you ever been married, Gio?”

“I have not,” he replies easily. “Nor was my mother, or my grandmother.”

“I’m sorry. I didn’t mean to bring up....”

“No, my friend. No need to apologize. It did not alter my path, I believe. We are all born, and we have a mother’s love, for a moment at least, or longer if we are so lucky.” He watches Duff’s eyes and senses a change. “My mother did not survive childbirth, you see. I was lucky to have a loving great-grandmother. She is the mother to whom I refer.”

Malone looks away, into the distance.

Sorvini continues slowly. “So, in response to your question, I have not been married.” Then he sighs and adds, raising his wine glass with a flourish, “But I have loved some beautiful women!”

Malone’s gaze returns to his friend, along with a small smile at this light comment.

"And your wedding, Duff, where will that be?"

"This depends on Christy's family. Probably at a justice of the peace, shortly after we arrive. If they can make arrangements in San Francisco, we could be married before you leave for home. Anna and Ruth could join us, with Alita and Lloyd. Bergen will stand up for me." He looks up as another passenger approaches.

"Mr. Malone, ... Duff, I would like a word with you." The little man looks nervous.

"Of course, Jonathan."

"We have had more meetings, my friends and I. Feelings among the passengers have changed, about news from the outside world."

"This sounds positive."

"We got over it, so to speak. If we're going to be broke when we get home, we want to know the details. We're tired of simply being angry, or hiding from it with cocktails. We don't want to give in to conditions we don't yet understand. We need to know what is really awaiting us. We have another few days before we reach San Francisco. Can you help us get information? Several of us have tried exchanging telegrams with family or colleagues, but we don't know what to believe."

"I'll do what I can, Jonathan. I'll contact my sources. Do you have specific questions?"

"We want to know what conditions are like back home. Will we be safe when we get to San Francisco? Are there riots? Then we want to know specifics. Let us begin with which stocks have fallen, and which may weather the storm? What banks have failed, and which have not?"

"We can certainly find out what life is like in America, San Francisco in particular. As for specific stock prices, or banks, that information may not be quite so accessible or useful, since it all seems to change so fast. And everyone owns different stocks. Would it not be best for individuals to look at what information we do have, and then call their people from San Francisco to check individual banks or holdings?"

"Certainly, if that's what we need to do. We'll see what we're working with, and then take the next steps."

As the man returns to his table, Duff looks over at Sorvini and wonders what they will find back in the States.

Malone has invited Alita and Lloyd to join them in his suite, as he and Bergen sort through the information.

"Let's give this some thought," Malone suggests. "I asked Roberts to level with me about how people are reacting in cities like Los Angeles and San Francisco. Are there riots, or looting? The odd thing is, he tells me that nothing much has changed from when we left, that the newspaper reports we hear about are greatly exaggerated. People jumping out of windows and such. If it actually happened, it was in New York City. But ordinary people seem to be all right. People are worried, of course, but under control."

"New York is a mess," Lloyd affirms. "My latest contact from Washington indicates that Wall Street is devastated." He adds, "Savings holders may not be in as much trouble as the investors, who are certain to be hit the hardest. While the markets affect nearly everyone aboard our ship, the vast majority of Americans -- over ninety per-cent, I'm told -- are not investors. They're worried about their savings deposits, but they're not directly affected by the stock failures."

Malone adds, "We can be sure, if the wealthiest people have been hurt the most, it will eventually affect peoples' jobs, but right now, outside of New York and Washington, it sounds as if we shouldn't expect disturbances on the streets."

"Our passengers are like a chapter from Schopenhauer," observes Bergen, "All the predictable stages. They ridiculed early reports, denying anything could damage the growing economy. When they realized it could happen, many panicked, arguing and racing to get back home before things got worse. We see our remaining people willing to accept the truth now, and looking for rational ways to deal with it."

"Let's talk about how we can provide rational ways to deal with this." suggests Malone. "We've agreed, we're not financial experts so we have no useful guidance there."

"As I see it, Duff, our role is still not financial. We continue to be communicators and helpers."

"As we were in Yokohama, providing the plan and the tools," nods Malone.

"That's what I think."

"Any other thoughts?" Malone scans the table. "Agreed, then. We'll report what we know, that the streets are safe, no riots, but that ordinary people are waiting to see what is coming next. Financial news is bad, but the atmosphere is safe and our staff will be at the pier ready to help with communications or travel plans, so they can find out for themselves where they stand. Then we will inform them of anything new as we approach San Francisco.

Chapter 44

They stand together at the starboard rail, wrapped in heavy jackets. Periodic blasts sound from distant foghorns, as mist dampens the early morning. When the ship alters course, a light crosswind chills their faces, then stills as they complete the turn and slip through the narrow mouth of San Francisco Bay, where visibility is surprisingly good.

Christy's hands grasp Malone's as the ship follows the shoreline, steering well clear of the distant ferry boats. Moving slowly, the *Malolo* seems to resist the reality that awaits them, allowing extra time for its passengers to gather themselves.

As the mist lifts further, they see old cannons on the bluff, and below, low piers that stretch into the water from the military base. They make a gradual arc toward their berth, seeing Alcatraz island squatting off the port side, like a small boulder in the middle of the bay. Off to the left of Alcatraz lies the much larger one known as Angel Island, where immigrants from Asia and the Pacific must enter the country.

Now almost dead in the water, the ship allows tugs to come alongside and nudge it to the pier. On the decks above, passengers crowd the rails as they always do, eager to get a first glimpse of home port after a lengthy absence. Traces of fog cling to the top of the hills, adding a ghostly touch as the wary travelers feel the land approach.

Duff and Christy spent a restless night, sharing hopes for the future and concerns for what awaits them. Finally they slept, arms wrapped around each other.

Malone recognizes that his assignment has ended with this fragmented group. That job is over. No announcement. No crescendo. Just a few personal thanks from individual passengers last night at dinner and during the dance-time. Knowing how anxious people are, he was quite touched by the quiet expressions of appreciation.

A part of him is shutting down, the part that has grown accustomed to reading the eyes and hearing the comments, and coming up with solutions, making things right. Another part is relieved and wants to simply get away, to take Christy and start over. But he knows that he really isn't looking for escape.

What's next? He will meet Christy's parents, and Mary, and arrange for the the brief marriage ceremony. *What will she think of him, this little girl? What do I know of being a father?*

He watches Bergen, steady at the top of the gangway, ready to go ashore and make certain that communications systems are in place. But Malone has no real duties now. Quietly, he asks, "What shall we do first? I'm afraid I feel a bit lost." They watch the passengers disembark, waving back at their shipmates. Christy squeezes his hand as he continues, more to himself than to her, "It's hard to accept. Bergen and I are no longer responsible. Our people are returning to their own lives."

"Is it really true, they are no longer 'our people'?" Christy quietly asks.

"They aren't," he nods, "and that's quite an adjustment. We must let them go."

"Not all of them, though," she reminds him. "Don't you let me go! We'll see Alita and Lloyd tomorrow, and Gio and Bergen at dinner tonight. Anna and Ruth will remain for our wedding, too, I hope. It's difficult to believe, isn't it? As anxious as we are about what has happened, the lives of those people waiting on shore may be very much as they were when we left. To them, maybe nothing has changed." They move closer together.

"Hello you two," Bergen returns, finished with his brief shore duties, now bundled in a heavy overcoat. "Sorry to interrupt, but I told the officers that I would deliver these to you, Duff. One is from the Commodore, I believe. The other forwarded by your department in New York."

Malone slips open the Commodore's envelope and reads it quickly. "I'm to call him later this morning, once we settle into the hotel. He will stay at the office until he hears from me. Bergen, you and I are to remain here for at least another week, maybe more."

"That's a start," sighs Christy. "Some adjustment time."

He opens the second one, removing a telegram enclosed from South Africa. Reading it, he closes his eyes and reads it again.

"Duff, what is it?"

"From my brother, Sandy. He says that mother is ill, and he is asking me to come home right away. She isn't expected to live more than a few weeks. That was several days ago."

"Then you need to go, Duff."

His face hardens, then he smiles over at her, "That's really a question, Christy. Do I want to see her? The damage was done long ago, and nothing has changed. But Sandy has told me something else."

"Is he asking you move back?"

"No, not that." He sees Christy relax slightly. "He's selling the mines. He wants to cash out and leave South Africa. He wants my help disposing of the house and other things."

"How do you get to South Africa?" asks Christy. "It must take forever."

"It's complicated, but I think there may be an answer from this airline owner, Trippe. He operates mail planes, and he may have something that carries passengers that far, stopping for refueling at delivery points along the way. Otherwise it's on tramp steamers that take a month or more each way."

They look over at each other and smile, carefully navigating down the gangway while holding hands like youngsters. "Well, here we are," grins Malone. "We seem to be going back into the real world."

"Yes, here we are," Christy returns his smile, a determined gleam in her eyes. "I can't wait to see my little girl. It's been so long. And mom and dad, of course."

Duff stops, holding her steady, "Hold on. Isn't that Gwen down there? And Captain Kimura, from Honolulu?"

"I don't know Captain Kimura, but that elegant woman is certainly Gwen." She waves and releases Duff's hand, quickly moving down to the pier.

"Hello, Mr. Malone. It's good to see you again."

"John, it's quite a surprise to see you. And Gwen!" Realizing that Kimura and Christy haven't met, he continues, "Officer, this is Christy Miller. She knows of our incident in Honolulu, with the DuPris couple. Now tell us, what are you doing here in San Francisco?"

Gwen responds for them, her voice strong but she looks tired, with dark circles under her eyes. "Officer Kimura has been very helpful, and has come upon some interesting information about Jason's death, and what led up to it."

"Can you tell us about it here, or shall we go somewhere and sit?"

"We're all booked-in at the Mark, Duff," she responds. "We can talk more easily there."

"Come to my suite around four o'clock. We'll order dinner in, and we can review everything in privacy." Smiling sheepishly, "We can also tell you about our wedding plans."

"Wedding? You'll tell me about them right now!" Insists Gwen, springing to life and taking Christy's arm. "We'll ride back with you in your car."

"If you will accompany Mrs. Gibson," says Kimura. "I'll remain here. I have an appointment to examine the cabin and meet with the communications people before the ship is fully cleaned from the voyage."

"It really wasn't difficult to figure out," Kimura begins, as the six of them sit at the large cherry-wood table, covered in linen and set with fine silver. Sorvini and Bergen are at opposite ends, like hosts, as the two couples sit across from each other. A tuxedo'd steward carefully serves generous portions of fish from the silver service followed by dabs of clear sauce studded with capers and herbs, while his assistant deftly pours the white wine.

"When Mrs. Gibson returned to Honolulu from Japan, she showed us the telegram she had received, advising that Mr. Gibson was booked to return to San Francisco on the SS *Cleveland*, then by train to New York City. When I contacted the Dollar Line about his passage, they indicated that he had moved his belongings on board the day before, but he missed the *Cleveland's* sailing. Then they showed me a message from the director of his board at Worldwide Bank. The communications office had held it for him." Kimura pauses to eat and take a brief sip of wine.

Gwen picks up his story, "Jason's bank director wired him and advised that there was no way they would consider a loan for Waikele Land & Pineapple. He said the idea was preposterous, given the two men involved, Thompson from Chumbley, and Knauss from Waikele. Thompson and his shell corporations are under investigation for fraud, and Knauss is a known crook."

"Yes, it was their mention of Knauss's name that led us to contact him at Waikele," continues Kimura. "He was quite new to Hawaii. Less than a year ago he came from Colorado to run the new company. He ran copper mines there. After a few months in Honolulu, he became known as a 'typical *haole*'. That is, an outsider who thinks he knows more than a backward native could ever know. He cut wages for his workers, and employed Mr. Oveida to coerce and intimidate them to stay in the fields, even though the pineapple crop was doing badly. They went into the Kaka'ako macadamia tree venture only to attract investors, trying to diversify in order to break into the two dominant fruit companies."

"So Knauss shot him?" asks Duff, incredulous.

"Oveida did. The man admits that he followed Gibson to the pier where the *Cleveland* was docked. Then he took Gibson to Bishop Street and made him phone his bank people for the loan. When they ridiculed the idea, Oveida phoned Knauss and told him. The bastard said to shoot him."

Gwen adds, "Mr. Knauss seemed to have no lack of brass and arrogance. He all but admitted to the police that Jason had insulted him, misled him about the loan, and he deserved to die. And Oveida was his willing gunman."

"Based on Knauss's surprising candor -- he seemed to believe he was too rich and important to be charged -- we got Oveida to confirm his role, and to fully implicate Knauss."

Wincing at the image, Malone wonders if the one bank might have influenced the New York financial collapse. "We read that Worldwide Bank had failed. How could that happen? And did that lead to other banks closing?"

"There were some unexpected pieces to the puzzle, Duff," Kimura lifts his hand as he continues. "While the bank failure had nothing to do with this loan, which was never completed, the highly publicized killing caused Worldwide's customers to panic, and to immediately begin withdrawing their funds. It's a major bank, so when people heard about it, that caused runs on several others, whose customers were afraid theirs would fold. Worldwide's board closed the bank, of course, as many have done, at least temporarily. Now they are sorting through more orderly settlements with their customers."

"You mentioned other pieces, John. Is there another?"

"I can add that, I believe," Gwen speaks softly, and looks as if she is sharing a shameful secret. "There is one other surprising part. We learned that in early September Jason began short-selling his personal shares in Worldwide. That's why he was hurrying back. I only recently understood what selling short means. He was literally selling shares in his own bank, that he didn't even own, hoping they would then lose value. When the value went down, he would buy them back at the lower amount, then return the stocks to the bank and keep the profit. He shorted nearly fifty-thousand shares, earning him millions. By using a Canadian shell-company to buy the stocks, his earning were tax-free. It's all terribly legal, I'm afraid. But so devious. What a bastard."

Chapter 45

21 November, 1929 San Francisco, USA

Dear Sandy,

This is a very difficult letter to write, for many reasons. First, because we have not seen each other for many years. Also, because I am about to touch places I have hidden away even longer, since I left home. I write to you on my return from a cruise assignment, having just yesterday read your news about mother's serious illness. I will not be returning to South Africa to see her.

As you must know, my feelings about mother and father are painful. A father we did not have, and a mother whose memory hurts and angers me to this day. I am glad that you have been with mother during her illness, and that you were direct about her condition. You are right, of course. She is no longer young, and her life was a demanding one.

After reading this, I hope you understand why I shall not return. My immediate reaction was to come join you and mother, a loyal son trying to be there before she dies. But I realize that it is far too late.

Perhaps it may not be too late to see her again before she dies. But for me, it is too late to change anything. The damage was done and is beyond fixing.

You describe how she changed some years ago, after nearly losing the mines. That she gave up alcohol, and with your help she held things together. That she has become "nearly a saint", helping Bantu mothers and children around Johannesburg.

I am afraid that I cannot feel sadness, or even a connection to our mother. I realize how difficult her life was, and how overwhelmed she must have felt when father died. I respect this, and am glad that she has become generous. But I cannot forgive those years of shame that she made me feel. My unworthiness, and hatred for her. Did you not feel it, too? We were just little boys, and she shouted that his death was our fault! Now I simply have no feelings for her.

I am glad, big brother, that you have come to terms with this, and are there to comfort her. Every human deserves comfort. While I am not pleased with myself for these harsh feelings toward her, I must acknowledge the truth. While I no longer feel shame about myself, and I have learned that my life does have value, the coldness remains within me.

With help, I have found happiness in my life, perhaps greater happiness than anyone has a right to. I have met a wonderful woman, who understands me in ways that I cannot explain. I hope to marry soon and take on a new life, as a husband and a father. As a married man, you must know these feelings.

I have enclosed my written authority to sell my share of the Johannesburg house and property, and any holdings I might have in the mines. I wish to keep nothing. As you see, it is my specific wish that my share goes to Cebo, and if the law does not allow him to own land, that it be held for him in the name of our solicitor until such time as ownership is possible. You tell me that the solicitor is a trustworthy and understanding man.

You say you and your wife are moving to Scotland, back to Elgin. Perhaps I will see you there, sooner than you might think. My new work is with an airline company, and we are likely to bring passenger airplanes to London, which is not so far away.

I wish you well, my brother, as you and your wife move to Scotland. I hope you understand my feelings about our mother. You have worked hard all your life, and you deserve a bit of respite. Perhaps we will meet and share our stories.

My love to you,
Duff

Chapter 46

February 25, 1932

Pete closes the gate quietly, so he won't wake Doris. She seems stronger here in Hawaii, in this little beach cottage at the base of Mount Leahi. Her breathing has settled, but he knows she lies awake almost every night. Sometimes it helps to read late before turning out the light. In truth, she misses sleeping in the same room as Mary. She reaches a deep sleep around three o'clock, just two hours before he is stirring, so he lets her sleep in.

It's a routine now. He throws on his old shorts and a faded pullover shirt, then slips out and goes to the bigger house where Duff has his coffee waiting for him along with his own dark tea. Together, they sit out on the lanai looking over the water, chatting until sunrise when the kids come down. Then the four of them, Pete, Duff, Mary and Theo, follow the beach path down to the cove. Mary loves it when they use her Hawaiian name "Malia"! It makes her feel special.

As they approach the row of palms, Pete lifts young Theo into his arms and Duff takes Malia's hand, helping each other down the sandy slope. While her dad sits on the large boulder, Malia tests the calm water with her toe, then runs back for a hug before she wades in. Duff looks over at Theo and Pete peering down into the black coral. Grandpa holds his little hand and points, probably telling him about the tiny sea creatures that inhabit the tide-pool. Even at two, Theo is fascinated by them, pointing his miniature finger, like Pete, and trying to say the words.

Duff looks back the way they came and grins in surprise, waving to Christy and Doris as they make their way down.

"Here, love, I'll take Malia for a few minutes." She walks over to the water, then reaches down and lifts her to come sit with Nana Doris.

Duff, hesitating, relinquishes her as he gives her a kiss.

Then he makes his way over to the tide-pool and grins as Pete holds up a tiny dark shell. "See this, Duff? I think we were eating these during drinks last night, over at Pio's house. "Opihi, I think they're called over here. We called them limpets in Long Beach."

"Did I ever tell you about the kind of delicacies we used to eat in Morocco?" Duff says, knowing that he has told Pete the goats-eye story dozens of times.

Christy and Doris watch the two men as they meander on the rocks with Theo, kneeling down to get a closer view of something. Christy smiles to herself and wipes her moist eyes with her hand, as Pete reaches over and puts his arm around Duff, giving him a fatherly squeeze.

#

AFTERWORD

The SS *Malolo* returned to San Francisco on November 20, 1929. Of the original 325 passengers, one hundred and eight returned with the ship. Over half left the *Malolo* in Hong Kong, arriving in America ten days sooner on direct voyages. The stock market stabilized briefly on November 23, before continuing its precipitous slide for three more years. It reached its lowest point ever, at 41 points, on July 8, 1932, an 89 percent drop from its pre-crash high.

Following the stock market Crash: The Securities and Exchange Commission (SEC) was established and the Glass-Stegall Act was passed. It separated commercial and investment banking activities. In 1933, the Federal Deposit Insurance Corporation (FDIC) was established to insure individual bank accounts for up to $100,000.

Lloyd & Alita Winston joined the board of directors of Pan American World Airways, and split time between their home in Georgetown and their cottage near Diamondhead in Hawaii. They both assisted in the expansion of airline transportation throughout the Pacific, with special emphasis on Asia. From their home in Honolulu, they frequently visited with Pan American's director of Pacific Operations, Duff Malone, and his growing family.

Count Giovanni Sorvini returned to Newark, New Jersey, where he expanded his dining empire to include San Francisco and Hawaii, introducing an Italian cuisine infused with subtle Asian influence and presentation. With the end of prohibition, he added imaginative tropical drinks garnished with fresh fruit. In 1938 he secured the contract to provide pre-cooked in-flight meals for Pan American Airways, en route to and from Hawaii.

Aubrey Kirsch returned to Hollywood and established

a popular new character in the talking movies, as Guy Lamont, sidekick to Whip McCord, "The Singing Cowboy". His wife, Toots, declined frequent offers to star in the new musical extravaganzas. Instead, she and Aubrey were married quietly in Reno, and she remains his makeup specialist and business manager.

Werner Bergen returned to Japan to work in Yokohama, where he became a paid consultant for Pan American Airways in its expansion into Japan, China and Australia. He also provided pro bono expertise for the city of Yokohama, as it continued to repair itself. He was recalled to America in 1935, to advise the U.S. Army on Asian languages and cultures.

Anna and Ruth Swanton returned to New York briefly, where Ruth assembled her client files in preparation for their move to the family cabin near Milford, Pennsylvania. Anna resigned her position as head librarian for the New York City Library, and applied for a volunteer position at the small lending library in Milford. They pursued their love of travel, enjoying Pacific cruises and spending time as Malone house-guests in Honolulu.

Gwen Gibson returned to New York and sold her house in White Plains. She moved into the Manhattan apartment and worked diligently with women and children who were found in breadlines or begging on the streets. She endowed a soup kitchen, working there nearly every night until it closed in 1934. With the depression ending, she transformed it into a dance studio for abused women, and girls from poor families.

Duff & Christy Malone moved to Honolulu, creating a small and comfortable home near Mount Leahi, overlooking a quiet beach and active tide-pools. Duff remained as Director of the Pacific for Pan American World Airways for twenty-two years, often hosting their landlord, Werner Bergen, and their good friends, Anna and Ruth, and Alita and Lloyd.

On her thirtieth birthday, Christy awoke to find a slip of paper pinned to her pillow, knowing that Duff was off on a flight to Sydney. It read:

Unconditional Love

Delicate frame

Fitting gently into mine.

Rounded back and curled-up toes,

Heavy-lidded loving eyes,

Finding more in me

Than others find.

Angels kissed your soft body,

That draws more from me

Than I could ever give.

Peaceful, soothing love,

As inside I am,

Inside I am,

Inside I am you,

And you me.

Aloha, Duff

The End

Credits

I acknowledge and credit the following for helping to establish a feel for the times, and a sense of what our characters were reading, of what moved them.

Rudyard Kipling, for his poem "If", [1910]
T.S. Eliot, for his poem "The Hollow Men" [1925]

Multiple songwriters for their song titles that are scattered through the book, providing background and texture for our story.

B.G. DeSylva and Vincent Rose
Charles N. Daniels and Richard A. Whiting
Irving Berlin
Irving King, James Campbell and Reginald Connelly
Isham Jones and Gus Kahn
Jean Schwartz & William Jerome
Jimmy McHugh and Clarence Gaskill
Ray Henderson and Mort Dixon
Richard Rodgers and Lorenz Hart
Ruggero Leoncavallo
Walter Donaldson and Gus Kahn

- Don McPhail

Acknowledgements

"The Millionaires Cruise" is completely fictitious, although there was an actual cruise for millionaires that sailed from San Francisco on the same date, September 22, 1929. For this story, I reduced the cruise to sixty days, from its actual ninety.

I have tried to accurately recreate the era, the places and the people, including the impact of trusts and investment syndicates on the culture. Certainly, 1929 bank closures were not triggered by a murder, nor a rush on the New York bank as implied here.

It should be noted that, when the millionaires' story came to light it seemed to present a unique, tragic event: hundreds of passengers leaving port one day as millionaires, and returning many days later, as paupers. In fact, as I worked with the undisciplined speculation of the Twenties, it was obvious that the real tragedy was the pain and suffering of millions of citizens that came later, from the terrible depression in the Thirties.

I thank my friends and football teammates at Menlo College, Dudley Buffa, a marvelous and successful author, and Jim Mashburn who was a teammate at both Menlo and Annapolis, for their encouragement. I thank Dudley, as well as another writer, mentor and friend Nan Phifer, and my wife Gretchen, as well as longtime friends Sue Mellberg, Dick Fregulia, Wade and Phyllis Meyercord, and Steve Grosvold for their very helpful editing suggestions and wise counsel. Special thanks to Budd Thalman, a friend who was the top sports information director at Annapolis during my two years at the Academy, for reading my manuscript and adding useful suggestions. I also thank Hawaii friends and ohana, Mas, Jan, Mary, Pris, Nane, and especially Scrappy, for providing insights and material over the years, about the cultures and the social history of Hawaii. Uncle Moke Ka'aihue and Auntie

Irmgard Aluli were clearly in mind during many of the scenes of Hawaiian grace and welcome.

Gretchen and I also thank Sheraton's Royal Hawaiian and Moana hotels for sharing their historic photos and items on display from the Twenties. Thanks to Filoli estate for their generous access to the Roth family library, containing information about Matson Lines, the Malolo and various ports of call. A special thanks to my brother-in-arms Ed Remington and his wonderful wife Joan, for their constant encouragement, and editing suggestions about Hawaii, Japan and China.

Thanks, too, to Judy, Scott and Jack, to my late friend Burton Sabol, and my late brother Bill, for always encouraging my writing. Burton and Bill, in their own different ways, taught me a great deal about feelings and personal growth, as they shared their strength with me at different times, while they each died rapidly, and far too young, from pancreatic cancer.

Most of all, this book is a tribute to our dad, William Riddoch McPhail, Jr., known to his friends as Mac, born in Elgin, Scotland in 1901, and raised in Johannesburg. He died from a massive heart attack in 1944, in Larchmont, New York. I was four then, and brother Bill was nine. Our mom, Kathryn Donovan McPhail, was thirty-eight. I will never understand how she was able to raise two energetic young boys, alone and grieving, on a nurse's salary. Dad was an executive with Pan American World Airways when he died, having also served for many years with American Express. While I never really knew him, I always wished that I had. Instead, I created a story that begins with his childhood in Johannesburg, where his parents were not at all like those I invented for this story. With this book, I have given him and our mom the chance for a long, successful and very happy life together.
Donald McPhail, Mountain View, California

About the Author

"The Millionaires Cruise" is the first novel by 74-year-old Donald McPhail, former freelance writer and marketing executive in the airline and hospitality industries. Born in Santiago, Chile in 1940, he was raised in the United State and piqued his interest in travel in 1959, when he first visited his father's home country, South Africa -- a place he loves and has visited many times since. McPhail attended Menlo College, and was an enlisted sailor for two years before qualifying for the U.S. Naval Academy at Annapolis, where he lettered in football and baseball for two years, before transferring to San Francisco State College. He graduated with a degree in international relations from SF State, with a minor in world literature. He was a marketing executive in the travel industry for over forty years.

Q&A With Donald McPhail

Why did you write "The Millionaires Cruise"?

I've been working at fiction for nearly twenty years, and it felt as if this story needed to be written. For one thing, I wanted to create a tribute to my dad. He died at a young age, and I wanted to project how his life might have been, so I created Duff Malone. Next, I wanted to write a novel, after writing corporate spin and exaggerations for so many years. In the eighties I studied with a brilliant writing teacher, Burton Sabol, learning alongside extraordinary teacher and memoirs writer Nan Phifer. Burton died of pancreatic cancer during our third year together. We both owed it to him, and to ourselves, to apply what he taught us.

Tell us about your favorite books or writers?

There are a several favorites, and my interests extend in a direct line back to early childhood, with Doctor Seuss and "Horton Hatches An Egg", and to elementary school and those orange-covered biographies of Lou Gehrig, Lewis & Clark, Thomas Jefferson and Clara Barton. As an adult, "Fifth Business" and "The Manticore" by Robertson Davies are my all-time favorites. I re-read them every few years. Davies was a gentle and wise writer, with quite a twinkle in his eye. He loved irony, and writing in what he called "the plain style", and not in a superior manner. Kesey's "Sometimes A Great Notion" is a brilliant, emotional and highly creative book. I read that the effort he put into writing this poetic novel had spent him, emotionally and physically, and it must have done. Steinbeck's "East of Eden" is a work of art and another brilliant book. He tells bare-knuckled truths, and in a beautiful, also very poetic way. As an avid reader, I admire good writers. Poets, sports writers, fiction, all kinds. My favorite courses in college were in world literature, about Goethe, Rilke, Holderlin and Yeats, Aeschelus and Sartre. And I have spent many years figuring things out -- whether sales and marketing strategies, or ironies such as why human nature can be so positive and yet we do stupid and contradictory things. Politics, politicians and materialism are so overwhelming in this era, that my next story is likely to take them head-on, and not as a subtopic as it was in "The Millionaires Cruise".

Any current writers?

There are a lot of favorite writers, whose new books I await eagerly. Donna Leon, Alan Furst, Olen Steinhauer, John LeCarre. I admire the characters and philosophies of D.W. Buffa, and I hunt for his books under his different pseudonyms. And Jane Gardam. Her books "Old Filth" and "The Man In The Wooden Hat" are original and wonderful.

What are you currently reading?

I just finished Alan Furst's most recent, "Midnight in Europe" and loved it, as I have all of his novels. Before that an incredible book, "Let the Great World Spin" by Colum McCann, and "Mary Coin" by Marisa Silver. Most recently I finished a series of books that my grandson loaned me. They were fascinating -- perceptively written by Dan Gutman, for kids and adults: "Honus and Me", "Satch and Me", "Roberto and Me". Other subjects were "Babe", "Ted", "Mickey", "Shoeless Joe". They all carry simple, healthy, rich messages. Great for us old ballplayers and baseball-card savers.

Do you have other interests?

I've always loved sports and music. They probably saved my life as a kid. I listened to music, and loved to sing in the choir at church, and then in high school. Joan Baez was a high school classmate in Palo Alto, and I'm proud to have sung with her on occasion. Never as an equal, of course, but through her generosity. I also traveled with the Naval Academy dance band, and was their token crooner for a few months. As for sports, I played football and baseball at a high level until I was twenty-five. I was second on the depth chart behind the extraordinary Roger Staubach when I left Navy and transferred to San Francisco State. Then I coached when I got older. Now I coach grandson Jack on his Little League teams in Palo Alto. And I do volunteer work. For nearly twenty years I have been on the board of directors for an incredible boys' school and residential treatment center, Hanna Boys Center in Sonoma. They help change the lives of seriously troubled boys, and I help raise money for them.

You were born in Chile and your father was from South Africa?

Like my character Duff Malone, dad was born in Elgin, Scotland and raised in South Africa. He went on to work for American Express for many years. He and mom, and my older brother Bill, were stationed in Santiago from 1938 to 1942, and that's where I was born. Since mom was an American citizen, I was automatically American.

Then we relocated to New York when he joined Pan Am. Though I had to formally drop my Chilean citizenship when I turned eighteen, my interests and perspectives have always been as an outsider of sorts. I'm an American citizen. I served in the military, two years as an enlisted sailor and at Annapolis for two years, and I appreciate our strengths as a nation. But I also see us falling short of our promise as a world leader. In so many ways, our idealism has been overcome by materialism and arrogance, and the need for power.

You worked in the travel industry. What did you do?

It was predictable, I guess, since my dad was with American Express and then Pan Am. I grew up hearing stories about him, which made him and the travel industry seem noble and heroic. I joined United Airlines by chance, when I heard of a part-time job while I finished college at San Francisco State. I was twenty-four, playing football and working nights. I did this for for two years, then was hired into sales when I graduated. United promoted me to national sales manager at corporate headquarters when I was twenty-seven, then I found that I enjoyed marketing. It included sales, of course, but also involved gathering data, analyzing and assessing it, then developing and carrying out strategies. Lots of writing, persuasion, image-building, squeezing the facts to create a better story. I worked at being a freelance writer in the eighties, all nonfiction articles, while I agonized over my first clumsy attempts at fiction. I retired a few years ago, and dedicated myself to writing this first-novel, "The Millionaires Cruise".

www.ingramcontent.com/pod-product-compliance
Lightning Source LLC
La Vergne TN
LVHW021638180125
801630LV00002B/214

* 9 7 8 0 6 9 2 3 6 6 1 1 0 *